Linda Gillard was born in England, but has lived in Scotland since 2001, mainly in the Highlands and Islands. She has been an actress, journalist and teacher.

Linda is the author of ten novels, including STAR GAZING, short-listed in 2009 for *Romantic Novel of the Year* and *The Robin Jenkins Literary Award* for writing that promotes the Scottish landscape.

HOUSE OF SILENCE and THE MEMORY TREE were No. 1 Kindle bestsellers.

Also by Linda Gillard

Emotional Geology

A Lifetime Burning

Star Gazing

House of Silence

Untying the Knot

The Glass Guardian

Cauldstane

The Memory Tree

Hidden

www.lindagillard.co.uk

TIME'S PRISONER

LINDA GILLARD

First published as an e-book 2024

This paperback edition 2024

Copyright © 2024 Linda Gillard

ISBN 9798876834157

Cover design by Jane Dixon-Smith

For Jean Perkins

The dead are invisible. They are not absent.

St Augustine

PROLOGUE

Now cracks a noble heart.

Hamlet

2018

The sick room was lit only by the dying embers of a log fire that made little impression on the ancient chill of a house built of stone and oak. In the failing light the elderly woman thought she saw a movement at the end of the half-tester bed. She attempted to raise herself from the pillows, then abandoned the struggle and sank back, panting. Gathering her strength, she murmured, 'Are you there?'

The answer came, weary but not unkind. 'I'm always here.'

'I can't *see* you.' The frail voice was anxious.

'Your sight is failing now. It was to be expected.'

The woman directed her voice to the end of the bed. 'But you'll stay? Until...'

'Of course.'

The invalid's thin lips contorted into a smile. '*Our revels now are ended...*'

'Not quite.'

'Soon though.'

'Yes. Soon.'

She tried to speak again but was prevented by a bout of violent coughing. When the fit had passed, she whispered, 'When I'm gone, you'll still be here.'

'Oh, yes. Part of the furniture.'

1

She nodded, as if satisfied. 'But there will be another. A successor. The matter is in hand.'

'I didn't doubt it.'

Her fingers clawed at the fraying quilt. 'You'll keep an eye on her?'

'It will be my duty and pleasure.'

'It's settled then.' She moved her head restlessly on the pillow, peering into the darkness. 'It's so dark now. Can't see a damn thing.'

'It's almost time.'

'I'm afraid.'

'Don't be.' The voice was at her side now, close to her ear. '*Our little life is rounded with a sleep.* And you said you longed to rest.'

'I do. I'm worn out... I'll shut my eyes, just for a few moments. But—' Suddenly fretful again. 'You'll stay?'

'Where would I go?'

Her wheezing laugh brought on another coughing attack. Staring blindly into the darkness, the woman lifted a skeletal hand in graceful salute. Summoning the very last of her strength, she whispered, '*Good night, sweet prince.*'

After a while, there came a response. Soft. Final.

'*And flights of angels sing thee to thy rest.*'

The death of Q. Brooke-Bennet was announced, with appropriate regret, by her literary agent. A brief statement said Queenie had died alone, peacefully after a long illness. She had no family, but friends were later informed that shortly before her death, the celebrated author had banished her nurse from the sick room. Under protest, Nurse Kemp had taken up a position outside the bedroom door, knitting, listening for the sound of Queenie's bell. All she heard was the muttering of a dying woman talking to herself and, if she wasn't mistaken, quoting Shakespeare.

When eventually her patient fell silent, Nurse Kemp knocked gently, then put her head round the door. The serene face was as white as the snowy mane of hair that framed its gaunt features. Experience told Nurse Kemp that Queenie would write no more. The long and eventful book of her life was now closed.

PART ONE

1

And thus the whirligig of time brings in his revenges.

Twelfth Night

2019

Jane Summers wished she could employ a secretary or at least an assistant, but neither her current postbag nor her income justified the expense. Sifting through a pile of envelopes, she recognised letters from elderly and far-flung fans and one from her solicitor bringing her up to date with the death throes of a long, unsatisfactory marriage. She recognised her agent's neat hand and surmised the contents would officially confirm a different kind of divorce between Jane and her publisher after twenty productive years. Fifteen out of a twenty-book series had been published, but the final five – all planned, one already written – would not now see publication. "Falling sales" decreed that the final instalments of *The Whirligig of Time* would be uneconomic to produce and difficult to market.

Jane could see there was a problem. Many readers who'd bought books early in the series were now dead. Some would now have sight problems. Few would be able to afford a hardback and most would wait for the paperback. That left libraries who preferred to spend their meagre budgets on Scandinavian crime and Tartan Noir, both more popular than Elizabethan whodunnits.

M J Somerville (aka Jane Summers) had had a good run for her money. She was neither surprised nor particularly aggrieved, merely disappointed that the series would not run its course. Jane's readers, however, would be heartbroken. There would be a deluge of outraged letters and emails, to which she would feel obliged to respond.

Jane wondered briefly if she could fake her own death, as Meg had done in *Heir to a Queen*, Book Four of *The Whirligig*, thereby avoiding cries of outraged disbelief on social media. It was difficult for readers to grasp that publishing was almost entirely about making money for the publisher. Rewarding reader loyalty, or indeed authors, was not a topic that cropped up in marketing meetings.

At fifty-one a pension was still a long way off and the divorce – civilised, if not amicable – would impoverish both parties. Jane would need to live frugally on backlist royalties. She might have to go back to writing book reviews and articles for history magazines to supplement her income.

Depressed, she set all the envelopes aside apart from one, which felt as if it contained several sheets. An effusive fan letter? Someone sharing a new theory about the mysterious death of Amy Robsart, or incontrovertible proof that Elizabeth I was a man?

Jane tore open the envelope hoping to find something that would raise her spirits. There were two letters: one from a solicitor forwarding another sealed letter addressed to *Ms Jane Summers*. This was unlikely to be fan mail. Jane opened the second envelope and withdrew a letter written in violet ink on good quality headed notepaper. It had been written over a year ago. She didn't recognise the bold, elaborate hand. Glancing again at the short covering letter, she tried to recall why the extraordinary name, *Quintilia Brooke-Bennet* seemed familiar. Abandoning the effort, Jane read the letter.

Wyngrave Hall
August 30th 2017

Dear Ms Summers
 If you are reading this letter, I am dead.
 I do not expect this information to upset you. You might well have wished me dead. I fear your mother did. I am pleased to render you some service at last, for I have long wished to make reparation to you. Even

though I do not consider I committed any wrong, I was certainly the cause of a great deal of unhappiness. However, I refuse to take any responsibility for your family's tragic loss.

In life, there was little I could have done. Your father refused all contact with me and after his death it was difficult to see how I might approach his only child in a spirit of reconciliation, especially as that child became a professional rival and stood in no need of financial favours. Your books sold as well as mine and there were many more of them. You had no need to cash in on my name, nor indeed my notoriety. In short, I had nothing to offer you and I was sure that once you realised who I was, you would not accept any gifts from me. _In life_.

In death – which is where you now find me – I wonder if the situation might be different? After all, I can derive no satisfaction from my generosity. I can receive no absolution and my conscience cannot be quieted since I shall never know the outcome of my plan. I have died leaving a great number of loose ends – anathema to a writer! – and I died not knowing if you would accept the two gifts I have bequeathed you. All _most_ unsatisfactory.

The first gift is my beloved home, Wyngrave Hall and its contents. You are a Tudor scholar, so I trust you will respect this ancient and beautiful house. I hope you might come to love it as much as I did.

Wyngrave Hall comes with a certain amount of money towards its maintenance. I suggest you sell my jewellery and one or two of the portraits should you need more.

My second gift is one that I hope will persuade you to accept the first. Ms Summers, I leave you an unsolved mystery! It concerns a sudden death. A murder. I have pondered this crime for many years, without result. Perhaps your younger, better educated mind will hit upon the solution.

More than this I am not prepared to say. Be assured, the mystery is worthy of your attention, but quite possibly insoluble. If you decide to take up the challenge, I doubt you will be disappointed.

And now for the small print…

The contents of Wyngrave Hall are yours but I do not gift the Hall to you outright. You may not sell it and should you decline to live there for at least half of every year, my solicitors are instructed to sell the house to benefit a list of charities. I require you to inhabit the house and become its chatelaine.

I have left a bequest to my erstwhile gardener and housekeeper, Bridget Thompson, since my death renders her homeless and unemployed. I have left another bequest to my nurse, Rosamund Kemp. Both women are acquainted with the many stories attached to the house but, to the best of my knowledge, they are ignorant of the mystery. Both observed my gradual decline. Had I discussed the matter with them, they would have assumed senile decay. (Though I am undoubtedly frail and sinking, I am still in possession of my faculties, as I hope this letter will attest.) So you must expect assistance to come from another quarter. I am confident it will.

Whether or not you take up my challenge, I wish you all the best in your endeavours, personal and professional.

I cannot apologise. I have always followed the dictates of a passionate heart, flouting convention and confounding expectations. No man behaving as I did would have been censured so severely. I decline therefore to ask for your forgiveness. Nevertheless, I was very sorry for your grievous loss.

If you should undertake to live at Wyngrave Hall, I hope and trust you will be very happy there.

Yours very sincerely,
Quintilia Brooke-Bennet

The hand that set the letter down was shaking. Jane stared at her trembling fingers, as if they belonged to someone else, then clasping one hand with the other, she sank into a chair and closed her eyes.

Queenie Brooke-Bennet.

Q.

That *witch.*

When her father died, it had fallen to Jane to arrange the funeral and sort through his possessions. Her mother, Felicity, had committed suicide in a hotel room when Jane was twelve, a fact Nigel Summers managed to conceal until Jane was eighteen. She'd been told her mother died suddenly of an unsuspected heart defect, something that could have carried her off at any time.

Jane had been aware her parents were unhappy. Doors slammed, her father raged, her mother wept, but no one explained and Jane, an only child, had no one to ask. She sought refuge in imaginary worlds, reading and eventually writing stories about people who seemed as real to her as her parents – possibly more real, because unlike them, characters in fiction made sense. Jane knew what they thought, even how they felt. If they did something unaccountable, she knew why. When Jane started to write her own fiction, she discovered she could control what people said and did, which meant her stories not only made sense, they were fair. The wicked were punished and the good rewarded.

At the age of twelve, Jane had learned life wasn't like that. It was bad enough not having siblings or even a pet, but to lose her mother, then have to watch her father sit slumped in front of the TV, whisky glass in hand, weeping silently, as if his only child did not exist, was too much. Life wasn't fair and made absolutely no sense, but *stories* made sense and, when you looked back, when you saw the big picture, *history* made sense too. Charles I got what was coming to him and the Great Fire of London was an accident waiting to happen.

Jane worked hard at school, resolving to become a historian and she duly obtained a First Class degree in History at St Anne's, Oxford. Nigel Summers failed to show up for her graduation and Jane was relieved. Her father was never quite sober and, though she knew at some level they must love each other, she also knew they had nothing to say to each other, not since Nigel had informed Jane that her mother hadn't died of a congenital heart defect, but an overdose of barbiturates washed down with vodka.

'*Why?*' Jane had asked repeatedly, sobbing. 'Why would she *do* that? I was *twelve*, for God's sake! Didn't she think about *me?*'

Nigel sat with his head in his hands, mumbling. 'I'm sorry, Jane… I thought you should know. You would have found out eventually… People knew, you see. Friends. Colleagues.'

'But *why?* Why would she take her life? Was she dying?'

'No.' Nigel looked up but didn't meet Jane's eyes. 'But her heart was broken… I think *she* was broken.'

'Who broke her heart? *You?*'

Jane saw him reach automatically for a glass that, for once, wasn't there. Remembering, he clasped his hands and stared down at his worn carpet slippers. 'Felicity and I grew apart over the years and I… well, I just didn't understand.'

'You were unfaithful.'

He exhaled. 'It wasn't what you're thinking, Jane. There *was* someone, but—'

'Is that why you became a drunk? Guilt?'

He looked at her then, his bloodshot eyes unfocused. 'I drink because I miss her. Because I loved her, but I couldn't save her. In the end, you see, she just couldn't bear living with me. Couldn't bear *living*. I *did* love her, Jane. But that wasn't enough.'

'Nor, apparently, was I!'

Clapping a hand over her mouth, Jane rushed out of the room, stumbled upstairs and into her bedroom, slamming the door behind her. She threw herself on the bed and sobbed, confident Nigel was too ashamed and embarrassed to intrude on her grief.

Was it grief? Or was it actually rage? Jane now felt she'd lost her mother twice.

Life was so unfair.

When, after his death, Jane went through her father's desk, she hoped to find a suicide note from her mother. In that she was disappointed, but locked in a drawer, she found a collection of letters written in violet ink. The hand was florid, obviously female.

The envelopes hadn't been retained and the letters were undated. They were addressed variously to *My Darling*, *Dearest* and *My Love*. Each was signed *Q* and the tail of the single letter was decorated with a pseudo-Elizabethan flourish.

Without reading them, Jane ripped every letter into tiny pieces, then gathered up the fragments and burned them.

Sylvia Marlow, National Treasure and *grande dame* (retired) of the British theatre sank into her favourite shabby, but comfortable armchair.

'Not many there,' Sylvia said, kicking off her shoes. 'I was surprised. But I suppose there aren't many of us left now.'

'Friends of Queenie? To be honest, I don't think it was ever a big club,' was her granddaughter's tart reply.

Dressed in funeral black, Sylvia looked older than her eighty-five years and the lines on her once beautiful face seemed more deeply etched. Her hair was thin now and white, though she liked to refer to it as silver. She'd worn the same hairstyle for longer than she could remember, pulling back her hair from her pale, luminous face into a *chic* and tidy *chignon* that had become less *chic* and less tidy with the passing years. Sylvia didn't care about her hair. She said people remember your smile and voice, not your hair, which had to disappear under wigs and not look "a fright" when the wig came off. Sylvia was right. Audiences had remembered her smile and voice for over sixty years.

Rosamund Kemp busied herself hanging up their coats and tidying away Sylvia's shoes so she wouldn't trip over them. Looking after the elderly was what Rosamund had done for most of her adult life, professionally and privately. Queenie Brooke-Bennet had been her last patient (Rosamund was inclined to think of her also as the last straw) but with her death had come a small, unexpected legacy. Rosamund needed to take stock. She would be forty at the end of the year, but so far there was no grey in her pre-Raphaelite halo of curling red hair, so inclined to frizz. There had been a few relationships, all short, none happy, though Rosamund was habitually and professionally cheerful, no doubt as a result of her work as a nurse. Her sense of humour was dark, but her smile was unfailing, as was her desire to sublimate her loneliness in hard work and caring for others. She knew there was always someone worse off, a thought she found perversely comforting because it meant she could never abandon herself to self-pity, an indulgence she understood and frequently observed in others, but privately despised.

Although an adult and professionally acquainted with death, Rosamund had felt the loss of her mother as a great blow, but she'd bonded with the grandmother who'd had to bury her daughter. At the funeral, a stoical Sylvia had recited some Shakespeare. Rosamund had never been a fan of the Bard and now she remembered only the first line: *Grief fills the room up of my absent child.* But she would always remember Sylvia's voice, her shining eyes and the way she'd smiled, half-mad with grief.

Sylvia broke into her thoughts now. 'It was a lovely service, even if there weren't many there.'

'Queenie would have *hated* it!' Rosamund scoffed. 'People standing up saying what a lovely person she was! You could almost hear hollow laughter coming from the coffin.'

'Oh, Ros, what an *awful* thing to say! She was your employer. *And* she left you some money.'

'For which I am duly grateful,' Rosamund replied, sitting down opposite her grandmother. 'But don't forget, I knew Queenie very well. She would have loathed the hypocrisy of people pretending she'd led a good life. She used to say she'd made more enemies than friends and the sparse attendance at her funeral bore that out.'

'Well, she would have enjoyed being the centre of attention one last time. I'm sure she hates being dead, poor thing.'

Rosamund regarded her grandmother. She was staring into space, as she often did nowadays, her pale eyes unfocused. Setting aside a familiar twinge of concern, Rosamund said, 'She's gone, Gran, and she was ready to go. She'd been ill for a long time and take it from me, she was the world's worst patient,' she added, trying to lighten her grandmother's mood.

Sylvia rallied as Rosamund had hoped. 'I bet she treated you like a servant.'

'Well, I was, wasn't I? But Queenie treated everyone like staff. Her GP, her solicitor, her agent. I've heard people speak more respectfully to their pets.'

'Oh, that was just her manner. Imperious. She thought it went with that aquiline profile, but her friends always knew her bark was worse than her bite.'

'Did you still think of her as a friend?'

'Not really, but we were close when we were young – and my word, we *were* young! Eighteen when we first met. *Centuries* ago!'

'Don't exaggerate.'

'Well, it feels like another lifetime. A different world… Queenie and I shared the same hopes and dreams. At one time we even shared the same man, though I didn't know, of course. But then our lives went in very different directions.'

Rosamund was tired, but she knew Sylvia wanted to talk. She also knew that much of what Sylvia wanted to say would be familiar, but she couldn't begrudge her the comfort of reminiscence. There came a point in the lives of the elderly when looking ahead became frightening and it was a relief to retreat into a past where there were no surprises. All is known because all is past. Rosamund supposed it must be something like the reassurance of returning to a favourite book. You can re-live the excitement, the emotional highs and lows, but there is no suspense, no uncertainty.

Bracing herself for the inevitable, Rosamund said, with her warm and habitual smile, 'Shall I make us a pot of tea?'

'Oh, that would be lovely. Thank you, darling.'

As Sylvia reached for a rug to spread over her knees, Rosamund pushed a footstool towards her, helped her lift her feet, then tucked the rug around her. Her final act of kindness before heading into the tiny kitchen was to ask, 'Why did Queenie give up acting? You started out together, didn't you?'

'RADA. Class of '52. We were holy terrors!'

'And then *you* acted for half a century.'

Sylvia laughed. 'Well, I didn't know how to do anything else, did I?'

'Sir John Gielgud called you the *Marvellous Marlow*.' Sylvia beamed as she remembered the accolade. 'But Queenie quit?'

'Oh, yes, quite early on. It was a great shame. Well, *she* didn't see it like that, but we all thought she was a great loss to the theatre because she had a special quality. Nothing to do with looks, because she wasn't a great beauty, but Queenie could make you *think* she was. She would have been a wonderful Cleopatra. Especially with that nose.'

Rosamund patted her grandmother's hand and said, 'I'm going to put the kettle on. Back in a jiff.' She headed for the kitchen, but Sylvia carried on talking, as Rosamund knew she would, raising her clear voice effortlessly, so she could be heard over the sound of the kettle boiling.

'We were posh, under-educated girls, expected to do nothing more than marry well, then sit at home breeding and hosting dinner parties. But Queenie and I had other ideas. *We* were going to be *actresses*! I think she had her sights set on Hollywood right from the start. She was never keen on the idea of starving in a garret, which I thought could be rather jolly. Queenie liked her creature comforts.'

'Was she actually any good?' Rosamund asked, leaning against the door frame as she waited for the kettle to boil.

'You couldn't take your eyes off her when she was on stage. And she had such a beautiful voice! I loved to hear her speak Shakespeare, especially in the dramatic roles. Comedy wasn't really her *forte*, though she could be an absolute scream offstage.'

'At the end her sense of humour was very dark. She could be quite cruel.'

'Oh, yes. She would say *wicked* things, and she meant to hurt, but she spared me for some reason. Perhaps because she didn't see me as any sort of rival. We were never up for the same parts and she was so much more glamorous. I thought she was ambitious, but she acted for only a few years before she married. Minor aristocracy. Only a younger son, but a good-looking boy. The marriage didn't last long. Queenie left him, then wrote a racy novel about a decaying aristocratic family.'

'That must have gone down well with the in-laws,' said Rosamund as she went back into the kitchen to make tea.

'People assumed it was barely disguised autobiography, but Queenie said she was just trying to do a Nancy Mitford. With sex.'

'Sounds like a recipe for a bestseller.'

'Well, it was more *Brideshead Revisited*. Lots of adultery and sexually confused toffs indulging in drink and drugs. It sold like hot cakes, of course, but the family took it badly.'

'You amaze me,' Rosamund said placidly, returning with two cups of tea.

'Her husband divorced her, but the book set Queenie off on a new and lucrative career. She wrote a sequel, then another. Eventually they were all televised.'

Rosamund handed Sylvia her tea and watched as she cocked her head on one side, like a bird, reaching for the saucer, apparently without looking at it. Sylvia took it, then hesitating briefly, she placed the cup on the coffee table at her side, spilling a little into the saucer, though Rosamund, always considerate, hadn't filled the cup. Little escaped her professional attention, whether it was a patient or her grandmother. As Sylvia reached for the handle of her cup, again without looking, Rosamund knew that soon she would have to say something. She'd hoped her grandmother would mention it first but knew that was unlikely.

Sylvia sighed and sipped her tea, evidently a little flustered, so Rosamund helped her settle again by throwing out another question.

'Did Queenie marry again?'

'Oh, yes, a couple of times, I believe.'

'But no children?'

'No, just a lot of young lovers, by all accounts. It was said, if you got involved with Queenie, you'd end up in court or in one of her novels. Or both. It was a risk quite a few were prepared to take.'

'Fortunately I shall never see myself caricatured in the pages of one of her books,' said Rosamund. 'But in the meantime, I'm out of a job.'

'There must be lots more elderly invalids you can look after.'

'Oh, yes, the agency will find me something. If I can face it.'

'Queenie's bequest will tide you over for a while, won't it? She must have thought very highly of you to leave you money.'

'I suppose so. Bridget said Queenie was quite fond of me. I said, "Whatever makes you think that?" and she said, "You're still here. If Queenie didn't like you, she would have driven you away, like the two nurses who quit before you". I was there for nearly a year. She was a long time dying, poor woman.'

Sylvia cleared her throat and said, 'Speaking of death—'

'Must we? I presume you're going to talk about yours.'

'Not exactly. But I'd like to let you have a little advance.'

'Advance?'

'On what you'll get when I die.'

'Oh, Gran, please don't talk like that. It's so morbid.'

'I want you to be able to plan your future. And I want to arrange the rest of mine.' Sylvia took a deep breath and said in a rush, 'I want to sell this cottage and buy myself a nice little flat. Cheap to heat and easy to maintain.'

'But there's no need to move! I can help out.'

'You do quite enough for me as it is,' Sylvia said briskly. 'And you'd need to do less if I moved.' She held up a hand to forestall objections. 'Oh, I know I manage at the moment, but the time will come when I can't, so I want to move now, while I'm still mobile and when I do sell up, I want you to have a little of the proceeds.'

'But Gran—'

'Oh, please don't argue, Rosamund! I shall get upset. You're all I have and you'll get everything when I die, but if you have some money now, I'll have the pleasure of seeing you spend it. Or save it. Whatever you prefer.'

'But how can you bear to give up your garden?'

'Easily!' Sylvia retorted. 'It's become a burden. It's too much for me now.'

'We could get a gardener to come in for a couple of hours a week.'

'Can't afford it.'

'Well, I could do it, if you tell me what to do.'

'*No*, Rosamund. You don't have time and even if you did, I wouldn't want you to spend it weeding my garden. I need to move and I *want* to move.' Sylvia's anxious eyes filled with tears. 'I need to… simplify.'

'Please don't upset yourself, Gran. If you really want to move, of course I'll help you. I just can't imagine you without your garden to potter in.'

'Peace of mind is more important to me now,' Sylvia said, setting down her teacup with a rattle. 'And independence. I have an absolute horror of being a burden to you.'

'You'll never be a burden! You're all I've got. You're my *family*.'

'Thank you, darling, but even if you don't regard me as a burden, I feel like one. And I…' Sylvia clenched her fists and said with unwonted vehemence, 'I just can't *bear* it!'

'Gran, I'll help you do whatever you want.'

'It's time for a change. A *big* change. We only get one life and I want to make the most of it, for as long as I can. Look at poor Queenie! Same age as me and dead now, after two terrible years fighting cancer.' Sylvia shook her head. 'There isn't a moment to lose, Rosamund.' She struggled to her feet and drew herself up to her full, but modest height. 'Life isn't a rehearsal. This is *it*. The show. The final act, as a matter of fact. My big moment,' she added, clasping gnarled hands to her chest in a girlish gesture.

Rosamund looked up and said, 'What's that crazy thing they say in the theatre when you want to wish someone luck?'

Sylvia chuckled and said, 'Break a leg!'

'Well, then,' said Rosamund, standing. 'Break a leg, Gran.'

Sylvia laughed again and flung her arms round her granddaughter. As Rosamund held her grandmother, she wondered if she knew she was suffering from AMD: age-related macular degeneration. Rosamund thought it likely. In which case, Sylvia's enthusiasm for Google had probably already informed her she was in the slow but inexorable process of going blind.

When Jane googled Wyngrave Hall, she turned up a *Country Life* article from the 1980s. It was an Elizabethan manor house in Essex and according to local tradition, a company of actors, said to include Shakespeare, had given a private performance within its walls when the London theatres were closed by plague.

Stunned by the scale of her inheritance, Jane rang Queenie Brooke-Bennet's solicitor, Laurence Putnam. He informed her that until such time as Jane accepted the bequest, one Bridget Thompson was acting as caretaker and would be happy to show her round.

'Miss Thompson is something of an expert on Wyngrave Hall. She's lived there for many years, firstly in a cottage in the grounds and latterly in the Hall itself, after she took on some housekeeping duties. Miss Thompson was employed originally as a gardener, I understand.'

'Are the grounds substantial?'

'No more than you would expect with a property of this kind. There's a walled garden, a small orchard, glasshouses and so forth. It keeps Miss Thompson busy, but she manages on her own. Are you a gardener, Ms Summers?'

'No. I can't even keep houseplants alive.'

'Ah. Some of the land could easily have been sold off as building plots, but Miss Brooke-Bennet refused to consider it. She said she wasn't prepared to have a building site on her doorstep. Or builders.'

'What is the house worth?' Jane asked, regretting immediately the bluntness of her enquiry.

'Well, it's not just a *house*,' Mr Putnam explained. 'There's the land and various outbuildings – all very run down at the moment, but they have potential for re-development. Miss Thompson's old cottage is somewhat dilapidated, but if modernised, it would have potential as a holiday let. Then of course there are the contents of the Hall itself. There are a number of portraits – some Tudor and Jacobean – and some very good furniture. Miss Brooke-Bennet also had jewellery which she expected you would sell.'

'Do you have a ballpark figure? I'm just trying to get my head round it all. Frankly it seems like some grotesque practical joke.'

When Laurence Putnam mentioned a sum, Jane dropped her mobile with a little yelp. As she bent to retrieve it, she heard him say, 'Of course, it would be worth twice that if it were in Surrey or Kent. Essex is commutable,' he conceded, 'but not – how shall I put it? – *desirable*. It's all relative of course and in this case entirely hypothetical. According to the terms of Miss Brooke-Bennet's will, you may sell the goods and chattels, if you occupy the Hall for half the year, but you cannot sell the property.'

'Yes, that's what she said in her letter, but I can't say I understood. Could you elaborate?'

'You can bequeath the *tenancy* of Wyngrave Hall to someone on your death, but you do not own it, nor can you sell.'

'I have no one to bequeath it to. I have no children, I'm an only child and I'm about to divorce.'

'I see… Well, there you find yourself in a similar position to Miss Brooke-Bennet. I understand she too had no family.'

'So what would happen if I died intestate?'

'Oh, I really wouldn't recommend it. If you do decide to accept the bequest, you would be advised to make a will, unless you wanted the proceeds of a sale to be distributed between Miss Brooke-Bennet's chosen charities after your death. But I do know it was her dearest wish that Wyngrave Hall should be passed on – in a personal way – to a relative or friend.'

'But I'm neither. I never even met her!'

'Is that so? I understood she knew your parents.'

'Oh, yes, she knew *them*,' Jane said, irritated. 'She knew them *very* well.'

'That would be the connection then,' Mr Putnam replied, un-ruffled. 'And of course your reputation as an author of Tudor novels must have suggested to Miss Brooke-Bennet that you might have a professional interest in the Hall.'

'Did you read the letter she wrote me? Do you know anything about the "mystery"?'

'No, she said nothing to me about that, I'm afraid. I just forwarded her letter. We'd discussed the legal issues, of course, but I know nothing of the more *colourful* detail.'

'Neither do I. Her letter was maddeningly enigmatic, like a publisher's blurb.'

'Ah. Well, she was a writer too, of course. But you say you never met?'

'Never. But I was aware of her reputation, personal and professional.'

'Miss Brooke-Bennet was undoubtedly what many people would describe as eccentric, but she was as sharp as a tack, even at the end. And she was a good age. Eighty-five. Her body failed her, but her mind never did. *She* knew what she was doing, even if we don't. But if I may venture a personal opinion… I knew the lady for many years. She could be difficult and often very rude, but I never saw malice. Perhaps the unusual nature of her bequest might lead you to suspect some sort of legal booby trap?'

'It does seem a bit like that. If I mess things up, millions go to some cats' home.'

'Miss Brooke-Bennet's charities are all connected with the promotion of literacy and education. She had no pets, as a matter of fact.'

'No pets, no family and so few friends, she leaves her home to a total stranger! What an extraordinary woman! Is there a shortlist of candidates? Who's next in line when I turn it down?'

'There are no other candidates, as you put it. If you decline, the house will be sold. Miss Brooke-Bennet wanted *you* to have it. It was my strong impression – I don't think I'm speaking out of turn here – that she wished you to be *happy* at Wyngrave Hall. I don't think she was setting any kind of trap. She viewed the house as a great gift. She said living there had been the greatest adventure of her life.'

'Adventure?'

'That was the word she used. And, as you're probably aware, no one would describe Miss Brooke-Bennet's life as *uneventful*.'

'Stranger than fiction, I gather. Well, thank you, Mr Putnam, you've been very helpful. I suppose I'd better go and view the house. That's the least I can do. You mentioned Bridget Somebody?'

'Thompson. She'll be happy to show you round and answer all your questions, but bear in mind the situation is a tad sensitive. Unless you wish to continue to employ her, Miss Thompson will soon become homeless. If you wish to consider maintaining the *status quo*, I have a glowing testimonial written by Miss Brooke-Bennet. Would you like Miss Thompson's number?'

Jane made a note of it and told Mr Putnam she would get back to him soon. When the call ended, Jane felt no less stunned than when she'd first read Queenie's letter. She assumed she must still be in a state of shock – shock compounded with the depressing realisation that if she were to bequeath Wyngrave Hall according to Queenie's suggestion, she could think of no one closer or more deserving than her agent. Her closest friends were now ensconced in France and Italy and she had lost two more good friends to cancer. Divorce had forced some friends to take sides. Losing a husband meant losing his family and friends and Duncan had always been the gregarious one. He enjoyed pubs and people. Jane loved books, work and long solitary walks on which she plotted her novels. Duncan had always said she should get out more, but until the conversation with Mr Putnam, Jane had never thought of herself as *lonely*. When there are scores of people in your head, vying for your attention, arguing, explaining, protesting, sharing their every thought and desire, how could you ever feel lonely?

When Duncan got home late from work (or, as now seemed more likely, an assignation with Sophie from HR) he'd say cheerily, as Jane tapped away on her laptop, 'Still talking to your imaginary friends? Did they say anything interesting today?' And without waiting for an answer, he'd head for the drinks cupboard, calling out over his shoulder, 'What's for dinner?'

Perhaps it *had* been a lonely life. She just hadn't thought of it like that.

Jane found herself looking forward to meeting Bridget Thompson and having someone to talk to about the seismic upheaval of her quiet writing life occasioned by the death of Queenie Brooke-Bennet.

She might even find a sympathetic ear since Bridget's future was currently as uncertain as Jane's.

He follows her around the Hall. "Like a lapdog", Queenie would have said, with withering scorn, though she knew he had no need to follow, nor be in any particular room. He is everywhere. And nowhere.

It amuses him to accompany Bridget as she removes dust sheets, draws back heavy curtains, throws open windows and lets in the light. It reminds him of old times, when the house teemed with life: families, servants, dogs, cats, even a parrot who outlived his master. All long dead.

His mind, but not his eye, follows Bridget into the room Queenie chose for her last bedroom. Not the one where she'd made love. The one where, as age and infirmity encroached, she'd sat propped up on pillows and written; the room in which she'd spent her last two years; the room in which she'd died.

Afterwards the bed was stripped efficiently by Nurse Kemp, the sheets bundled up and passed to a weeping Bridget for laundering. Now the mattress is covered with a worn and faded patchwork quilt. Bridget found it in a glasshouse and guessed it had been used to keep frost off tender plants. Or possibly the gardener.

She'd washed it several times, then spread it on her own bed, not caring about the holes. Now it lay on Queenie's bed, hiding a wine-stained mattress: an offering to an employer who would accept nothing from Bridget in life, not even friendship.

He does not enter Queenie's room but cannot prevent the perambulations of his mind. This emptiness, this anguish is what he always feels when they die. And they do always die. Of few things can he be certain, but death is one. Perhaps the only one, though Queenie used to rail against the exorbitant demands of the taxman.

Will Wyngrave have a new occupant? Someone has always come. Sometimes not for months, even years, but eventually someone always comes to join him in his Hell. Someone assumes the stewardship of Wyngrave Hall. Even then, he might have no audience. Some sense something uncanny but refuse to engage or even acknowledge what instinct tells them. Most remain unaware. The lonely are the first to realise and they assume they're going mad. Children also notice but are ignored, their claims dismissed by doubting parents as juvenile fantasy.

Queenie had assured him she'd done her best to make suitable arrangements. Usually it was a matter of chance whether he acquired someone who would wish to further his cause, or simply keep him company. Queenie said she'd pinned her hopes on a woman, not young, to whom she owed much. Not money. Some tragedy, she implied. Queenie was uncharacteristically vague and he assumed she was ashamed.

This woman was a specialist and might be able to help. Knowledgeable and clever, she was able to create and therefore possibly solve puzzles of the most complex kind. But, he had argued, only someone prepared to *inhabit* Wyngrave Hall would be of any use to him. Ownership meant little. Since he could never leave the confines of the Hall, it seemed reasonable to assume the solution to the mystery of his continuing presence lay within Wyngrave itself and enlightenment must therefore come from that quarter. If there were answers, they must be contained within these walls, beneath these stones, borne in the dust of ages on the very air he no longer breathed.

Here. Here the answer must lie.

Bridget has laid fires and now arranges flowers. Evidently someone is expected and Bridget Thompson – a woman of the earth, not the spirit – is preparing Wyngrave for its audition. He feels something unfamiliar… A kind of stage fright, though he will make no appearance. Frustration, then anger rise, both are soon quelled. Over the centuries he has made his peace with them. Mostly.

Bridget surveys the room, then tweaks an arrangement of flowers she grew in a garden he sees only from the window. The anger again… If he knew this garden in life, he has no recollection of it now. Few memories at all.

Bridget looks at her watch and heads towards the massive oak front door. She lifts the iron latch and, as it swings open, a shaft of sunlight falls across the uneven flagstones, illuminating the dust motes she has disturbed.

The door bangs shut and he hears the great iron key grate in its lock. If he had a heart, it would sink.

There is nothing to do now but wait. To hope would be foolish. He must wait, with neither hope nor expectation, as he has waited for centuries.

2

I count myself in nothing else so happy
As in a soul remembering my good friends.

Richard II

Bridget Thompson had offered to meet Jane at Colchester station and drive her to Wyngrave Hall. Jane had accepted gratefully. She very much wanted to see the house she would be rejecting and hear the inside story of the magnificent gift a total stranger wanted her to have.

Was it a gift? Since Jane could never sell, it felt more like an obligation: a property that would be expensive to run, need specialised maintenance and in which she was required to live. Hardly a gift, unless you wanted to inhabit a decaying historic building for the rest of your days, as Queenie had done.

The idea certainly didn't appeal to Jane, a life-long flat-dweller. Much as she enjoyed researching her novels, she'd never thought as she wandered round historic houses, "How nice it would be to live somewhere like this". She knew it would be cold, damp and dark, even in summer. Bookcases wouldn't fit because the walls weren't perpendicular. Doors and windows wouldn't shut properly and occupants would be assailed constantly by draughts. Jane wondered how an old woman of eighty-five had borne it, but Queenie had grown up without central heating and was no doubt made of sterner stuff.

The marital home was on the market and though it would be a wrench, Jane was eager to make a new start. The flat they'd owned for twenty years had never become a family home, so she hadn't had to deal with an "empty nest", but if she was to live alone now, she declined to sit contemplating the empty shelves Duncan's vinyl collection had filled, or the space his shabby leather armchair had occupied. A new home was essential. An ancient manor house in darkest Essex was not what she had in mind.

Jane could live and work anywhere with internet access. She owned a substantial collection of research books. She saw her agent once a year for a convivial lunch, but mostly they kept in touch by email. Jane's closest friends now lived abroad and reunions, though joyous, had been rare. With time differences, email was more convenient than the telephone, so Jane found herself in the odd position of sharing the minutiae of her friends' lives, while feeling as if she no longer knew who they were.

Jane imagined they felt much the same about her. She'd found it impossible to describe the rift with Duncan and when she announced her divorce, her friends had been shocked. Their regular exchange of news felt like friendship, but it wasn't really. Alison hadn't mentioned breast cancer until hers was deemed terminal. Susie hadn't mentioned her son's drug addiction until he went into re-hab. Maeve had presumably been too embarrassed to admit she'd fallen in love with Giacomo, twelve years her junior. Until she received an invitation to a wedding in Lombardy, Jane assumed Giacomo was just another racy episode in Maeve's colourful love life. Short of cash and with a deadline looming, Jane declined the invitation and watched the wedding video online, crying because the groom was so beautiful and the bride looked so happy.

As the rain fell at Alison's funeral, Jane wondered what their hundreds of emails had been about. Work, mostly. Research, drafts, edits, advances, sequels, prequels and awards. Just *work*. Real life was something you shared over the second bottle of wine. Death you didn't share at all.

Do you ever really *know* people, Jane wondered? Your dying friend, your cheating husband, your philandering father? As the flat Essex countryside sped past, Jane stared through the grubby train window, wishing Susie or Maeve were accompanying her to view Wyngrave Hall. The trip would have been a hoot and the pub lunch afterwards where they compared notes would have been (as Maeve would say) *epic*.

But it was probably just as well Jane was going alone. Maeve and Susie would insist she accept the bequest. So would Alison, if she'd lived. 'Life isn't a first draft, Jane. This is *it*. The definitive edition, with or without a happy ending. Make sure you *live*, my darling!' The last email, before she'd become too weak even to dictate.

Maeve had taken Alison's advice to heart and now enjoyed *la dolce vita* with a large number of noisy and devoted relations. She would have no sympathy with her risk-averse friend, which is why she knew nothing of Jane's astonishing inheritance. Nor did Susie. One day, the bizarre story would make an entertaining email and Jane would be chided gently for her cowardice.

As the Essex countryside became a blur, Jane rubbed tired eyes and found they were wet. Reaching into her bag for a tissue, she could almost hear her friends, dead and alive, as they argued and cajoled, like bickering ghosts.

Bridget Thompson was waiting at the station and stepped forward to introduce herself. Jane had sent a link to her website where Bridget would find a few photos, none of them recent, but good enough for identification purposes. She'd replied, 'You can't miss me. I'm tall.' Indeed she was. Very tall, almost six foot. She was what the Edwardians might have called "a handsome woman". Tanned from working outdoors, she looked fit and strong. Her dark curling hair was cut short and showed only a little grey. Thick brows arched over intelligent blue eyes. When Bridget greeted Jane, the proffered hand was dry and callused, but her smile was warm. Jane liked her immediately and relaxed a little.

Jane followed as Bridget led the way out of the station. Trotting across the car park to catch up, Jane wondered if she should have worn more sensible shoes, but she had no interest in touring the grounds. She was merely curious to see Wyngrave Hall. The home of the home-wrecker. She thought it might be shabby and it would probably seem depressing: the house of an old, friendless recluse, all but forgotten – for who read the novels of Q. Brooke-Bennet now? Jane had researched Queenie's life online. (Can one stalk the dead, she wondered?) She read interviews in which Queenie was portrayed as selfish and ambitious, characteristics that would go unremarked in a man. Journalists seemed scarcely able to conceal their disdain for their subject and, reading carefully, Jane could see the feeling was mutual. Despite herself, Jane felt a grudging respect for Queenie who had been asked to drop *Quintilia* in favour of the genderless *Q* on the grounds that books by men were taken more seriously and were more likely to be reviewed. Queenie pointed out a girl's name hadn't done her friend Evelyn Waugh any harm, but she eventually conceded defeat because she needed the money.

Sadly, little had changed in the intervening years. At the start of her career, Jane had been persuaded *M J Somerville* would sell more books than *Jane Summers* or even the more elegant *Jane Somerville*. Whilst women would happily read books by men, men were apparently reluctant to read books by women, and so *M J Somerville* was born. Jane learned to smile graciously at signings when customers handed her a book and said, sounding vaguely affronted. "I didn't realise you were a *woman*." Just once, in the early days, Jane had said sweetly, "I'm so sorry. Would you like your money back?", but the manager at Hatchard's had overheard the exchange and had a quiet word.

Bridget's car had seen better days. As she got in, Jane hoped the seat was cleaner than the floor which was littered with twigs, spilled compost and sweet wrappers.

'Sorry about the mess,' Bridget said. 'I have to transport stuff in the car. I gave the seat a good wipe.'

'Please don't worry about it. It's very good of you to give up your time to show me round. I hope this won't disrupt your routine too much.'

'I don't really have one now, not since Queenie died,' Bridget replied as they pulled out of the station car park. 'I get a caretaking retainer, but no one pays my salary any more. I'm just keeping the garden ticking over until I know what's going to happen.'

'Do you live in?'

'I do now. I used to live in a cottage in the grounds, but it was in very poor condition. Queenie eventually offered me rooms in the house to save herself the expense of maintaining it. I missed my independence, but she was already losing hers. I was having to do a lot more for her, so it made sense for me to move in. It's a shame about the cottage though. It would make someone a lovely little home. I used to see deer on the lawn. A badger occasionally.' As she indicated left, Bridget said, 'We turn off the main road here, then it's minor roads, then *very* minor roads all the way to the Hall. It's not actually far from the station, but the journey's slow and uncomfortable, especially in winter when the muddy tracks freeze.' She swerved to avoid a pothole. 'Sorry about that. There will be plenty more, I'm afraid… Do you know much about the Hall?'

'A fair amount about its history which I've researched online.'

'I'll try to answer any questions you have, though I'm no historian. But you are, I think?'

'Well, I'm a historical novelist, which isn't quite the same thing.'

'The Tudors?'

'Yes, I write historical whodunnits.'

Bridget nodded. 'Queenie had a lot of your books. They look well-read too. Maybe that's why she thought of you for the Hall.'

'It's certainly *one* of the reasons,' Jane replied, staring fixedly though the windscreen.

Bridget shot her a sideways glance and saw at once that there was a story to be told, but Jane wasn't about to share it. They drove on in silence until Jane said, 'Do you know anything about a mystery attached to the Hall?'

'Mystery?'

'Queenie left me a very odd letter in which she talked about a mystery, but it was all very cryptic.'

Bridget smiled. 'She did like to be mysterious. And she loved secrets – hers and other people's.'

'Does the house have a priest hole? Or a secret passage? Are there any legends of people being walled up alive?'

'Queenie never spoke of anything like that, but we didn't go in for a lot of chat.' Bridget was thoughtful for a while. 'She once said Wyngrave was haunted. She'd had a few cocktails and I'm not sure she was being entirely serious. Hard to tell with Queenie. But I never saw anything and I've been there for years.'

Jane turned and looked at Bridget. She thought she sensed some uneasiness. 'You said you've never *seen* anything but perhaps you heard something odd?'

'Oh, no, nothing like that.'

'But… there's something?'

Bridget smiled. 'If you live with a crazy old lady for years, some of it's bound to rub off, isn't it? Like dogs and their owners.'

'Was Queenie crazy? The letter she sent me was very strange, but it seemed perfectly lucid.'

Bridget hesitated, then said, 'No, I'm being disloyal. She wasn't crazy at all. Queenie was herself – alert, intelligent, articulate – until the morphine got the better of her.'

'But she believed the Hall was haunted?'

'Who knows what Queenie believed? She *said* it was, but I thought that was just to discourage house guests. She resented any kind of intrusion and hated entertaining.'

'*You* don't think Wyngrave Hall is haunted?'

'Well, I've never seen or heard anything.'

'But…? Don't worry, ghosts won't alarm me because I don't be-lieve in them, but I'm interested in people who do. My job has taken me to a lot of supposedly haunted properties where Grey Ladies – they're always grey, aren't they? – are said to walk, bemoaning their fate. Some owners talk it up for publicity, but others are absolutely convinced their ghost is real and not at all sinister. It's quite touching to see their attachment to the idea.'

'So you don't believe in ghosts at all?'

'No. I can't even claim to have an open mind, which is perhaps not very useful in a writer. But I'm interested – academically, I sup-pose – in whether Queenie or anyone else believed Wyngrave Hall was haunted. Whatever you say won't discourage me from taking up Queenie's bequest because, to be perfectly frank, I'm very unlikely to give up the convenience of a London flat to live in an Elizabethan manor house at the end of one of these awful roads. In any case, I'd be more frightened of rats and mice than ghosts.'

'How are you with bats?' Jane shuddered and Bridget failed to suppress a grin. 'I manage to keep the mouse population down and there are no rats, but the bats are protected. I can't touch them and wouldn't want to.'

'But there *is* something that bothers you, isn't there? And it's obviously not bats.'

'No, I love the bats.' Bridget was silent for a moment, then said, 'You asked me if the Hall is haunted. I have no reason to believe it is, but if you'd asked me if *Queenie* was haunted, well, that would have been harder to answer.'

Jane turned and stared at Bridget's profile. 'Now you have my attention.'

'Queenie lived the life of a recluse. I cleaned and mended things, kept the freezer stocked, saw to her meals. There were no visitors. Queenie said everyone was dead, which wasn't actually true. Nurse Kemp's grandmother was an old friend. They were at drama school together but lost touch.'

'Nurse Kemp was the last to care for her?'

'That's right. Queenie and I lived at opposite ends of the house and rarely saw each other. She preferred to leave me notes, so I kept out of her way. To all intents and purposes, Queenie lived alone. But...' Bridget paused to consider 'There was something about her manner...' She shook her head. 'I'm probably reading too much into it.'

'I doubt it. You're not the type.'

'You're right, I'm not. Okay, since you asked... When he was young, my brother Sean had an imaginary friend called Robin. Sean liked to play on his own – had to really, because I was nine years older and refused to play with small boys.'

'Maybe that's why he invented Robin.'

'Probably. So Sean played on his own, but he never seemed lonely or even solitary. Because he *wasn't* alone. Not really.'

'And that's how Queenie struck you?'

'Yes. So when she hinted that the Hall was haunted, I could almost believe it was true, because it seemed true for *Queenie*.'

Jane nodded. 'That was one of the things about her writing. She made you see what she saw. It's a kind of telepathy. All good writers can do it. So you think Queenie might have created her own Robin. A constant companion.'

'Well, she never *said* anything about him.'

'You think he was male?'

'No, not necessarily, but Queenie never had many female friends. She seemed to have a knack for alienating them. Sleeping with their husbands, I expect.'

'So I've heard,' Jane said grimly.

'All I'm saying is, if Queenie invented an imaginary friend, I think he would be male.'

'That makes sense. It's probably just her name, but when I think of Queenie, I think of Elizabeth I. The aged monarch surrounded by sycophantic male courtiers.'

'She died alone though. Wouldn't even let Ros Kemp sit with her.'

'That's strange. Most people dread dying alone.'

'Maybe she wasn't,' Bridget said simply. 'Perhaps she thought her friend was with her at the end.'

'And you know nothing about him, not even that he was male.'

'Nor that Queenie believed in him. It's just an odd feeling I used to get.'

'You'd known her for many years and you strike me as an observant sort of person. Intuitive. Someone who picks up on things.'

Bridget smiled. 'Queenie once said, "Not much gets past *you*." That was the nearest she ever got to paying me a compliment.'

'In that case maybe there *is* something in it. The imaginary friend, I mean. I think we can dismiss ghosts.'

'It was the way she'd smile sometimes. For no apparent reason. And then her eyes would mist over... I thought it must be an old lover. Someone special who died a long time ago.'

Jane immediately thought of her father, but struggled to believe Queenie could have cherished Nigel's memory for forty years. She dismissed the idea. If Queenie chose to reminisce, she would have been spoiled for choice.

'Nearly there,' Bridget announced as she turned onto a muddy, rutted track. After a few minutes she hauled the wheel round and drove through open wrought iron gates, then along a curving drive. Jane leaned forward eagerly but Wyngrave Hall was obscured by tall shrubs and trees on both sides.

As Bridget drove slowly over the gravel, Jane was aware of feeling something more than curiosity. She was excited to see the ancient home of Queenie Brooke-Bennet, one that, in an alternative universe perhaps, could have been hers.

As she parked the car, Bridget craned her head and cast an experienced eye up at the sky. 'Rain on the way, I'd say. Would you like to see the grounds first?'

'Sorry, Bridget, but I'm no gardener. I'd just like to see the house, if you'd be so kind.' Jane sensed her disappointment and added, 'If the weather holds, you could show me round later?'

They got out of the car and approached the house. As she looked up and surveyed the front of Wyngrave Hall, Jane noted the silence that enveloped the Hall. No traffic was audible, there was no sound of neighbours strimming or children playing and no dogs barked. As her ears became attuned to the silence, Jane realised there was in fact a tapestry of small sounds: a breeze rustled through leaves, birds sang from treetops and chimneys, others twittered in hedges. A faint hum could be traced to bees visiting early summer flowers. Jane couldn't remember the last time she'd seen a bee, let alone heard one.

She had visited many properties like Wyngrave Hall, mostly owned by the National Trust and restored to reflect buildings of the Tudor and Jacobean age as they were at that time. They didn't look new, but nor did they look neglected like Wyngrave Hall, its pale, almost colourless stone eroded by centuries of weather. Even the massive oak door looked bleached with age. Jane was startled by the harsh call of a crow. Looking up, she noticed several red roof tiles were askew and a tall barley sugar chimney leaned precariously. Jane thought of Queenie in her last days, frail and withdrawn, living in one room, knowing her beloved home was gradually falling into ruin; knowing time had run out for her to repair it; knowing time had simply run out.

Standing beside Jane as she surveyed the building, Bridget said, 'There's a lot to be done. Queenie and I devised a programme of renovations, then she was diagnosed. She lost heart after that. We carried on working on her ideas until she was no longer up to it. It provided a distraction, but she genuinely wanted the house to be safe and comfortable for whoever came next.'

'It's beautiful. Estate agents would describe it as *mellow*, wouldn't they, but to me it looks so... *sad*. Faded. And fragile.'

'Like poor old Queenie. The march of time. It's been a constant battle and perhaps we're losing, but I still love the old place.'

Aware she'd been disparaging Bridget's home as well as Queenie's, Jane said, 'It must have been a wonderful family home once.'

'Oh, yes. It cries out for people.'

'Well, there's only me, I'm afraid. *If* I took it on,' Jane added hastily. She turned to Bridget. 'Are you interested in staying on as a tenant?'

'If I could keep my old job, yes, I'd love to stay on at Wyngrave and I'd love to see our plans put into practice. They were mostly mine anyway. And *something* needs to be done if the poor old place is to survive another five hundred years. Or even fifty.' Bridget pointed at the climbing plants twining round the mullioned windows. 'Those climbers aren't doing the fabric of the building any good, but Queenie wouldn't let me touch them.'

'They're magical! They make the Hall look like something out of a fairy tale. The thickness of those trunks! They must be so old.'

'You've come at just the right time for the wisteria.'

'The dangling white flowers?'

'The flowers come before the leaves. You don't often see the white variety. The lilac version is more common. I must get up there and pull down some of that ivy before it takes over. There's always so much to do at this time of year.'

'Queenie's plans… How was she going to fund them?'

'She was going to spend her life's savings because, as she said, she had no one to leave money to. She was also going to sell some paintings. I don't know if any are particularly valuable, but there are a lot, some contemporary with the house.'

Jane continued to gaze up at the building, wondering already about the views from the upper windows. 'It's so *big*, Bridget! It would be ridiculous for me to take it on, just me on my own. As you say, the house needs a family.'

'I didn't say family, I said people. The Hall would divide up quite easily into three or four units without spoiling the integrity of the house. Queenie wasn't interested in sharing her home. She said living with the past was company enough, but I always wondered about turning it into a house-share for single women. People do that sort of thing now, don't they?'

'Yes, they do. Few women can afford to live alone. I've always thought it was a very sensible solution, if you could find the right people.' The first drops of rain began to fall. 'You were right!' Jane exclaimed. 'Here comes the rain. I imagine the roof leaks?'

'Not a *lot*,' Bridget replied with a smile. 'It depends on the direction of the wind. But there are some strategically placed buckets.' As the rain began to fall in earnest, she said, 'Come on. Time for the tour.'

Bridget headed for the front door, fishing in her backpack for the large iron key. As she was about to insert it, she turned. Jane was startled by the intensity of her shrewd blue eyes. 'This door was made five hundred years ago. The oak it was made from would have been two or three hundred years old. Maybe more.' She laid a hand reverently on the wood. 'This door is *history*.' Without waiting for a response, Bridget bowed her head and inserted the huge key into the lock. She turned it, pushed the heavy door open and indicated with her hand. 'After you.' Jane stepped across the threshold, into the Great Hall.

She thought she was prepared. She'd researched the history of Wyngrave and made notes, as was her habit. She'd examined the blurred black and white photos. All useful research, she'd persuaded herself, for fiction, not life. As she stepped into the dim flag-stoned hall and felt the heat of the log fire embrace her; as she inhaled a mixture of woodsmoke, beeswax and lavender; as the deep silence of centuries enfolded her, Jane Summers was quite certain she did not believe in ghosts.

Something else she did not believe in (and M J Somerville would have scorned to write about) was love at first sight.

30ᵗʰ June 2019

Hi Susie & Maeve

Sorry for the long silence but life has been complicated and very challenging. I haven't felt like writing about the divorce but it's all over now. I'm single and we have a buyer for the flat. Duncan has moved in with his girlfriend, so I'm on my own, having a massive clear-out which is deeply therapeutic. I've realised I don't use or even look at much of the stuff I own, so most it is going, apart from my books. Good riddance to all the junk!

The other reason I've found it hard to write is, I've had some news that will no doubt strike you as very strange. Good news, I think, but I'm still not quite sure. Time will tell, I suppose.

In the last few weeks I've often thought of Alison. When she knew she was dying, she used to say, "But you must live!" And I knew I wasn't living, not really. You must have known too. I pretended it was a lack of funds, a lack of time and energy, but I knew I was in an old, tired marriage. I think I guessed Duncan was seeing someone when he started being nicer to me and paying compliments. Maeve, you once said that was an infallible sign. When they change for the better, you said, "They've either found God or a mistress." Well, it wasn't God.

When I wasn't sobbing into my G & T, I tried to see the divorce as an opportunity. A new start. Then a real opportunity presented itself. The weirdest thing! Brace yourselves... A famous author I've never met died and left me a Tudor house in Essex. Not mock-Tudor. Tudor!! It's called Wyngrave Hall. I can't bring myself to tell you how much it's worth, but it doesn't actually matter because under the terms of the bequest, I can never sell.

Wyngrave Hall was the home of a writer, Q. Brooke-Bennet, famous in her day. Notorious, in fact. She knew my parents and my mother edited some of her early work. Long story short – Queenie left the house to me because of the connection with my parents. So far, so fairy-tale, but there are conditions to my ownership. Not only can I never sell, I must live there for at least half the year.

I was all set to turn it down because of the ludicrous conditions attached, not to mention a sitting tenant who's been there for years. But I went to view it, just out of curiosity, and when I saw the house, I changed my mind. Completely and immediately. Alison would have whooped with laughter. I wish she could have been there. I wish you all could have been there to see me make an absolute fool of myself, falling in love with a house. I haven't lived in a house since I was a small child! But I've accepted the bequest and – ta-dah! – I'm going to be Mistress of Wyngrave Hall. (Good title for a book.)

Queenie also left me some money for the maintenance of the Hall and I'm going to need every penny. I've decided to retain Bridget (the tenant) and continue to employ her as gardener/handywoman. She seems very nice, efficient and knows the house really well.

I shall have two further tenants. We'll almost be a women's commune. Alison would have approved. I'm also planning to earn some income eventually from a cottage in the grounds. Which is just as well. My editor has rejected the remaining Whirligig books and now we're "in negotiations" about a new series and a new pen name, both of which make my heart sink, but I do need the cash.

So I'm going to be a very upmarket landlady. The Hall is already divided up informally into three units. The upstairs area, which is the largest and has views of the grounds and woodland beyond. (That's mine.) Then there's downstairs where Queenie lived once she became too infirm to manage the stairs, and there's the "staff wing", as Bridget calls it, where she's lived since the old cottage ceased to be watertight.

I asked Bridget how I could go about finding someone to live downstairs. She said depending on how much rent I want, she already knew of someone nice and reliable: a woman who'd worked at the Hall, nursing Queenie in her last illness, but the nurse came with "baggage". I assumed it was going to be a child, but it was her grandmother, who is losing her sight. Both women needed to move and the nurse was looking for somewhere suitable for both of them as she'll probably end up being the old lady's carer.

So we all met for lunch at Wyngrave and got on famously. Such interesting women! Poor soon-to-be-blind Sylvia is a retired actress and performed with all the greats. After her second gin she regaled us with scandalous anecdotes! She looked so happy, holding court. So did her granddaughter as she watched.

So it's all settled. There will be four women living at Wyngrave Hall, aged between 39 and 85. At the moment I'm excited, hopeful and very nervous. This is the craziest thing I've ever done, but really, what did my future hold? I was all set to move out of one London flat into another – smaller and cheaper.

Out in the country (but only 20 mins from Colchester Station) there will be little for me to do but write, and write is what I really need to do now to get my career and finances back on track. Fortunately my editor wants me to stay with the Tudors. I was dreading she'd ask me to move into Regency romps or Medieval time-slip, but she's happy for me to stay with mysteries. She wants me to come up with a crime-busting duo, an Elizabethan Holmes and Watson. I'm fighting for a m/f couple but my editor is unconvinced. I'm not giving up yet. I wondered about a midwife or female herbalist. The latter would know all about poisons.

Have I gone completely mad? Possibly. But if it all goes wrong, I just move out, the solicitor sells the Hall, evicts the tenants and I go back to flat-hunting.

Wish me well, my dears, and come and see me in my new home! I don't really know what I'm doing with my new life, but I'm fairly sure Alison would have called it "living".

All love
J
xxx

PART TWO

3

Why this is very midsummer madness.

Twelfth Night

Thus, to my astonishment, I found myself mistress of Wyngrave Hall.

It took a while to sink in that I was not "just visiting". Even surrounded by cardboard boxes labelled in my own hand, I couldn't help thinking my presence at the Hall was part of a long and particularly arduous research trip. Over the years I'd visited many Tudor and Jacobean houses in various states of preservation and dilapidation. What I'd never done was stay in one, let alone one that had been converted to a twenty-first century home.

I wasn't interested in many of Queenie's books, but her bookshelves would solve a problem I had long wrestled with. My books had of necessity been double-shelved in our flat and Duncan predicted that one day the floor would give way and my book collection would descend on the elderly couple below.

Queenie had bookcases in almost every room and she had set aside one room upstairs as a library, which I decided to use as a study. I got rid of my tatty Ikea desk and sat, awestruck, at a huge Jacobean table that was too heavy to move, even with Bridget's help. So it stayed where it was and I sat there in front of my laptop, feeling incongruous, gazing out distractedly through mullioned windows.

The garden was laid out before me. Gravel paths followed a geometric pattern and led to benches and arbours resting against crumbling brick walls where climbers and fruit trees had been trained: a fig of great age that looked like the Giant's Beanstalk and an apricot that had started to fruit prolifically since our summers had become warmer. Over the walls I could see the orchard where Bridget had allowed the grass to grow longer. Miniature fruits were starting to swell. Beyond the orchard I could see the mossy remains of an old moat, empty now but for a trickle of water in winter, Bridget said, followed by swathes of snowdrops and daffodils, then primroses in spring.

Some might have said the paths needed weeding, but I knew Bridget did this regularly and anything left to grow was in fact meant to be there. There were thymes and chamomiles and an invasive daisy with an unpronounceable name that I was determined to learn. I'd mastered Latin mottoes for work, so surely botanic Latin couldn't be too much of a stretch?

I wandered around the house, often accompanied by Bridget, making notes of jobs to do, things to be moved, things to be sold, things to be given away. The Hall might not be mine to sell, but the contents were. Queenie had left me some money, but when that ran out, I'd have to live on the rent from my tenants and whatever I could earn from my books.

So the urgent need to launch a new series nagged at me, but what better inspiration could I have, living in such a setting? Nevertheless, I was constantly tired and irritable, angry with Duncan that I had to re-invent myself as a singleton and angry with my publishers' insistence I reinvent myself as a writer. I felt as if I was in free-fall, wondering when and how I would land and who, apart from me, would pick up the pieces.

I turned to Bridget for companionship as well as advice and she proved invaluable: calm, practical, as solid and handsome as a piece of Jacobean furniture. In the presence of Bridget's quiet confidence and good sense, I coped, but if she was in Colchester doing errands, or if she spent the day outdoors working in the garden, I was left to my own devices in a very old, mostly dark house, where the only sounds I heard apart from the tap of my laptop keys were the ticking of a longcase clock and the crackle and shift of logs on the fire we lit every day in the Great Hall as back-up for the ineffectual central heating.

We looked forward to the arrival of Sylvia Marlow and her granddaughter, Rosamund. I'd been concerned that Sylvia would find it difficult downsizing from her cottage of thirty years to an en-suite bedroom and communal living areas, but she was all for a clean sweep and liked to regale us with the principles of Swedish death cleaning which, she assured Rosamund, would simplify "clearing up" after her demise. To listen to Sylvia, you would have thought death was imminent. As far as we knew, it wasn't, but blindness was. Rosamund said Sylvia's enthusiasm for death cleaning was her grandmother's way of getting rid of books she could no longer read, photo albums she could no longer see and ornaments she dare no longer dust. Nominally preparing for death, Sylvia was in fact bracing herself to face the approaching darkness.

Had I faced up to my future with as much courage and style? It was to be very different from the one I'd planned. Some might say I'd gone to extraordinary lengths to avoid the lonely life of a middle-aged divorcée. Others would perhaps admire my positive and creative attitude to the huge upheavals in my life, personal and professional. But it was some time before I admitted to myself that I disliked spending a day working at home on my own, not because I feared to be alone in the ancient house, but because I feared I *wasn't.*

The silence at Wyngrave Hall was strange after decades of co-habi-tation and twenty-four hour London traffic, but it didn't bother me. The idiosyncratic noises the house made – creaking floorboards, rat-tling windowpanes, the penetrating tick of the clock – soon became familiar. I developed a fondness for them. Newly divorced and frankly lonely, it was almost as if I wished to engage in a dialogue with the ancient house. If I sensed anything, it was reassuringly inanimate. It was just the fabric of the building adjusting to weather conditions, or the comings and goings of its new mistress.

Once I recognised all the noises the house made, the soft coun-terpoint to my very quiet life was almost comforting. Occasionally I would think of the generations of families whose tread had made the oak stairs sag, whose boots had worn the flagstones smooth. I was constantly aware of the history of the house and its previous owners, but none of this accounted for the sensation I had of being *watched.*

Do we all possess this animal instinct to some degree? Perhaps it's more developed in women than men, as a sort of primitive survival mechanism. If I'd felt watched all the time, I would have ascribed the sensation to being surrounded by the many portraits that adorned the walls. Some sitters had gazed directly at the artist, so their eyes appeared to follow me as I moved around, but others stared into the distance, preoccupied with their own importance. But the sense that I was being watched, the feeling I was not alone, was intermittent. It came and went, like a cat wandering in and out of the room.

To begin with it was just a vague feeling. Even when it became more than a feeling, I didn't set any store by the evidence because I assumed the culprit was Bridget.

One of the many treasures Queenie left behind was a magnificent chess set. I've been a fan of the game since I read *Alice Through the Looking-Glass* and I persuaded my father to teach me "the game of kings". Playing chess together was one of the few things we'd shared. I always suspected he let me win, but he claimed I was eventually such a good player, he had no need to give me an advantage.

I left Queenie's set on display in the Great Hall where I could appreciate the workmanship that had gone into the pieces. One day as I walked through the hall, I happened to glance down at the chess board and noticed that a white pawn had been moved forward, as if to initiate a game. I was amused that Bridget had made this opening gambit and I couldn't resist bending to move a black pawn in response. Later she responded with another move, so I did likewise. This went on for a couple of days and each time I passed the board, white had moved, often devastatingly, and I was soon struggling to stay in the game. Pieces gradually disappeared from the board until one morning, I found my poor King lying on his side, vanquished, while the White Queen towered over him. It was checkmate.

Perversely delighted by my defeat, I followed a smell of frying bacon and found the victor in the kitchen, making breakfast.

'Good morning, Bridget. Hail the conquering hero! Or should I say heroine?'

She looked up from the hob. 'I'm sorry?'

'Congratulations on your win. It was a jolly good game. I haven't played in years. That's no excuse though. You beat me soundly.'

Bridget's face looked blank. She turned back to the frying pan, poked her rashers and said, 'Sorry, Jane, I still don't follow. What game?'

I knew then. Well, I didn't *know* exactly, it was more a sort of creeping dread. Nevertheless, I persisted with my inquiry, knowing already it was futile.

'Chess. The board in the hall.'

'Oh, that! Yes, Queenie used to play. On her own. I always thought I should learn so I could give her a game, but I never got round to it.'

'You don't play?'

'No. Do you?'

'Yes. But I just lost.'

Bridget laughed. '*Can* you lose if you're playing yourself?'

'You didn't move the pieces at all?'

'Wouldn't know where to move them to.'

'And you haven't been… dusting.'

'Afraid not. That rarely makes it to the top of my To Do list. I've cooked too much bacon. Would you like some?'

'No, thanks,' I said feeling queasy.

'There's tea in the pot.'

'Thanks, but I've just remembered an urgent call I need to make. I'll have breakfast later.'

As Bridget piled bacon onto her plate, I fled through the house, ignoring the chess pieces in disarray and took refuge in the library. I closed the door firmly behind me and sat at my desk, staring blindly through the window. My heart was beating fast and I could feel a tension headache coming on. I closed my eyes and listened to the tiny sounds of the ivy and wisteria scratching at the windowpanes as the wind agitated them. You can't see the wind, but you can see what it does…

I opened my eyes. There had to be a rational explanation.

Evidently I had played both black and white and had somehow managed to forget moving the white pieces. I'd also managed to play a winning game far beyond my experience and expertise. Black had been thrashed and apparently I had done the thrashing.

There *had* to be a rational explanation, even if the rational explanation was that I was going mad.

If Bridget and I hadn't already discussed Queenie's imaginary friend, I might have broached the subject of my unease with her, though somehow I doubt it. There really was no way to tackle it without sounding deranged. Bridget might give notice and I feared I couldn't make a go of Wyngrave without her inside knowledge and support, so I kept my wild imaginings to myself.

I am not by nature fanciful. Some reviewers have claimed I'm too much of a historian to be a good storyteller and it's true, I am happiest re-imagining the lives of historical figures, people who lived. I'm much less comfortable inventing characters, but that appeared to be what I had done.

I tried to dismiss my misgivings and resolved to settle down to work. I can be untidy, but at the end of the day, however late, I clear up and put my current research books back on the shelf. I collect my papers together, placing them in neat piles. It's all part of a ritual that allows me to emerge gradually from the all-engrossing world of the book.

There's one characteristic I've developed after many years of working with ancient and valuable tomes: I never leave books open, unless I'm actually working on them. At the end of the day, I habitually shut all books to protect them from light, dust, insects, damp air and spillages. So when one morning I approached my desk and found my *Complete Works of Shakespeare* lying open, I simply wondered why Bridget of all people had been consulting it. I knew I hadn't left the book open because I don't do that, and I've always taken particular care of my *Complete Works* because it was a school prize, of sentimental value to me.

I concluded Bridget had wanted to look something up. A crossword clue? She was not a fan of the internet, so she might consult a book rather than Google, but I'd never seen her do a crossword. Bridget didn't often sit down and when finally she did, she would sprawl in an armchair in front of the fire and fall asleep within minutes.

I said nothing. The library doubled as my study, but it was to be a resource for all to use. Bridget entered to light the fire and, at the end of the day, check the windows. I knew I was going to have to be less territorial if communal living was to work.

Again, I said nothing when I found Milton's *Paradise Lost* open on the seat of one of the library armchairs, but a seed of doubt was sown. Milton? *Bridget?* When the next day an expensive leather-bound edition of Montaigne's Essays lay open on the floor, I decided I must say something at an appropriate moment. I'd concluded Bridget must be studying for an Open University degree and, whilst I deplored her untidiness, I was pleased to think we might have more to discuss than Wyngrave and its gardens. But still I deferred.

Things came to a head when I approached my desk one morning and found an Agatha Christie open and lying face-down on top of my papers. It was *The Body in the Library*. Incensed, I snatched up the book and closed it.

I resolved to speak to Bridget, but even as I made the decision, I felt apprehensive. Nothing in my experience of her led me to believe she was a reader, but the culprit *had* to be Bridget simply because there was no one else, not unless I was sleepwalking at night and littering the library with open books.

But I wonder now... Did I know, at some level, even before Sylvia and Rosamund moved in, that Queenie's imaginary friend might *not* be imaginary? Perhaps I did, or I maybe I suspected, but I wasn't going to admit it. Not to Bridget.

Not even to myself.

I was brooding in the kitchen over a pot of coffee when Bridget came in from the garden. She'd removed her boots in the scullery and padded over to the sink to put the kettle on.

'Are you after coffee?' I asked. 'I just made a pot. You're welcome to share.'

'Thanks,' she said, sinking onto a chair next to me at the table. She poured herself black coffee and downed it quickly.

'Tough morning?' I asked.

'Not too bad. The weeds are growing fast. The thing is to get in quick with a hoe.'

'If you say so.'

Bridget smiled. 'Do you even know what a hoe is?'

'Of course I do!' I snorted. 'The Elizabethans used them. If it was around in the sixteenth century, I know about it. It's the twenty-first I find challenging.'

'Me too. By the way, I don't use chemical weedkillers, so you'll have to tolerate a few weeds or get a new gardener.'

'Fine by me. Aren't weeds good for bees?'

'When they flower. You know about bees then?'

'The Elizabethans kept them and made mead,' I said, pouring us both more coffee. 'Queen Elizabeth had her own recipe.'

'At the end of the summer, I'll take you upstairs and show you the Ghost Garden.'

'*Ghost* Garden?'

'It's just what I call it. It's a garden that's no longer there. I don't know when anyone first noticed it. Maybe the drought of 1976? The big lawn – bane of my life – used to be an Elizabethan formal garden.'

'A Knot Garden?'

'That's right. It was dug up to grow food in World War One, then it was turfed over for good after World War Two. I don't think anyone knew about it until the lawn started to die back in the hot weather, then this beautiful pattern started to emerge. The grass dies where the paths used to be. If you stand at the library window after a spell of dry weather, you can see the outline of the old garden. Then when the rains come, it disappears again.'

'And you called it the Ghost Garden?'

'Well, somebody did, before Queenie's time. We just inherited the name, along with all the other Wyngrave baggage. But the knot garden's magical, the way it comes and goes. We know it's there, but it can't be seen.'

I got up and put my empty mug in the dishwasher, thinking about the "Wyngrave baggage". Without looking at her, I said as casually as I could, 'Bridget, have you been doing some studying?'

'No.' She sounded surprised. 'Why do you ask?'

'I wondered if you'd been working in the library.'

'No. I go in there to tend the fire and I check all windows last thing at night, but that's all.'

I closed the dishwasher, leaned against the sink and said, 'So you haven't been browsing at some of the books?

She shook her head. 'I'm not much of a reader, to be honest. I'd never touch Queenie's books anyway. I suppose they're yours now, but the same applies. Queenie and I had a big fall-out over her books.'

'Oh? What happened?'

'Nothing as far as I was concerned, but she accused me of leaving open books lying around, which I would no more do than leave garden tools— Jane, are you all right? Did I say something—'

Groping for a chair, I moved back to the table and sat down. 'I'm fine. It was just a surprise... when you said that. Such an odd coincidence.' I closed my eyes, took a deep breath, then opened them again. I tried to smile. 'You see, *I'm* finding books left open on my desk. And on chairs. Even the floor.'

'Books you use for work?'

'No. That's how I know it's not me being untidy.'

Bridget scoffed. 'You *aren't* untidy.'

'Exactly.'

'Well, it's not me, Jane.'

'I wish it were! That would solve the mystery. Do we have a cleaner yet?' I asked in mounting desperation.

'No. It's on my very long *To Do* list.'

'So the only people going in to the library are you and me?'

'Yes.'

'Wasn't there an electrician recently?'

'Last week, but he didn't do anything in the library.'

'And I doubt he'd be a fan of Montaigne's *Essays*,' I added gloomily. 'When did Queenie accuse you of... disturbing her books?'

'Years ago. I still lived in the cottage then, but I'd started to do jobs for her indoors. She couldn't really cope, so I became a sort of housekeeper. She was always very particular about her book collection.'

'Writers are. Books are precious things to us.'

'I realised that, and I was pretty miffed at the accusation, but when I told her it wasn't me, she just accepted it. Apologised, in fact, and never mentioned it again. I'd forgotten all about that row until you mentioned your books... So it's happening to you too?' I nodded. 'That's weird.'

'If you think about it long enough, it's worse than weird. You're *sure* no one else has used the library? Mr Putnam hasn't been snooping around, checking up on the place?'

'No, and only you and I have keys, so no one gets in without one of us letting them in. I keep all the doors locked during the day because people assume an old house like this contains valuables. I suggest you do the same, Jane. You can't be too careful. Burglaries happen in broad daylight nowadays.'

'Don't worry, you don't need to convince me about security. I'm finding it quite scary, adjusting.'

'There's bound to be an explanation,' Bridget said. 'Something we haven't thought of,' she added, without meeting my eye.

There was a long silence in which, I was sure, we both failed to think of anything resembling an explanation. Eventually, I asked in what I hoped was a casual tone, 'Have *your* things ever... moved about?'

'No, never.'

'Maybe it's a poltergeist,' I said cheerfully. 'You know, annoying, but harmless. If you believe in such things.'

'Do you?'

'I *didn't*.'

There was another long silence. Bridget folded her arms and scowled at her empty coffee mug, deep in thought. When her head suddenly shot up, I waited, hopeful and expectant.

'Do you sleepwalk?'

'I never used to.'

'Sometimes people sleepwalk, do things, then go back to bed, none the wiser.'

'Yes, I considered that, but I don't think I'd pick up an Agatha Christie, even in my sleep. I'm not a fan.'

'Which one?'

'I'm sorry?'

'Which Agatha Christie?'

'*The Body in the Library*.'

Bridget laughed out loud, then looked sheepish. 'Sorry. I have a warped sense of humour.'

'So does the poltergeist, apparently. Well, I won't keep you any longer. I'm sure you want to get back to the weeds. But if you see anything else untoward, could you let me know? Anything odd. I promise I won't think you're crazy.'

'And you'll tell me too?'

'If you promise not to laugh.'

She smiled. 'I'll try.'

'I don't think we should mention this to Sylvia and Rosamund, do you? Sylvia's got quite enough to cope with, losing her sight, and I wouldn't want either of them thinking I'm paranoid. Or unhinged.'

'I won't mention it. See you later.'

As she headed for the door, I called, 'Bridget, did Queenie ever seem *frightened*?'

'No, never. Well, not until she got the cancer diagnosis. That rattled her, but I'd say she was more angry than frightened. Worried about pain, of course, but once they knew it was terminal, her pain was easier to manage. Medically, I mean.'

'So although you said she was possibly *haunted*, she never actually seemed frightened to you?'

'No. Definitely not.'

'Well, that's *something*,' I replied, though exactly what it was, I really couldn't have said.

Unsettled, irritated, I decided to avoid the library for a day and settled down to a tedious job I'd been putting off: going through Queenie's papers. Bridget had made a start by sorting everything into three boxes labelled *Wyngrave Hall*, *Writing* and *Personal*. She said Queenie didn't allow anyone to write her biography because too many people would be hurt. She'd destroyed a lot of incriminating evidence, but she hoped that at some point someone would re-assess her work, so she'd maintained a chaotic archive that might appeal to a PhD student looking for a colourful thesis.

There was naturally some overlap between *Writing* and *Personal* and Bridget had left it to me to sort through Queenie's papers for the final time. I started with *Personal* because it was the smallest box and I thought it would be the most interesting.

Bridget had collected letters together with rubber bands so they were sorted by correspondent, not date, but Queenie had kept all personal letters in their envelopes, neatly slit open with a paper knife. Most of the envelopes were hand-written and Bridget hadn't indicated the name of the correspondent. Finding out who the letters were from was clearly my first job. As I removed them from the box and laid them out on the floor, I recognised one hand with a jolt that felt like a small electric shock.

There was a small pack of letters, perhaps ten, all uniform, all written in black ink on what looked like Basildon Bond. I didn't need to look inside the envelopes to see who they were from. These letters were from my mother.

When the shock waves had subsided, I removed the rubber band and looked at the postmarks. All the letters had been sent during a period of a few months, the months before my mother took her life. The last letter was sent three weeks before she died. Overwhelmed, I set them down.

Felicity had never had reason to write to me – she died when I was twelve – and I had never seen or held a letter from her, not even her suicide note, but I knew her handwriting from birthday cards and inscriptions in treasured books. To come across letters from her should have been a cause for joy, but they were letters addressed to Queenie. What could they be other than letters in which she begged the other woman to relinquish her hold on Nigel so the marriage could be saved? Perhaps she even hinted she was cracking up.

I couldn't bear to read them. Why on earth had Queenie kept them? Even if she'd wanted to gloat in triumph at the time, surely once Felicity had died, Queenie would have destroyed the correspondence. She must have felt bad about how things ended and if she'd destroyed other embarrassing material to protect people, why had she kept these incriminating letters, letters I was bound to find and which Queenie knew would upset me?

It can't have been malevolence. Queenie had left me Wyngrave Hall as her attempt at atonement. Yet she'd kept my mother's letters and knew I would find them…

I gathered up the letters, took them to my bedroom and, shaking, got into the ancient half-tester bed. I sat bolt upright against the dark wooden bedhead, steeling myself – for what, I didn't know.

I thought about the solidity of the carved oak surrounding me, the consummations, births and deaths my bed had witnessed. With four centuries of history at my back, I braced myself and, with shaking fingers, I took the first letter out of its envelope.

I got no further than the first two words. Confused, astonished, I checked the address at the top of the letter. It was my childhood home. I picked up the envelope and peered at the inscription: *Miss Q. Brooke-Bennet*, written in my mother's hand. There could be no mistaking sender or recipient, yet the first letter began, *My darling*.

Shaking violently now, I held the sheets of paper in both hands and forced my eyes to travel over the words Felicity had written to her lover, pleading with her not to end their affair. The first letter, carefully written, promised undying devotion and limitless freedom. The last, an erratic scrawl, berated Queenie for her long silence and hinted darkly at desperation and suicide. In contrast with the effusion of the letters themselves, each was signed, simply, *F*.

I placed each letter back in its envelope, arranged them in date order, then bound them together with their rubber band. I placed them on my bedside table, then lay down under the duvet. I stared up at the window, watching through the lattice of glass diamonds as the pale sky darkened. I listened to the calming sounds of the oak boards creaking, doors opening and closing downstairs, grateful for any distraction, anything that would stem the torrent of my thoughts, which was, in fact, only one thought.

My poor, poor father…
I'm so sorry.
I didn't know.
Why didn't you say?

Anno Domini 1603
Lamentation the First

Alas, I am condemned. No help, no hope doth remain, for I have made enemies, mighty and dreadful.

I dare not say thy name, nor even write it, for who might be listening at the door? Who might enter of a sudden and deprive me of the comforts of my poor candle, my precious paper and ink?

My earthly life I prize at naught. It is but a trifle. I live to protect thee, my dearest love. I live in hope that we might meet once more; that I might see my son again.

Art thou yet living? And is thy name known to my tormentors? I have not uttered it, nor shall I, not even in the sanctuary of my narrow bed. I had rather dash out my brains on these walls that imprison me. But what if I should lose my wits, as I fear I am like to do? Or contract a fever and, raving, call out thy name, thus condemning thee to share my fate? Or a worse.

In silence lies thy safety. So silent shall I be.

4

The web of our life is of a mingled yarn, good and ill together.

All's Well That Ends Well

I must have fallen asleep. When I woke, I couldn't think where I was. Frightened, I sat up and switched the bedside light on automatically, for company. I hadn't done that for a long time, but I remembered that for years after my mother died, I would never go to sleep in the dark. Dark was death and light was life. That's how I saw things when I was twelve.

My eye fell on a photo of young Felicity holding me as a chubby toddler. We were both laughing. My father must have taken the photo. Perhaps he'd made us laugh. I had none of him on display and few had survived the cull of personal belongings after his death. I was surprised to find he'd kept all his wedding photos and many others of Felicity. In my ignorance, I assumed he must have saved them for me, but after she died, he never married again, never even dated anyone as far as I knew. It seemed likely now he'd never stopped loving her.

I closed my eyes again. Was there a single thought, a single assumption about my parents – about *Queenie* – that I wouldn't have to revise?

I'd railed mentally at Queenie for leaving my mother's desperate love letters for me to find, then realised she would have no idea Nigel had protected me from the truth. Even if I hadn't known as a child the cause of my mother's despair, Queenie probably assumed Nigel had told me as an adult. She, with her own lax morals, would never imagine that Nigel might choose to protect his wife and shield

55

a grief-stricken daughter from the very awkward truth – and at his own expense.

But why had he kept Queenie's love letters, the letters I'd found after his death, but hadn't read? Had he wanted me to read them? Was that how I was supposed to discover the truth about my mother's suicide? Or did he just want me to know that Felicity died for love? That for her, life without it was unbearable?

I would never know, but Queenie knew why Felicity had taken her life and she'd done what she could by way of reparation. She'd left me Wyngrave and the money to preserve it. She'd also left me my mother's letters. In the light of Felicity's suicide, I supposed Queenie had felt unable to destroy them and she could hardly return them to my bereaved father. Perhaps Queenie wasn't quite the heartless monster I'd taken her for. Nor was my mother the hapless victim of Nigel's imagined philandering.

I sat motionless on the bed, but the room appeared to rotate and I began to feel physically sick. I needed to eat, but instead I considered packing a suitcase, leaving a note for Bridget, calling a taxi and running away to a very distant hotel – somewhere in the Highlands, or perhaps Cornwall. I consoled myself with this fantasy for a few moments, then realised my plan of escape was thwarted by the imminent arrival of Sylvia Marlow and her granddaughter. Running away was not an option. I was mistress of Wyngrave Hall and for now it was my home. It was my duty to greet my new housemates and make them feel welcome. I believed fervently it was what my father would have expected of me. Somehow that helped. It drew me slightly closer to a man I had apparently never really known.

Besides, how could I possibly run away? I hadn't solved Queenie's mystery.

Rosamund Kemp sent her grandmother off to stay with friends while she packed what still remained in the bungalow, then delegated the removal to a man with a van. She arrived in her Mini which she said contained her own worldly goods and we unloaded a surprising number of cardboard boxes and bin liners from the little car. 'They're like the Tardis,' she said proudly. 'So much bigger on the inside.'

Rosamund no longer looked the pre-Raphaelite beauty I remembered. Her auburn curls were now scraped back into a practical ponytail and she looked tired. The big clear-out at the bungalow had evidently been emotionally taxing. I imagined it had been even worse for Sylvia, but Rosamund claimed her grandmother had been surprisingly ruthless sifting through a lifetime's belongings.

She supervised the unpacking in Sylvia's bed-sitting room and we did our best to make it look welcoming. Rosamund had requested that any spare bookcases or shelves be put in Sylvia's room. 'Not for books. We got rid of those for obvious reasons, but she's brought a lot of photos. Mementoes of shows and people she's worked with. First Night cards from special people and a few awards too. She might not be able to see them very clearly now, but they mean home to her. She used to sit and look at them. Now she likes to sit and hold them. I suspect she actually talks to the photos. There are some lovely ones of my mum. In fact, you can hardly tell which are Mum and which are young Sylvia. Both so beautiful. Peas in a pod.'

Bridget and I had brought down a revolving mahogany bookcase from the library which we thought would hold a large amount of stuff in a small space and give Sylvia a changing display. We also moved a small dresser from the kitchen. Its narrow shelves were ideal for photos and bric-a-brac. Bridget had raided the garden for flowers and set out several vases so that the room was filled with scent. I'd found a Victorian découpaged screen and set it beside Sylvia's single bed, in case she wanted to subdivide the room. We did our best to make it look homely, but Bridget shook her head and said, 'There's not a lot of space. I mean, it's a good-sized room, but Sylvia's stuff fills it.'

'She'll *love* it,' Rosamund assured us. 'She was always complaining about the bungalow being too big. Don't forget, she's used to making a tiny dressing-room into a home-from-home.' Bridget still looked unconvinced but Rosamund said sternly, 'If my grandmother had gone into a care home, she would have been allowed one suitcase of belongings. Trust me, Sylvia will think this is Heaven, especially when she sees Queenie's little fridge.'

'That was Queenie's?' I asked, surprised.

'I told Bridget to hang on to it when you were clearing out.'

Bridget smiled. 'I always wondered why Queenie wanted a fridge in her bedroom at the end.'

'Champagne, darling,' Rosamund boomed, in imitation, I supposed, of Queenie's imperial manner. 'She kept it stocked with mini bottles of champagne and canned Margaritas. I also managed to squeeze in some milk for our tea, which saved me a trek to the kitchen. It will be ideal for Sylvia. She likes to be independent. She'd never dream of asking anyone to make her a drink, so I thought she could keep milk and a few cans in her own little fridge and have a travel kettle. It can all go behind the screen if she wants to keep the sitting area nice.' Rosamund surveyed the finished room and nodded. 'I bet Sylvia says it reminds her of some cosy theatrical digs, which she absolutely *loved*. You'll see. Actors are brilliant at playing house.'

When Sylvia moved in twenty-four hours later, her lined face looked tired and apprehensive. Bridget and I hovered at a discreet distance while Rosamund led Sylvia into her room. We heard gasps of astonishment alternating with squeals of delight, then a gushing exclamation: 'Oh, it reminds me of my wonderful digs in Stratford! We had a screen *just* like that! It was quite charming, but Elsie Stephens draped her clothes all over it. Too lazy to hang anything up. And you say I've got all this to myself?'

'And I'm just next door,' Rosamund replied. 'In my old room.'

'The one you used when you were nursing Queenie?'

'The same. Knock on the wall and I'll hear you.'

'Look at that lovely window! I can open it and listen to the birds. You see, I shan't miss my garden at all ... And *look* at this vase of flowers... Oh, and another. It's like a first night! Flowers everywhere!' We heard Sylvia's voice trail off into a choking sob and Bridget and I looked at each other anxiously, then Sylvia blew her nose and said, 'This is absolute *Heaven*! I don't know what I've done to deserve such kindness.'

'Check out the contents of your mini fridge,' Rosamund replied briskly. 'And you'll find glasses in the dresser cupboard. I'm summoning Jane and Bridget now. Time for a celebration, I think.'

She appeared in the doorway, beaming with relief and mouthed 'Told you so,' then she beckoned us in. Sylvia turned round to face us holding a bottle of champagne, her face wet with tears. 'Oh, my dears, such a wonderful welcome! Thank you! I don't know what to say...' She thrust the bottle into my hands. 'Jane, will you be mother?' Without waiting for an answer, Sylvia turned away to fetch glasses from her dresser while I set about opening the champagne.

We muddled along quite happily, tired, but companionable. In the beginning everyone was very polite, but soon we began to relax and enjoy each other's company. I got used to Rosamund's dark sense of humour and the tart comments that so amused Bridget, but which Sylvia, out of long habit, ignored. Rosamund's teasing humour allowed Sylvia to feel one of the girls: an equal, despite her advanced age and failing sight. Bridget and I quickly learned that Sylvia would far rather be the butt of someone's jokes than an object of pity.

On fine evenings we gathered in the garden where we'd often find Sylvia sitting on a bench with a rug over her knees, listening to the birds. She was convinced they communicated with each other and said she wished she could learn their language. 'But I know now when it's about to rain. They tell each other, just before it starts. It's uncanny. You hear that song and you know it's time to bring the washing in.'

I would bring out a tray of drinks and Sylvia always acted surprised, as if the nightly ritual was a special treat. If it was wet or too chilly to sit out, we would sit by the fire in the Great Hall. Sylvia would occupy the fireside armchair, happily roasting one side of her face, while the rest of us kept a respectful distance from the crackling logs.

Sylvia had her own television and I'd designated an area off the kitchen, once known as the Housekeeper's Room, for communal viewing, but in fact we usually spent our evenings together in the Hall. Rosamund was always knitting something and we would chat about possible improvements to Wyngrave, or listen to Sylvia's apparently inexhaustible fund of showbiz stories, all entertaining, some slanderous.

But the silence was just as companionable. It wasn't really silence. Logs would shift and spit while Rosamund's knitting needles beat a tiny, constant tattoo. Sylvia and I were always the first to retire, leaving Bridget and Rosamund to watch the fire as it dwindled to ash.

Sylvia's first theatrical love was Shakespeare, so we shared an interest in the Elizabethans and she started listening to audiobooks of my Tudor whodunnits, which she said kept her up late at night. Sylvia wore her learning lightly, but it soon became apparent that over the years she'd amassed a lot of knowledge about Elizabethan actors and was keen to research the history of the house, another interest we shared.

One night when we were sitting round the fire, Sylvia said, 'Jane, I've been meaning to tell you, I came across a lovely story about an actor who vanished during a performance of *Hamlet*.'

'Vanished? You don't mean here?' I asked.

'Yes! Disappeared and was never seen again.'

'Abducted by aliens,' said Ros, not looking up from her knitting.

Sylvia ignored her. 'The story goes that Shakespeare himself stepped into the breach. Well, it *was* one of his parts. The Ghost of Hamlet's father.'

'The actor playing the *ghost* disappeared?' Bridget laughed. 'How very appropriate!'

'Shakespeare's company did put on performances in private houses,' I said. 'Though I haven't found any evidence they ever performed at Wyngrave.'

'But it *could* all be true?' Sylvia asked eagerly.

'It's possible.'

Ros picked up her knitting pattern and studied it. 'But it's only slightly more likely than being abducted by aliens.'

Undaunted, Sylvia said, 'I don't really care if it's true. I love a mystery! The actor playing the ghost of a murdered King completely disappears... It's perfect!' She sat back in her armchair and sighed. 'Such a pity Wyngrave isn't haunted.'

Her wistful comment elicited no response from the assembled company, not even Ros, but Bridget looked up, caught my eye, then quickly looked away again.

One evening I was sitting at the kitchen table, studying my lists, when Rosamund appeared. As she took the kettle to the sink, I stood up and said, 'I'm going to open some wine. Would you like a glass?'

'Sounds great. Thanks. I'm not sure I can find the energy to make tea – and I'm not even working at the moment. Why am I so tired?'

I took glasses out of the cupboard and set them on the table. 'Everything's new. A bit stressful. And I think we often don't know how tired we are until we stop.' I took a bottle of wine out of the fridge and unscrewed the top. As Rosamund sat down at the table, I indicated my lists and said, 'There's so much to do here – renovations, I mean. I've been trying to decide what order to do things in. And how to raise the money.' I poured two glasses of wine and slid one across the table.

'Sell a kidney?'

'I was thinking of Queenie's jewellery, but I think the portraits will raise more. I really need Bridget to hold my hand. She's the one with all the good ideas.'

'But you're the one holding the purse strings. Where is Bridget?'

'Early night. She said she was knackered. She's been clearing the ground to dig our wildlife pond.'

'That sounds strenuous,' Rosamund said, sipping her wine.

'Impossible without a vicious machine called a rotovator.'

'Is that what the noise was?'

I nodded. 'Boudicca had nothing on Bridget wielding this thing. It's something to behold. She's cleared the top level, but underneath she's going through it quite carefully with a fork.'

'Must be back-breaking work.'

'It is, but Bridget has always wanted to make a pond. Apparently they're brilliant for wildlife. We think there might have been a pond there in Tudor times. A stew pond, where they bred and fattened fish for eating.'

'Well, I must get off my butt and go and help her tomorrow,' said Rosamund. 'I need the exercise.'

'Has Sylvia gone to bed?'

'Yes. She was sitting by the remains of the fire, fast asleep, but I woke her up and suggested she'd be more comfortable in bed. And warmer. She feels the cold, even in summer. Poor circulation, and now she can't see very well, she doesn't get much exercise. She's frightened of falling, but hates using her stick.'

'She never complains though. About *anything*. Which is pretty amazing when you consider what she's having to deal with.'

'I used to think she was the last word in resilience,' Rosamund said, her expression serious for once.

'Used to? Is she struggling now? I'm sorry, I didn't realise.'

'Jane, I know you haven't known her long, but has it struck you that she's… deteriorating?'

'No, not at all. I thought she was happy here.'

'She is. Very.' Rosamund lifted her glass and drank. 'But I'm sure something is bugging her.'

'Apart from going blind, you mean?'

'Well, there's no way of knowing what effect that might have, I suppose. Does she seem confused to you?'

'No… Sometimes a bit nervous, perhaps, but I put that down to exhaustion. Negotiating a new property and new people. At her age. I mean, it's not easy for any of us. Even Bridget has got to adjust to new *people*.'

'It's still early days, I suppose,' Rosamund agreed.

'But even if Sylvia does become ill eventually, we all knew the score. That was part of the deal. Perhaps I should say *ideal*. We wanted to create a mutually supportive household of single women. It was actually Bridget's idea, not mine.'

'Was it? I didn't realise.'

'That was how she persuaded me to take it on. At the moment I'm not even the owner of Wyngrave Hall, merely the custodian, so I'm feeling my way. But do feel free to talk honestly about any difficulties that arise. Personally, I'm really enjoying Sylvia's company. I'm very glad Bridget introduced me to you both. But I can see the future looks worrying for you.'

'It's not even Sylvia I'm worried about if I'm honest. It's me.' Rosamund paused and I saw her brace herself. 'Big birthdays have that effect on you, don't they?'

'Have you had a significant birthday? And you didn't *tell* us?'

'It's later this year. I've sworn Sylvia to silence because I don't really feel like celebrating.'

'Oh, I understand, but take heart. You're still the youngest and you always will be.' I topped up our glasses. 'Perhaps *that's* what's bothering Sylvia. Keeping a secret?'

'It's certainly not one of her key skills.'

'I expect she finds it hard, especially as you're all the world to her.'

'And that's quite a responsibility.'

'I bet. I also bet Sylvia loves parties.'

'She does. She likes to dance and after she's had a few, she sings, in a husky baritone.'

'Sounds like another reason for a party.'

'We go to more funerals than parties, these days. Me in my professional capacity, Sylvia burying her mates. It's really depressing. So is turning forty.'

'Don't ask me about fifty.'

'You don't look fifty.'

'And the rest!'

'I would have said you were mid-forties.'

'Thanks. I do dye my hair though.'

'Oh, stop apologising! I've spent most of my life wanting to look like you. Slim, brunette—'

'*Chilli Chocolate.*'

'Shut up. Your hair is lovely, the way it shines and swings. Like a shampoo ad. Mine looks like I've had a serious electric shock.'

'It's *beautiful*, Ros. And so unusual.'

'It's a pain. I'd cut it short, but that looks even worse. It's easier to keep it tidy for work when it's long.'

'Well, I'm told that after sixty, cussedness sets in and you don't care any more.' Rosamund gave me what Sylvia would have called an old-fashioned look. 'Look at it this way, you're still in your thirties and we've got ages to plan a party.'

Ros smiled. 'You missed your vocation, Jane. You're a natural organiser.'

'No, that would be Bridget. *This*,' I said, indicating the A4 pad and wine glass, 'is just a displacement activity. I'm supposed to be planning a series of Tudor novels, but this is what writers do.'

'What is?'

'Renovate a Tudor garden. Plan a wildlife pond. Anything rather than write. We're also good at mending, dusting and cleaning ovens. All displacement activities.'

'Is it actually painful, writing? Something like talking to a therapist?'

'Worse. At least in therapy someone is listening and you know your therapist is on your side. Your laptop just sits there looking blank and bored. If it had arms, it would fold them and snarl, "Entertain me." Don't laugh,' I said in mock outrage. 'Writing's *awful*. Until it isn't.'

'Like nursing. You do it because you have to. I mean, no one does it to get rich, do they? Being a nursing auxiliary is the hardest work you can do for the least money.'

'You sound like you really need a party... Shall we? A small one? We could call it our housewarming party if you want to keep quiet about the big four-o.'

'Sylvia will blab, but still, it's not a bad idea. Embrace the inevitable.'

'Now, now. You're still the baby in the family. Oh... I'm sorry, was that a bit tactless of me? Are you depressed about forty because you haven't started a family yet? But *you* know all the science. Forty is no great age these days.'

'No, it's not that. I have no interest in children. Giving birth, I mean. No, it's *nursing* that's the problem... I think I've had enough. Or rather, I think I've had enough of nursing the elderly. Enough of people dying on me. I'll be looking after an old woman for the rest of her life – and that is what I *want* to do. But I'm not sure I can do that as well as my job. And if something has to go, it's got to be the job. At least while Sylvia is alive.'

'Do you get Carer's Allowance?'

'Yes, but there's a limit to how much you can earn on top of that.'

'I suppose once Sylvia has lost her sight altogether, you'll become a fulltime carer?'

'Probably, though she'll hate that. We're lucky she's got time to adapt, but I think I'll have to be around. It's not just the blindness, it's her age and... well, just *Sylvia*.'

'She needs people, doesn't she?'

'It's only since we moved here that I've realised how much she missed out, living alone. You and Bridget have been amazing.'

'She's a joy! Still so much energy!'

'She plans to live long enough to dance at my wedding.'

'And sing?'

'Oh, probably. But that isn't going to happen,' Rosamund said with some finality. 'A big wedding, I mean.'

Something prevented me from doing a knee-jerk contradiction and spouting about late starters. It wasn't just that I would sound like a middle-aged divorcée trying to cheer myself up. I looked at Rosamund's weary, pretty face and registered that despite the cherubic curls and mischievous eyes, she looked older than forty. Treading carefully, I said, 'Nursing is surely something you can only do if you love it. You're no longer feeling the love. And there is such a thing as burn-out.'

'I've buried too many patients. I know it goes with the territory, but in the end, it takes its toll. Always being with the old, frequently the dying.'

'Rewarding, but completely draining, I should think.'

'Some make a good end. Many don't. You see people at their best and at their very worst.'

'And *you* have to come home to another needy old person, delightful as she is.'

'And very grateful.'

'Yes, but there's no respite, Ros. You've got no life of your own, though I hope we can change that a bit. Bridget and I are available and Bridget never goes anywhere, so I really think you could commit yourself to doing things. Getting out. I'm almost always at home except after a book launch, so there would usually be someone around. In any case, we could arrange things so that there was.'

'You're very kind.'

She remained glum and silent, so I said, 'What do *you* want to do, Ros? Really?'

'Stop worrying about Sylvia,' she answered promptly. 'Don't get me wrong. Things are so much better for her since we moved here. She thinks she's on holiday! She's brighter and quicker and her language skills are back up to speed. You've given her a second chance.'

Embarrassed, I said, 'Queenie took a chance on me. I wanted to share that in a meaningful way.'

'Well, you've certainly done that.'

'Ros, if you gave up nursing – for now – could you study? Or write a book?'

'*Me?*' she scoffed.

'A practical guide for carers? We're all having to deal with an ageing population, so it's a hot topic.' She didn't reply. 'If you gained more qualifications, would that mean more money later?'

'When she's dead, you mean?'

'I suppose that is what I meant. But perhaps you *should* plan for... afterwards.'

'I certainly should. And that's my problem. At eighty-five, Sylvia could live for another ten, even twenty years. People do nowadays. I would be fifty, too old to return to work. *And*, God forbid, she could die tomorrow. You see my problem. But as I'm her sole heir, I would be able to take my time to think about the future. Queenie left me a bit of money, which was very nice of her. I should use that wisely. She would certainly have approved of further education and maybe writing a book.'

'She'd also approve of cases of champagne, according to Bridget.'

'I go round and round in circles, trying to decide what's best. For me. For Sylvia... She's happy enough at the moment, but frankly, it's all downhill from here. Blindness. Failing health. Mobility issues. But don't tell her I said so.'

'She already knows. And she's fighting it. I've got her doing armchair yoga. I looked for it on YouTube and showed her how to find it on the TV. She loves it.' Ros looked at me, stricken, and tears started into her tired eyes. I leaned across the table and put my hand over hers. 'Oh, don't get upset! It was just a little idea I had. Was I wrong?'

'No, I just feel so guilty! I know I shouldn't, but I do. She's lost everything but me. Now she's even losing her *sight*. Whatever I do, it never seems *enough*.'

'And that feeling is probably why you became a nurse. But even that isn't enough, is it?' She didn't reply, but she didn't need to. I released her hand, sat back and stared at my wine glass. 'My mum died when I was twelve. It was suicide.'

'Oh, Jane, I'm so sorry.'

'The reason I'm telling you is, I know how you feel. *I* wasn't enough. And what I've done since she died has never seemed enough. The guilt is endless. I didn't even look after my bereaved father.'

'Not your job. You were twelve.'

'I meant later, when I was an adult. We were strangers when he died and I realised – very recently – that he must have been lonely. And that's one of the reasons why he drank.' Rosamund asked no questions, but listened, her face intent. 'I haven't had a mum since I was a child, so looking after Sylvia, making her happy is pure pleasure for me. I can do things for her that I never got to do for my mum, or *with* my mum, so please don't feel guilty if we share the care. I'm very glad to do it. It's a privilege.' I surveyed the old kitchen with its huge refectory table and said, possibly too loudly, 'Isn't that what's so bloody brilliant about this place? People being kind and generous and accepting – and funny!' I reached for the bottle. 'Oh, don't you just *love* women?'

Rosamund stared at her glass as I refilled it. 'Yes, I do… And I really wish I could tell Sylvia.' She looked up at me then, with a hint of challenge in her eyes and I knew at once what she meant. Perhaps I'd always known. 'I knew it wouldn't be a problem for *you*,' she continued. 'And I'm pretty sure Bridget knows. But Sylvia doesn't.'

'What you mean is, you haven't *told* Sylvia. She might well have guessed. And if she hasn't, I really don't think she'd be bothered. Sylvia has lived and breathed theatre for nearly seventy years. She's worked with all sorts. She laughs and says *Liquorice Allsorts,* doesn't she?' Rosamund smiled and I felt a wave of relief. 'It would take a great deal more than your love-life to shock Sylvia. I think she'd take *anything* in her stride.' Unbidden, the Wyngrave poltergeist sprang to mind. 'She just wants you to be *happy*.'

We sat in silence for a while, but it was companionable, not awkward. Eventually Rosamund said, 'You could be right. Sylvia might already know. She doesn't miss much, even though she's half-blind.'

'And she has no real confusion or memory issues, which is good at her age.'

'She says actors die with good memories because most of them refuse to retire and carry on learning lines. She still has a head full of quotes. It's amazing.'

'I think her memories are a comfort to her. They're certainly a great source of entertainment for *us*.'

'And that's what she wants to be. That's what she was missing.' Rosamund shook her head. 'I really wasn't a good audience.'

'Well, you weren't a *big* audience and actors love a full house. And you've heard all her stories before. But to be fair, some of them do bear repeating.'

'It's the way she tells them.' Rosamund smiled, remembering shared hilarity, then her face clouded over again. 'She *is* happy, but I'm sure something's bothering her.'

'But if she hasn't *said* anything—'

'That's just it. It's what she's *not* saying. She's not letting on about something.'

'Well, if you find out what it is, do let me know. It's probably just some little niggle we can sort out. Try not to worry about it.' Rosamund looked unconvinced. 'If you *must* worry, worry about turning forty.'

I was rewarded with a grin and she raised her glass to me. 'To forty. And beyond!'

Sylvia's anecdote about the disappearing actor encouraged me to do some more research and I decided to take another look at the portraits. I couldn't quite bring myself to think of them as "my" portraits, though they were and I felt an odd weight of responsibility towards them, almost as if they were people: dependents and minor members of the Wyngrave Hall family. The sitters were my house-mates, people I saw every day, like Bridget, Rosamund and Sylvia. Their eyes observed me as I moved around the house.

Queenie Brooke-Bennet, or perhaps earlier owners of Wyngrave Hall, had collected a number of portraits associated with the Wyngrave family. There were several late sixteenth-century paintings depicting the De Vere family and I'd decided that these were the ones I would sell. Sir Gervase De Vere was top of my list. I assumed the artist had attempted a flattering portrait. Nevertheless, with his small eyes, thin lips and pale, bloated face, Sir Gervase looked like my idea of an Elizabethan gangster. Something told me you wouldn't want to make an enemy of this man. The expression in his eyes conveyed no humanity, just the complacency of wealth and privilege.

I disliked the portraits of the sons almost as much as the father's, though the artist had evidently had more attractive material to work with. Ferdinand and Oliver De Vere could never have been called handsome. A certain coarseness of feature denied them beauty and both men had inherited their father's hard mouth, but they were still a striking pair: dark, saturnine, confident. Possibly ruthless. These were the new men: the thrusting, middle-class, mercantile de Veres, marrying their way up the social ladder.

I could see how they might have appealed to Queenie's sense of drama, but I'd relegated most of the de Vere family to a spare room where Bridget and I stored things of value that I didn't want to keep. We called it the Sale Room. Thus had the de Veres come down in the world. Their portraits were now surrounded by boxes of books, tea chests of china and trunks of old linen. Of the pictures I could live with, I put some in the Great Hall and hung the rest upstairs in the Long Gallery.

My judgement was subjective rather than artistic. Two small portraits, neither bigger than a large tea tray, had spoken to me: both Wyngraves, of different generations. One depicted a young woman, Lady Edith Wyngrave, neé de Vere, pale and jaundiced-looking – though who would look healthy peering out at the world through layers of old varnish? Her round, startled eyes gave her a doll-like appearance, though if I stared at the painting long enough, I thought I could discern something more. Anxiety? Fear, even.

I chided myself for being fanciful. Perhaps she was sickly or pregnant. At a time when pregnancy was often a death sentence, fear can never have been far from the thoughts of a married woman of childbearing age.

Queenie had elected not to hang the portrait of Edith's husband, Sir Walter Wyngrave, an effete and elderly aristocrat, and I could see why. The artist had certainly captured a personality, but not one I felt inclined to spend time with. Judging from his likeness, Sir Walter had not been overburdened with intelligence. His mouth was slack and thick-lipped and his eyes looked vacant. Surveying the portrait as whole, I thought Sir Walter's clothes far more impressive than the man himself, so he remained in the Sale Room, where he stood in a corner, facing the wall, as if he'd committed some misdemeanour.

As I passed Edith's portrait in the Gallery, I would sometimes stop to regard her solemn prettiness, wishing I could interrogate her about her life. Was the portrait painted on the occasion of her marriage to Wyngrave, many years her senior? It surely could not have been a happy alliance. There was something in Edith's expression – resignation, perhaps, or a sense of duty? – that told me she knew she'd made a bad bargain. Was it even her bargain? Had she been sold off by her father, Gervase de Vere? Her youth, health and happiness in exchange for money and position as the mistress of Wyngrave Hall? Happy or otherwise, the marriage was neither long nor fruitful. Samuel Wyngrave was the only issue and Edith had not long survived his birth.

I'd found Samuel's portrait stacked in a cupboard with several others. These pictures were so varied and mostly so undistinguished, I guessed they'd been set aside for the frames to be re-used since those were all in good condition.

It was difficult to make out Samuel's features, so very dark was the overall appearance of the painting. Four centuries of dirt and ageing varnish had created a thick veil through which the young man's eyes peered at the viewer. I'd initially set him aside in the *For Sale* pile, but something made me retrieve the painting and examine it more closely.

The portrait depicted a very young man, perhaps still a teenager. Even through the layers of varnish, I could see his face radiated a sensitivity conspicuously lacking in the young De Vere portraits, but this was a later, Jacobean picture and by a different artist. Samuel looked a gentle, artistic soul. I could imagine him writing poetry, or singing, accompanying himself on the lute. The De Veres' pastimes would, I was sure, involve riding horses very hard and killing a variety of animals. They looked like men with blood on their hands. I hoped none of it was human.

Despite the condition of the paintings, I decided to hang mother and son in the Gallery until I'd decided whether to keep them. I resolved to have both portraits cleaned and all of them valued. But even as I googled *Fine Art Restoration*, I knew I probably wouldn't part with Samuel Wyngrave. He already felt like a friend.

As the thought crossed my mind, I thought of Queenie and her imaginary friend... Was I going the same way? Already? Was there something very odd about Wyngrave Hall? Enter at your psychological peril? Then with a hammer blow of insight, I realised my fondness for young Samuel, the attachment I already felt towards his likeness, was possibly a frustrated maternal instinct. Women my age had teenage sons, young men who might provide some consolation and company at the end of a marriage.

Children hadn't happened for Duncan and me and he had never shown any interest in finding out why. I'd never felt particularly maternal and had a tendency to become wrapped up in work, so years of childlessness drifted by until one day I accepted that a door was now permanently closed, a door I'd never really tried to open.

Now, single at fifty-one, living with women who until recently were total strangers, I contemplated the portrait of Samuel Wyngrave, a young man who had never known his mother and found myself hoping he'd been loved and valued as something more than the heir to Wyngrave Hall.

Had Lady Edith known love in her short life? Surveying the portrait of her husband, it was hard to believe, if she had been loved, that the feeling would have been reciprocated. Had Edith been any more to Sir Walter than the provider of an heir? He hadn't married again. Did that suggest he was inconsolable? He had a son, wealth, position and the domestic comfort of Wyngrave Hall. Did such things console a Jacobean gentleman on the death of a young wife and the end of a marriage?

I considered the end of my own and its consolations. It was surely no loss to lose someone who no longer loved me, who was prepared to deceive me with another woman. No real loss, but there was an *absence*, a gap I struggled to fill, despite my acquisition of Wyngrave Hall, a mysterious benefactor and new friends, real and possibly imaginary.

Always short of material for my sadly neglected blog, I posted the results of my research into Wyngrave Hall, hoping this might generate some ideas for the new series I'd promised my publisher. To amuse Sylvia, I researched her disappearing actor and found a colourful story, no doubt apocryphal, and posted it online...

Legend has it that William Shakespeare himself once performed at Wyngrave Hall. We shall never know if the Bard himself made an appearance, but we do know his company performed here, probably in the Great Hall. Shakespeare is said to have played the Ghost of Hamlet's father here and he is known to have played that significant part elsewhere. Nicholas Rowe, Shakespeare's first biographer, mentioned that Shakespeare's rôle as "the Ghost in his own Hamlet" was "the top of his performance."

Local tradition has it that Shakespeare stepped into the rôle of the Ghost at the last minute when the actor playing the part failed to appear backstage. At the time there was a rumour he'd been murdered. Did he perhaps abscond with the box office takings? The mystery remains unsolved, but we do know Shakespeare decided to concentrate on playwriting, so All's Well That Ends Well.

Unusually for a house of its great age, there are no tales of Wyngrave Hall being haunted...

I stopped typing and re-read my last sentence. For a moment my finger hovered over the delete key. Was I superstitious? Surely not. Queenie's imaginary friend was just a hunch of Bridget's and I'd simply over-reacted to a few disordered books. And beaten myself hollow at chess. Without realising it.

There wasn't any *real* reason to believe Wyngrave was haunted.

Not until Sylvia dropped her bombshell.

Lamentation the Second

What blessings have I now that I should fear to die? Better a thousand times to die than live thus tormented.

I am barred, like one infected, from the crown and comfort of my life, first fruit of my womb: my infant son.

I dwell in darkness, all cheerful light kept from me, but for my little candle. Pale ghosts and frightful shades are all my acquaintance now, but even they cannot banish friendly sleep.

Come, sleep, and close mine eyes, weary now with weeping. Since sleep is but the shadow of death, wherefore should I fear to die?

Death do your worst. I fear you not, for the Bible sayeth, the Last Enemy that shall be destroyed is Death.

5

Stage direction: Enter the Ghost

Hamlet

Sylvia was sitting by the open window in the Great Hall, our "public area" and the nicest room in the house. Bridget and I had worked hard to make it comfortable for everyone and, despite its size, cosy.

Sylvia loved to chat. There wasn't a great deal else she could do and she was often to be found there, sitting by the log fire or by the window. She never appeared to gaze at the fire, as we did, and her eyes always seemed to be averted from the view of the garden, but that was because Sylvia could see little if she looked straight ahead. She could observe firelight or a sunset in her peripheral vision, but mostly she listened. Sylvia said she had an "absolute horror" of losing her hearing. She knew and accepted she'd one day be effectively blind, but she didn't think that would cut her off from the world, from Rosamund in particular, who was sensitive to Sylvia's every need, often before it was perceived by Sylvia herself. "Oh, you read my mind!" she would announce, delighted.

Deafness – even being hard of hearing – was something Sylvia would not countenance. She liked to believe (and it might have been true) that as her eyes deteriorated, her hearing improved. She sat at the open window, listening to the birds, looking bird-like herself, with her head cocked to one side. 'Listen to the chaffinches!' she exclaimed, delighted. 'They do sound cross! And isn't that a pheasant I can hear squawking in the distance?'

I hadn't registered any of the birds, just the blissful quiet as I arranged flowers on the broad window-sill next to Sylvia, so she would be able to smell them. Rosamund had mentioned how much her grandmother loved cutting flowers in her old cottage garden and so Bridget and I endeavoured to arrange fresh flowers in Sylvia's room and any of the areas she liked to sit. It was one of those little things that I would never have done for myself, but which now gave me great pleasure. Even though I just placed them haphazardly in jugs and vases, Sylvia was appreciative and quick to identify something new.

'Is that the last of the wallflowers? How divine.'

'Don't thank me. Bridget picked them for you and told me to put them in a jug. She said you'd enjoy the scent.'

'Indeed, I shall. I'll be burying my nose in them all day. The colours are glorious, aren't they? Like Elizabethan doublets! I remember a production of *Much Ado* where the designer said he wanted us to look like a bed of wallflowers. I believe we did too. I wore a saffron velvet gown. Yellow should have been a nightmare with my colouring, but this was *saffron...*' Sylvia would gaze, smiling into space, and I knew she could see herself and the company in their rich velvets.

Sylvia was blessed with a good memory. She appeared to suffer no hearing loss, nor did we have any fear for her reasoning. Even though she'd received little in the way of formal education, she appeared to know a bit about most things and be interested in everything. She was as sensible, as intelligent, as sane as the rest of us, so when she finally voiced her concerns, I didn't know what to say. It was as if the ground beneath me was giving way.

I was arranging some roses on the windowsill for Sylvia, when she struggled out of her armchair and picked up the stick she scarcely needed for support, but which gave her confidence. She tended to twirl it in front of her in a buccaneering fashion, to make sure there was no obstacle in her way. She came and stood beside me at the open window and hooked her arm through mine.

'Jane...' Sylvia lowered her voice and inclined her head towards me. Being much taller, I bent my head to hear what she might be about to say. I needn't have bothered, because she said in a stage whisper that could have been heard at the back of the Theatre Royal,

Drury Lane, 'Is that man *ever* going to finish his measuring up, or whatever it is he's doing?'

I was glad Sylvia probably couldn't see my gaping mouth. I looked over my shoulder and quickly round the room, not in search of some silent tradesman, but to check that we were in fact alone. I knew Rosamund was out and Bridget was in the garden, so we were – of course – alone.

'There's nobody here, Sylvia,' I said, my voice not quite steady. 'It's just us.'

'Has he gone then?' she asked.

I could think of nothing more sensible to say than, 'Yes. We're alone. Where… Where do you think you saw him?'

'In the corner. I'll say this for him, he does keep out of the way, but it's a bit *inhibiting*, isn't it? And I really think he ought to have finished by now, doing whatever it is he's doing. Not very much, if you ask me! I've tried striking up a conversation with him, but he didn't respond. Is he Polish? They usually speak very good English. Anyway, he just disappeared. I didn't see where he went. Very rude, I thought. I was just trying to be friendly as he seems to be here for the duration.' Sylvia paused, but I said nothing. 'Oh, dear, have I spoken out of turn?'

'No, not at all. I just… I don't know what to say,' I admitted.

'Forget I mentioned it. He's no trouble. Just a bit odd, that's all.'

'Sylvia, what can you see? I mean, what does he look like?'

'Well, I can hardly see a thing, so there's not much point asking me! But I'm always aware of him when he's in the room. It's a dark *presence*.'

'Dark?'

'Yes. He looks to me like he's dressed in black. Is he? And his hair looks dark too. Darker than yours. Am I right? I like to think I can still distinguish *colour*.'

'Sylvia, why don't you sit down again? I think we should have a chat.'

As she sat obediently, I pulled up a stool and sat beside her, playing for time, trying to adjust to what she'd told me. What could I possibly say? If I pretended I didn't know what she was talking about, I would make the poor woman feel she was going mad. If I explained there were no tradesmen currently employed at Wyngrave, but we *might* have a poltergeist, I would look as if *I* was going mad. I resolved to stick to the truth as far as possible.

'Sylvia,' I said calmly, 'I'm sorry, but there's no one there.'

'Oh, not now, but he'll be back later. He seems to work very odd hours.'

'I mean, I don't employ anyone. The electrician, the plumber who did your *en suite*, they've all finished now. So it's just... us,' I said, conscious I'd already abandoned the truth.

Sylvia was silent a moment, then said, aghast, 'Are you suggesting I'm *seeing* things?'

I hesitated, then said, 'Perhaps it's to do with your condition.'

'Nonsense!' Sylvia scoffed. 'He's about the only thing I *can* see clearly! When he stands still, that is. He has a tendency to flit in and out of the room. I don't know what he thinks he's doing. He reminds me of a director I worked with who really didn't have a clue, but he wandered round the rehearsal room, watching us from different angles. He used to say, "Don't mind me, I'm invisible." He *wasn't*, so it was all rather annoying. Your chap reminds me of him. Thinks he's invisible!' Sylvia snorted.

'You must be *aware* of someone, but...' I swallowed and said, 'I'm afraid it's not someone real.'

'Are you saying *you* don't see him?'

'No, I don't.'

Sylvia sat in silence for a long time. I feared she might cry, but she placed her hands in her lap, folded them neatly and sat looking quite composed. 'So,' she said, heavily. 'I can see someone no one else sees.' I didn't answer. I couldn't. 'Ros and Bridget haven't said anything?'

'No.'

'Well, either I'm seeing a ghost, or I'm losing my marbles, it's as simple as that. And I know what Ros would say, because she's a scientist, through and through. What do *you* think?'

'You seem completely *compos mentis* to me.'

'Thank you, Jane, dear, but that means I'm seeing a ghost.'

'I wonder if it's something to do with the AMD?'

'The eye specialist talked about hallucinations, but you're supposed to see patterns and colours, not people. Personally, I think a ghost seems much more likely, especially when you consider the age of this place.'

'You seem to be taking it very calmly, Sylvia.'

'Do I? Well, I suppose that's because it's not the first time.'

'You've seen things *before?*'

'Occasionally. Most old theatres have a resident ghost, or at least stories about ghosts and many people say they've seen them. It's not that surprising, is it? Some theatres are very old and sometimes people have died on stage, or backstage. Theatres are fearfully dangerous places, you know! People say ghosts come back to haunt their old stamping ground and I can well imagine it. You know how old actors hate to retire! Anyway, I didn't have to imagine it.'

'You *saw* a ghost?'

'A couple of times – and there was nothing wrong with my vision then. But I was quite young. Impressionable. Maybe I imagined it, but I didn't think so at the time. Actors are a superstitious lot, but we're also sensitive. And open-minded. You have to believe in magic, the *possibility* of magic, otherwise how could you get through a half-empty matinée on a wet Wednesday?' Sylvia got to her feet with an effort. 'I suddenly feel rather tired. I think I'll go and have a lie down.' She picked up her stick and said, 'You won't mention this to Rosamund, will you? I don't want to worry her. If I *am* going bonkers, she'll find out soon enough.'

'I don't think you are, Sylvia.'

'Bless you, neither do I, but if I tell her there's a ghost and I can *see* him, she'll definitely think I'm going ga-ga. So I think say nothing, don't you?'

'Maybe that would be best.'

'Thank you. And thank you for not laughing at me. I appreciate that. And all the lovely flowers,' she added with a catch in her voice. 'Gorgeous! I thought I'd miss my old garden, but I certainly don't miss the work. And I was always ham-fisted when it came to picking flowers for the house. I do so appreciate your efforts, Jane. Thank you.'

She hobbled off in the direction of her bedroom, sweeping her stick before her, then she stopped and turned. She appeared to be staring at the fire, but I knew she was peering at me. 'You will tell me, won't you? If *you* see anything.'

'Yes, of course,' I replied, not at all sure I would.

'Good.' Sylvia tossed her head to one side, then the other, as if searching the Great Hall, then she trudged off to her room, her head bowed.

I got through the day, keeping busy. I folded washing, cleaned the kitchen and emptied my Inbox – all the things you do when you're trying to convince yourself your world isn't falling apart, that life will go on, even when your husband says he wants a divorce, or your best friend says this Christmas will be her last. Washing must be folded and kitchens must be cleaned, otherwise you would just lie in a tearful heap in the middle of the floor, waiting to be found.

But Sylvia's revelation had changed things. I'd been able to dismiss my own delusions (the menopause can be blamed for a multitude of sins), but even allowing for Sylvia's increasing blindness, her age and an imaginative disposition, it was hard to ignore what she'd said.

With my chores done, I still couldn't settle to work, so I re-searched conservators in London. The Hall might not be mine, but the paintings were, and I thought they should be cleaned before I decided whether to keep them or sell them. Sylvia and I avoided each other discreetly for the rest of the day and when she opted for an early night, I decided I would do the same.

I headed upstairs with a mug of chamomile tea and looked into the Long Gallery, where it seemed much colder, but there was no fire and the windows were currently uncurtained. My thoughts turned to an unseasonable but comforting hot water bottle. Well, why not? I turned and headed back and the Gallery echoed as my heels tapped on the ancient floorboards. I paused in front of a portrait and waited, but I had no idea what I was waiting for. There was suddenly an odd noise. We were always hearing odd noises at Wyngrave, but I turned and called out, 'Is anyone there?'

There was, of course, no answer. I cast my eyes round the dimly lit Gallery, half expecting to see someone, but I was alone.

Except that I knew I wasn't. The sensation of being watched – or watched *over* – was surely becoming more intense. I told myself I wasn't afraid, and to prove it, I strode to the darker end of the

Gallery and stood in front of Samuel Wyngrave's portrait, which I hoped would have a calming effect. In the gloom, it seemed as if a little smile lurked at the corners of his mouth, but I must have imagined it. A trick of the inadequate light.

Too tired to make that reassuring hot water bottle, I clutched my cooling chamomile tea and hurried through the Gallery, heading for the safety of my bed.

I closed the bedroom door and leaned against it. Why? Was I barricading myself in? But ghosts can walk through doors. Well, they do in movies.

I gazed round the oppressively dark, oak-panelled room and took stock. Perhaps I was having a breakdown. I'd been through a lot lately. It must surely have taken a toll.

Or maybe the whole thing was just a dream. I would simply wake up to find myself in my old London flat, having dreamed I acquired a haunted Elizabethan manor house.

Feeling nervous, but longing for sleep and oblivion, I began to undress. I stared at the ornately carved sliding wardrobe doors – beautifully re-purposed oak panels – but declined to open them. That surely meant admitting I felt afraid. Suddenly overwhelmed, I sank down onto the bed, my shirt half-unbuttoned and heard my own voice say, 'It's not Queenie, is it? It's not her I can sense. It's *you*... But who the hell *are* you?' I asked angrily.

There was no sound and nothing in the room moved, I'm quite sure of that, but I did sense something. Something like a tiny click in my head. A lightbulb moment of realisation.

'You're not *in* this room, are you?' Relief washed over me, followed immediately by something else. Curiosity? 'Do I have to invite you in?' I listened to the silence and said, 'Queenie knew you, didn't she?'

That click again. Another piece of the jigsaw slotted into place.

'She was your friend. And... you miss her, don't you...? Oh, *listen* to me! I'm talking to an invisible man! I don't even know if you *are* a man! This is pitiful!' I put my hands up to my face and covered my eyes. 'Get out of my head! I'd rather you were in the room. I'd rather *see* you than feel *invaded* like this. Please. For Queenie's sake!'

There was another click, as if my ears had popped, then the temperature in the room dropped rapidly, as if all the windows had blown open, but the curtains were quite still. The temperature kept falling and I began to shiver, with fright as well as cold. I scrambled into bed fully clothed, sat propped up against the ancient wooden bedhead and hauled the duvet up to my chin. Drawing up my knees to form a further barrier, I braced myself. As the wardrobe doors began to slide apart, I opened my mouth, intending to scream but, as in a nightmare, nothing came out.

But an apparition did.

He was male. Elizabethan. Dressed in black. It was as if one of the portraits in the Gallery had come to life and was standing at the end of my bed, executing a bow. Then it spoke.

'Madam, a thousand apologies for the unorthodox entrance. I had no wish to alarm you, but that is where the door used to be. I see the original architecture as well as the new, plus all the hideous accretions that mercifully have now been removed. Remembering which door to use can be a challenge, even for an actor.'

I didn't reply. I couldn't. I just clutched the duvet and blinked, like a traumatised owl.

He must have thought I hadn't understood. 'Exits and entrances,' he explained with a wave of his hand, indicating the wardrobe and the bedroom door.

My shattered brain shifted into gear and I heard a small, unsteady voice recite something I'd learned by heart at school.

'All the world's a stage
And all the men and women merely players.
They have their exits and their entrances
And one man in his time plays many parts.'

Queenie's imaginary friend beamed. 'I can see we're going to get along famously.'

The small voice spoke again. 'Who *are* you?'

'My name is Horatio Fortune. *Was.* In so far as I still have a name, that is it,' he said irritably. 'Madam—'

'My name is Jane Summers.'

'I know.'

'How do you know?' I asked, alarmed.

'Queenie told me.'

'Queenie knew you?'

'Very well. I was with her at the end.'

The room seemed to sway, then settle. 'I don't understand. Ros – Nurse Kemp said Queenie died alone.'

'Technically, she did. Nevertheless, I was present when she died. Her thoughts turned to you as she prepared to embark upon her final journey. *To that undiscovered country, from whose bourn no traveller returns.*'

'But you *have?*'

He shook his head. 'I never left. But I've been hoping to.' He sighed. 'For a very long time.'

I looked at his clothes and my historian's eye assessed the black velvet and white lace. 'Four hundred and twenty years to judge from your clothes.' Good grief, was I showing off? *To a ghost?*

'Oh, this old thing,' he said with a nonchalant flick of his short cloak. 'I've had this for years. Years and *years*. Though it's a moot point, I suppose. The originals were made four centuries ago, but in their present… incarnation,' he said carefully, 'I think we would have to describe them as *ageless* rather than *aged*. Certainly they're now beyond the depredations of time and ill use. As indeed am I. But these garments were not that old when I put them on.'

'Which was?'

'1603. The twelfth of June. It was a fair day. To begin with.'

'You've lived here for over four centuries?'

'Not *lived*. I have been resident. In. This. House,' he said with steely emphasis. 'I cannot even step outside.'

'Your… situation. Is it eternal?'

'Not necessarily, it just feels like that. But I fear my incarceration will continue until—' He paused, then looked at me, as if considering.

I shrank down into the bed, pulling the duvet higher. 'Until?'

'Until I find out who murdered me. And why.'

I sat bolt upright. 'Oh my God! You're Queenie's unsolved mystery!'

'Your humble servant, madam,' he said, bowing again.

'I'm dreaming, aren't I? This is one of those awful dreams where you're absolutely convinced you're *not* dreaming, but actually you *are*.'

'You're not.'

'I know.'

'Good. I'm glad we've cleared that up.'

I shivered violently and thought longingly of the hot water bottle that never was. 'Can you do anything about the temperature? It's freezing in here and I'm sure that's your doing.'

'Indeed, but there's nothing I can do about it. I bring my own chilly micro-climate. Would you prefer me to leave?'

'Yes! I mean, no. Actually, I don't know what I mean. I think I need you to stay until… until I've adjusted to the fact of your existence.'

'Ah.' His smile was frigidly polite. 'We could be in for a long night.'

It was a pleasant smile, not in the least alarming. For a ghost. As I gradually got used to the greyish colour of his skin, I was able to appreciate that Horatio Fortune must once have been a fine young man: tall, athletic, his black hose revealing leg muscles accustomed to riding, sword fighting and not, I imagined, a great deal of sitting about. He was clean-shaven, as you would expect of an actor who had to don different beards. His hair was dark, but greyish, which might have been the result of premature aging, but since his skin was also ashen, I began to wonder if ghosts were basically monochrome. Horatio Fortune must surely have been more colourful when he was alive, but in death he looked like a character from an old black and white TV programme, where the picture lacked definition: grey, dramatic and slightly fuzzy.

As I gazed at him, details remained elusive. No sooner did I try to focus on the cut of his doublet or the hang of his cloak than these things would blur, almost dissolve into the background, as if his person was fluid, even gaseous.

'*O, that this too, too solid flesh would melt, thaw and resolve itself into a dew!* Mine did eventually.'

'Good grief, can you read my thoughts?'

'Only if I make a particular effort. I wouldn't bother normally. Most people's thoughts are exceedingly dull, demonstrating a preoccupation with the belly and bowels, but your head is stuffed full of quotations. Just like mine. In any case, madam, you can depend upon my discretion. If I were able to read a lady's thoughts, I am too much the gentleman to exploit the skill.'

Unsure how to respond to this polite, but unsettling reassurance, I too took refuge in good manners. 'Would you like to sit down? Not on the bed,' I added quickly. 'You're making feel me nervous, looming over me like that. You seem very tall for a ghost.'

His eyes widened. 'I wasn't aware there was a standard height for phantoms, but if you prefer, I shall be seated.' He took up a position on a chair placed against the wall and folded his arms. 'But pray, do not concern yourself. I have no need of rest.'

'You never get tired?'

'Tired, no. *Tetchy*, yes. But after the first fifty years or so, you don't register what the living call exhaustion. Entities like me give a new meaning to the phrase, "dead tired".' As he treated me to a mirthless smile, I realised he had the tragi-comic demeanour of a stand-up comedian. He looked away and spoke softly, as if to himself. 'But there are days when I fear I shall be trapped at Wyngrave Hall to the last syllable of recorded time. That apprehension, that *dread* can feel upon occasion like a deep weariness.' He looked up, as if he'd just remembered my presence. 'But, no, I am never tired. Not in the way you mean. Would that I were. Then I might sleep.'

'Who *are* you?'

'I was Horatio Fortune. *A poor player, that struts and frets his hour upon the stage...*' He spread expressive hands. '*And then is heard no more.*'

'You were an actor?'

'Until my life was cut short.'

'And it wasn't an accident?'

'*Murder most foul*, unfortunately.'

'You're sure?'

'I remember a massive blow to the head. My last conscious thought was, I'd miss my entrance and the closet scene would be ruined.'

'You were performing?'

'I was offstage, waiting to make my entrance. As the ghost of Hamlet's father, ironically. I've often wondered if I was condemned to this miserable existence because I died playing the ghost of a murdered man. Type-cast at the point of death, I now find myself in a long-running show – even longer than *Coronation Street*.'

'What can you possibly know of *Coronation Street*?'

'Queenie never missed an episode. We used to watch a lot of television together, especially Agatha Christie – though that was always a little too close to home for my liking. Blunt instruments in the library, and so forth. But Queenie was quite the Elizabethan in that respect. She loved a puzzle.'

'Is that why you speak the way you do?' He gazed at me, momentarily at a loss. 'You speak a hybrid form of English that ranges across four centuries. It's… dizzying.'

'That's partly the television, I suppose, but mostly it's all the people I've lived with.' He tilted his head to one side. 'Can I say that? I haven't *lived* for four hundred years. Perhaps I should say, all the people with whom I've shared Wyngrave Hall. Since almost everyone ignored me, there's been little for me to do apart from listen to small talk. And learn.'

'So you're a walking history of the English vernacular.'

'Why, thank you, I suppose I am. But not just English. I've picked up a smattering of other languages too. There was a devout couple in the seventeenth century who used to converse in Latin. *For fun*. I also speak fluent Texan.'

'*Texan?*'

'Wyngrave Hall had an American owner in the 1930s. A delightful old gentleman who used to conclude his pronouncements with, *The good Lord willin' and the creek don't rise*.'

I gasped, laughing despite myself at the Southern drawl. By now I'd concluded I *must* be dreaming and was beginning to enjoy myself.

The ghost was evidently glad to have an appreciative audience. 'To begin with, I thought the poor man lived in perpetual dread of flooding, even though the moat had been dry for more than a century. Eventually I realized it was just a manner of speaking. *In Texas*. He was a dear chap. William Robert Cartwright III, known to his friends as Billy Bob. I miss him, even though he never acknowledged my existence. *Do* I exist? Well, you know what I mean. Queenie was one of the few who recognised me. I shall not look upon her like again.'

'So Queenie believed in ghosts?'

'She believed in *me*.'

I was suddenly aware of a constriction in my throat that made speech difficult. 'And the others? Your... hosts?'

'Mostly they couldn't see me. Others just ignored me. You might be interested to know that being ignored is even worse than being invisible.'

I struggled for a moment with the unfamiliar concept, then said, 'You died during a performance, you say?'

'I assume so. After the blow to the head, my recollections are hazy and few.'

'Where were you performing?'

'Here, of course.'

'*No!*'

'As Lady Macbeth said, *What – in* our *house?*'

'Oh, for Heaven's sake, murder is hardly a joking matter!'

'I'm glad you think so. I certainly didn't die laughing.'

'Who killed you?'

He shrugged. 'No idea. Nor do I know his motive. A lot of backbiting went on in our company and there was some *vicious* professional jealousy, but I don't believe any man would have killed to further his career. And it wasn't as if I was a bright particular star in that theatrical firmament. My death would hardly have opened the door of opportunity for a rival. No one ever talked of Richard Burbage and Horatio Fortune in the same breath, and no one ever will.' The strained smile again. 'I was ambitious. What actor isn't? I sought renown, but none of us looked to the future. We prayed the plague would spare us for another season and hoped the Puritans wouldn't close the theatres. But it would have been gratifying to be remembered, as Burbage is now remembered. Or Robert Armin. Or even that irritating exhibitionist, Will Kempe.'

'For all their fame in their lifetime, they're now just footnotes in history.'

As he considered the phrase, Horatio regarded me, his dark eyes stark against the grey pallor of his face. 'Is that not sufficient epitaph for a man like me, a lowly player? Now my only ambition is to find out who murdered me. And why.'

I felt strangely moved by his plight. 'Perhaps solving your mystery would constitute a footnote in history. It would certainly be a footnote in the history of Wyngrave Hall.' He looked unconvinced. Decidedly morose, in fact, and possibly a shade greyer. 'I wish I could be more encouraging, but after four centuries—'

'Dear lady, do not trouble yourself! I am but poor company, for to say true,' he said, laying a hand on his velvet-clad chest, 'My soul is exceeding sorrowful and I should therefore take my leave.' He glanced over his shoulder. 'I shall depart in the same manner in which I arrived, if that meets with your approval?'

'Yes, of course. But... if you should come again, would you mind knocking before you enter?'

'Gladly. Madam, I am your most obedient servant.' He bowed again and retreated backwards into the wardrobe, where he paused for a moment, looking ridiculous. Then the sliding doors began to move, apparently of their own accord, and obscured him from view.

I remembered then the final exit of another dead person: my last sight of Alison's coffin as it slowly disappeared behind a curtain, journeying to that *undiscovered country*. The others said they looked away, but I made myself watch. Because seeing is believing.

I sat quite still, cocooned in my duvet and the blanket of silence that had descended. After a few moments, to my utter dismay, I burst into extravagant tears. Burying my face in the pillow, I sobbed. For my husband and my marriage, for my old flat where everything stayed where I left it, for my father who'd lived a lie, for my mother who'd died for love. I cried for poor Alison, for the friends I never saw and the babies I never had. I howled because I'd lost almost everything that ever mattered to me and now, apparently, I was losing my mind.

When there were no more tears left to shed, I slept, dreamless and deep.

Lamentation the Third

The serving woman is forbidden to speak to me. I address her and enquire if it is a fair day or a foul, or if she has word of my son, but she delivers my meagre victuals and empties the slop pail in silence, her head bent in fear. No eye looks into mine. No voice answers. If I did not write this journal, certain, I should go mad.

Yet is this prison full of noises. I hear sounds outside my door. Whisperings at the keyhole. Footsteps. The shift of waiting bodies, bent on revenge. They listen. Listen for a name. Thy name.

Surely imagination plays me false. This whispering is but the scrabbling of rats and mice, my only companions.

I shall I think on thee, dear love, and when I do, all losses will be restored to me, all sorrows end.

But in sooth, I fear I am not in my perfect mind.

6

'Tis the time's plague when madmen lead the blind.

King Lear

When I woke the following morning, I assumed I'd had a very weird dream. When I sat up and found myself still fully dressed, memory gradually returned. I sank back on my pillows and stared at my wardrobe doors, horrified.

When I felt a little calmer, I reached into a pocket for my phone. I quickly established that Google does not list local exorcists. Further research revealed that the Church of England offered a spiritual Rentokil service that would evict ghosts and troublesome spirits or try to persuade them to leave. Unlike Rentokil, the only way I could contact these clerical rat-catchers was by contacting my local minister who would put me in touch with someone suitably trained and very discreet.

I googled my local church, made a note of the minister's name and number, then lay in bed for some time, stunned.

Setting aside for now incipient insanity, I had apparently been presented with a cold case: a four-hundred-year-old murder. But it's not a murder until you've found a body. Is it murder if the *victim* claims he was done to death? I was used to concocting mysteries without recourse to DNA, even occasionally without a corpse, but even my most enterprising Tudor "detectives" had never interviewed a murder *victim*, so I had little to draw on.

Was it a murder? Was there any four-hundred-year-old evidence? I tried to remember what I'd been told, or *thought* I'd been told. Horatio Fortune lived at a time when people could be put to death for stealing a hawk, so was it perhaps simply some sort of execution? But he said he felt a blow on the head. Perhaps he was lying. Why would a ghost *lie*? Maybe when he was alive Horatio Fortune wasn't a very nice person and someone had a grievance against him.

But *murder*?

It was a dream. It must be. All a dream.

I reached for the pad I kept by my bedside and opened it at a fresh page. An idea for a new book had simply come to me in a dream and it was an absolute corker! I started to jot down a few notes, then looked up anxiously at the wardrobe doors.

Unless…

Unless Horatio Fortune was real – well, a real *ghost* – and a friend, not at all imaginary, of Queenie Brooke-Bennet's and his murder was the mystery she expected me to solve.

I didn't know whether to laugh or cry, but I'm a writer, so I did what writers do. I made notes, because at fifty-one, your memory isn't what it was, especially when you've just seen a ghost. Actually, nothing was what it was. My mother. My father. My marriage. Queenie. Wyngrave Hall. Work was the only thing that hadn't changed, the only thing I could navigate by. Words still meant what I meant them to mean. I could still earn a living writing whodunnits and while I worked, I could ignore the apparently insoluble mystery of the death of Horatio Fortune.

When I wasn't working, I turned to the renovation of the house and garden and the procrastinator's great comfort: lists. Bridget and I had two daunting master lists labelled *Inside* and *Outside*. *Inside* read:

Safety (esp. Sylvia)
Insulation
Valuation of portraits, jewellery, furniture, etc.
Value/clean/sell paintings
Inventory of jewellery – value and sell
Rot (woodworm?) in attic
Quotes for underfloor heating (or renovate CH?)
Refurbish old cottage as holiday let

The *Outdoors* list was even longer. To her credit, Bridget was prepared to tackle anything in the cause of saving me money or increasing biodiversity. That list read:

> *Fix roof*
> *Dig pond*
> *Clear and repair paths*
> *Repair/replace summerhouse. (Convert to writing hut?)*
> *Repair glasshouses*
> *Re-roof apple store*
> *Revive kitchen garden and grow food*
> *Wildflower meadow?*
> *Keep bees?*
> *Plan small Sensory Garden for Sylvia*

There was no dispute over where we should start. As there were no urgent safety concerns, making the roof watertight was our most pressing problem, especially as this was a job Bridget couldn't do and was best tackled in the summer. I say there were no safety concerns, but I had put my foot through rotten floorboards at the top of the house. When the wood was examined by specialists, they said all the old elm floorboards should be replaced with reclaimed boards to create a new floor.

Removing ancient floorboards was something Bridget thought she could tackle on days when it was too wet to work in the garden and I was happy to let her as it saved me some money. It was a slow and filthy job, but not difficult. The oak joists were sound and supported Bridget's weight, but she had to wear a mask and goggles to protect herself from the huge clouds of lime plaster dust that arose. She was delighted by all the evidence of wildlife that had made its home under the floor. An early find was a rats' nest that incorporated hundreds of tiny shreds of textiles, probably Tudor. Evidently earlier inhabitants of Wyngrave Hall weren't all human.

Remembering Horatio Fortune, I realised they still weren't.

It was on my conscience that I'd told Sylvia I would inform her if I saw anything untoward.

And I certainly had.

Of course, when I made the promise, I hadn't expected to see anything and any odd occurrences could be attributed to my over-active imagination. But now I *had* seen something. Someone. Someone who conformed to Sylvia's description of what she claimed she'd almost-seen several times.

Apart from the assurance I'd given her, it surely wasn't right that I let the poor woman labour under her misapprehension: that she was the only one who could see a ghost. Even if it was just a shared delusion, the point was, it was shared. I benefited from this comfort (was that really the word?), but Sylvia didn't. Sharing things – good and bad – had been one of the principles of trying to live together at Wyngrave. Before Sylvia and Rosamund had moved in, we'd all discussed it as a group and no doubt given it much private consideration. We wanted to achieve the seemingly impossible: respect the private lives and space of the occupants, while providing the strength and security of female support. We would all be around if needed, but not until then.

The fine principles of Wyngrave's supportive sisterhood were already under pressure, besieged by doubt and disbelief. Sylvia had shared her truth, not realising how problematic it would be. Already we had agreed to keep something from Rosamund and Bridget, yet I knew Bridget was prepared to believe in Queenie's "imaginary friend". And now I had *met* him.

I was aware I was breathing heavily, possibly in danger of hyperventilating, but where could I go to calm down, to feel safe? Sylvia saw her man in the Great Hall where I knew he'd moved my chess pieces. My bedroom? Horatio (was I going to use his *name*?) agreed to knock before entering next time. (*Next time?*) No, my bedroom was now out of the question. Some things are sacred. If he asked to enter my room, I would just say no. The library was the obvious place. At least there I was unlikely to be disturbed by any of the others. I could just sit at my desk and pretend to be working. It wouldn't be the first time.

So I headed for the library, sat down and gazed out the window, trying to focus on the reassuringly solid figure of Bridget as she walked up and down with the mower, robotic in her regularity.

Soothing stripes appeared on the lawn as dandelions, clover and daisies disappeared. Sorry, bees, but we're planning a wildflower meadow, something Bridget would only have to cut twice a year. What use is a lawn, especially in the heatwaves predicted for future summers, droughts that will parch the grass and reveal the Ghost Garden?

Ghost.

I should talk to Sylvia. It wasn't fair she should suffer alone, nor should she have to worry needlessly about the onset of dementia. But was it better to worry about dementia than seeing ghosts? Sylvia had seemed more concerned about losing her mind than being haunted. So for that matter was I. Bridget said the only thing that ever frightened Queenie was cancer. Perhaps I was wrong and ghosts were... all right?

It seemed certain now that Queenie knew of Horatio Fortune's existence and wanted me to succeed where she had failed. Somehow I was meant to find out who'd killed him. And why.

So now there were three of us: Queenie, Sylvia and me. It wasn't dementia. Could it be collective hysteria? No, because Sylvia had no idea about Queenie's imaginary friend, nor the mystery of Wyngrave Hall that I was supposed to solve, and I'd had no idea Sylvia was seeing things.

Two women definitely saw someone, and another woman (now dead) might have.

Did that make it true?

Not really. Perhaps Horatio was a forgotten memory of mine. I'd researched Elizabethan players and somehow the name *Horatio Fortune* had embedded itself, unbeknown to me. That plus Sylvia's legend of the disappearing actor.

But why would *Sylvia* see him, especially as she could see very little?

I was going round in circles, not calming down at all. The fact remained I'd told Sylvia I would level with her. I certainly wanted her to be straight with me. All the time there were two of us, I didn't have to ask myself if I was going mad and if the only way to get Horatio Fortune to leave was to find his killer, then Sylvia might be a useful ally. In any case, there was surely safety in numbers.

I should talk to Sylvia.

I would take her a gin and tonic to cushion the blow. I would take two.

Doubles.

Sylvia was sitting in the orchard, wearing a big straw hat. Ancient cider apple trees and largely unproductive pears and damsons were kept because, Bridget said, there had never been the will or time to grub them up. She and Queenie had thought the trees worth keeping for their autumn foliage, the shade they cast and the delight of their blossom, which kept the bees happy.

Bridget talked a lot about bees and always in a serious way. At heart a city-dweller, even I knew bees were in trouble, and if bees were, then so were we. Bridget had suggested we start keeping our own. Beekeeping was something I actually knew about, thanks to my historical research. If it meant replacing the drone of the lawnmower with the drone of bees, I was all for it. For now, my pressing problem was to let Sylvia know of my approach through the long grass of the orchard.

She was sitting on a wooden bench that encircled an old tree and appeared to have closed her eyes. As I approached, as noisily as possible, Sylvia's eyes opened and she gazed about her, moving her head quickly back and forth. 'Surely I hear the chink of ice! Jane? Is that you? Do come and join me. I'm listening to the birds. That blackbird! It's glorious!'

'Yes, it's me. It's good to see you enjoying the sunshine. I thought you'd like a gin.'

'Ooh, thank you, darling. You're so thoughtful.' She took the glass with both hands, keen not to spill a drop. 'Have you finished in the Word Factory for today? I meant to tell you, Ros got me your latest audiobook from the library. Very gripping! But I don't listen outdoors. I like to hear all the natural sounds and look at things. For as long as I can,' she added. 'Then, when I can't actually see them any longer, I'll still be able to see them in my mind's eye. That's Shakespeare, of course. We say it now without thinking about it, but it's what Hamlet says when he thinks he sees his dead father... Oh, dear. Listen to me running on.' Sylvia scowled. 'And I was *determined* not to talk about ghosts.'

'That's all right. Quite helpful really, because that's what I came to talk to you about.'

'So you came fortified with gin and tonic. Very wise. I hope you poured one for yourself.'

I raised my glass to her. 'I certainly did. Cheers.'

We drank, then Sylvia said, 'I rang my friend Rupert after we spoke. He's the one who was a minister before he retired.'

'Does he believe in ghosts?'

'He must. He's worked in that field. Very discreetly.'

'Exorcisms?'

'They don't call them that. That's just Hollywood hype. Rupert was much more low-key. *Very* Church of England,' she added solemnly. 'He said he *had* to keep an open mind because most of the cases he dealt with seemed quite genuine.' Sylvia lowered her voice. 'He's seen things you wouldn't believe.'

'Oh, I might actually.'

'Really? I thought you'd be a sceptic. Like Horatio.'

I sat very still, clutching my glass. 'I beg your pardon?'

'You know, Hamlet's old friend. He refused to believe a ghost was walking the battlements until he'd seen it for himself.'

'Oh, *Horatio*. Yes, I see.'

'So you do believe in ghosts?'

'No, I don't think so. But I might have seen one.'

Sylvia's spare hand flew out and reached for my arm. '*Here?* At the Hall?'

'Yes.'

'When?'

'Last night.'

'Good God! Were you frightened?'

'I was at first. Very.'

There was a long silence in which we both took a hefty swig from our glasses. Sylvia swallowed and said, 'Well, we can't *both* be going ga-ga, can we?'

'No. I think Wyngrave is haunted.'

'*Do* you?' Despite herself, Sylvia sounded thrilled.

'I think it's been haunted for a very long time.'

'But you didn't know when you moved in?'

'No. Queenie gave no indication. But I have reason to believe she knew.'

'Really? And she didn't sell her story to the papers? That wasn't like her,' Sylvia added with a snort of laughter.

'Perhaps she thought she'd be dismissed as a crazy old woman.' I heard myself and apologised immediately. 'Sorry, Sylvia, but I think you know how it must look to outsiders.'

'Of course I do! I shouldn't have spoken ill of the dead. Poor Queenie. If she *knew*, but had no one to tell…'

'She didn't say anything to Ros at the end? Deathbed ramblings?'

'No, Queenie sent her away. Wouldn't have her in the room. Said she wanted to be alone.'

'Well, according to my source, Queenie *wasn't* alone.'

'*Source?*' Sylvia asked sharply. The conversation was slipping away from me. 'Jane, did you say source?'

'If I tell you, you'll think I'm completely bonkers.'

She shook her head. 'I won't. People who *are* bonkers have absolutely no idea. Trust me, darling, I've known a few.' She lowered her voice to a stage whisper. 'One was a Knight of the theatre, now deceased. A great relief to all concerned.'

'My source is… the ghost.'

Sylvia let out a little squeak and her hand flew to her mouth. 'He *speaks*? Was it the same man? Tall, dark and for all I know, rather handsome?'

'The apparition I saw answered your description.'

'Oh, Jane! Somehow it all seems so much *worse* now I know it's not just me! I have no choice but to believe because – well, because you're so *sensible*.'

'I had an idea something wasn't right. More than an idea. Some strange things had been happening, but you find excuses, don't you?'

We sat in gloomy silence as the sun sank lower in the sky. The blackbird continued to sing his heart out from the top of a barley sugar chimney.

Sylvia sighed. 'What are we going to do?'

'Haven't a clue. But I don't think we should say anything to the others, not until we have to.'

'I agree. Rosamund won't believe us anyway. She'll just laugh, then tease us mercilessly.' Sylvia was thoughtful for a moment, then said, 'I don't suppose we could just ask him to leave?'

'He wants nothing more than to leave, but he's tied to this place. He's been stuck here for centuries.'

'Poor thing. I wonder if I *should* have a quiet word with my friend, Rupert?'

'Is he local?'

'No, and as he's retired, he could only act in an advisory capacity. But he could probably put you in touch with someone who could help you get rid of it. Oh, listen to me! I'm sounding like a back-street abortionist.'

'But that's just it, Sylvia. I'm not sure if that *is* what I want to do. Do I have the right to evict a harmless ghost who's lived here for over four hundred years? Doesn't he have as much right to be here as me? More! I don't even *own* the Hall. I'm just a tenant. Like you.'

'Oh, I didn't realise you were sub-letting.'

'I'm not.' Perhaps it was the gin, but I suddenly felt very confused. 'Sorry, Sylvia, but it's all rather complicated.'

'I beg your pardon, I didn't mean to pry. But if you're just a tenant, Jane, who is your landlord?'

'I'm not absolutely sure. I think it might be the ghost.'

I needed an opinion on my portraits. I knew I must sell some, but I also wished to keep a few. But which? I'd already made an emotional choice, but it was based on what the paintings looked like now, obscured by centuries of filth and varnish. It also took no account of what the portraits might be worth. I didn't know if I could afford to make emotional choices.

I was also curious. I'd been learning and writing about the Tudors for most of my adult life, but I'd never owned so much as a drawing from the period. I had studied portraits looking for characters in my fiction. I'd examined clothes and jewellery, but I knew nothing of painting itself, neither how it was done then, nor how it was restored now.

But I knew that, in comparison with clothes, books and furniture in the sixteenth century, paintings were cheap. They were also largely anonymous. A portrait might tell you the name, birthdate and age of the sitter, what honours he'd acquired, what his particular areas of prowess were, but of the artist there would most likely be no mention. If it was a copy, there would be no mention of whose work was being copied. All that mattered was the appearance of the sitter, which might or might not be a realistic representation, as Henry VIII and Philip of Spain discovered, cursing the artists who'd portrayed Anne of Cleves and Mary Tudor as those ladies wished to be perceived.

The artists' anonymity isn't quite as odd as at first it seems. We don't know who photographed the subject on the cover of *Vogue* or *Time* magazine. If it has been photoshopped, we have no idea who did it, nor do we care. All that matters is *who* features on the cover. The Elizabethan attitude to portrait painters was similarly dismissive.

Finding and selling art appeared to be a lucrative business, so I was out of my depth, used as I was to rubbing threadbare shoulders with other impecunious authors in the British Library. Fairly randomly, I invited conservator and art dealer Jesper Olsen to Wyngrave. Mr Olsen, despite his Scandinavian name, spoke with no accent and had an evident passion for his work. He responded immediately to my enquiring email and when we spoke, said he was particularly interested in portraiture. As Bridget sensibly pointed out, 'You've got to start somewhere,' so I thought I'd start with Jesper Olsen.

Lamentation the Fourth

Oftentimes I yield to the sin of despair and consider whether I might hasten mine own end. Yet what need is there? I know it will come ere long. The cords that tether me to this earthly life are thin now and frayed. Soon I shall be free.

When last I walked in the sun it was almost harvest time. Now I feel the approach of winter in my weary bones, yet have I no fire. I starve for lack of nourishment. I have no water with which to wash, scarce enough to drink.

Why does my husband not kill me? If I needs must die, why cannot my death be quick and merciful? Must I die in darkness, like a creature in its burrow, breathing this noisome air? Even traitors see the sky before their execution. They enjoy the good offices of a priest and go to their doom shaved, shriven and fit to meet Their Maker.

Shall I be allowed to make confession at the end? Or shall I just die like a dog?

7

A merrier man,
Within the limit of becoming mirth.
I never spent an hour's talk withal.

Love's Labours Lost

I happened to be upstairs, looking out over the gravel drive when a car pulled up. On time exactly, Mr Olsen got out, stretched a long frame and approached the front door, looking about him. I don't know what I'd been expecting. My experience of the art world is restricted to looking at portraits and exchanging occasional emails with helpful people at galleries. I suppose I expected to see someone who looked like an estate agent. A smart suit, but with a more flamboyant tie.

Mr Olsen didn't look like an estate agent. He looked rumpled. Not rumpled as if he'd just got out of bed, but comfortable. Relaxed. As if he had all the time in the world, time to bend and smell a late rose, even though it was raining. I'm sure Bridget would have said that was an encouraging sign. As Olsen approached the house, I could see his linen jacket didn't match his trousers, but they were both an intense blue. He looked older than his website had led me to expect, but as large amounts of money might be changing hands, that inspired confidence. I headed downstairs.

We have no doorbell, only the huge solid iron door knocker shaped in a ring which really takes two hands to lift. Undaunted by its weight and age, the postman will knock heartily, but people unused to the house produce a timid sound that only those with good ears can hear. Sylvia would delight in calling out, 'Someone nervous at the door,' but today as I passed her in the Great Hall, she said, 'An authoritative knock! Mr Olsen sounds as if he knows his way around sixteenth-century door furniture. Shall I make myself scarce, Jane?'

'No, you're fine. We'll be going up to the Gallery to look at the portraits. But you're very welcome to join us, if you can face the stairs.'

Sweeping past her, I hauled open the oak door and said, 'Mr Olsen? Good morning.'

He extended a hand and took mine firmly. His eyes were the same colour as the linen. 'Ms Summers, how d'you do?'

His tanned face was as creased as his clothes, but the lines looked as if they'd been acquired smiling into the sun, not scowling into his phone. His sleek, short hair was an indeterminate colour, probably blond once, now greying, almost white where it turned up in front, wayward, like a schoolboy's.

'Welcome to Wyngrave. Do come in.' Closing the door behind him, I said, 'I could wish for better weather for you. Brighter, I mean. All the portraits are upstairs in the Gallery because that's where we have the best light, but some of the pictures are very dark.'

He produced a slim torch from a drooping jacket pocket. 'I came prepared. As my grandmother used to say, "It's like looking for a black cat in a coal cellar".'

Sylvia, half-hidden in her wing chair by the fire, leaned forward. 'My mother used to say that!' She got to her feet, extending her hand. 'How do you do, Mr Olsen? I'm Sylvia Marlow. I live here, but I have nothing to do with the paintings. They're all Jane's. I'm afraid I don't even look at them because I no longer see very well.'

Olsen wasn't thrown by Sylvia's oblique look as she shook his hand and I doubted she could see he was examining her face.

'Forgive my impertinence, but are you *the* Sylvia Marlow? The actress?'

Sylvia produced her musical laugh. 'For my sins, yes, I was once an actress. I expect you thought I was dead.'

'Not at all. But your presence is much missed.'

'You're very kind, but how does a young man like you know of me anyway? You must have been watching some old films on television.'

'Well, in the first place, Miss Marlow, I'm really not that young. In the second place, *you* haven't changed at all.'

'Rubbish! I'm as old as Methuselah.'

'And in the third place,' Olsen continued, ignoring her, 'You made a great impression on me when I *was* young. Just a teenager, in fact.'

'Good Lord! What was I playing?'

'Gertrude.'

'Hamlet's mother?' Sylvia looked confused. 'But I only ever played that part on tour. Abroad.'

'In Elsinore. Or Helsingør, as we like to call it.'

'We performed outdoors in front of Kronborg Castle,' said Sylvia remembering. 'By the sea... You *saw* that production?'

'It was the first time I'd seen Shakespeare in English, but I already knew the play.'

'Because you're *Danish!*'

'My father was. My mother is English and she took me to see the play. She loves Shakespeare and was always quoting him to me. She'll be thrilled when I tell her I've met you. I'm so pleased to be able to thank you for your performance, Miss Marlow. It was truly memorable.'

'Oh, please call me Sylvia!' she said, clearly touched.

'Then I hope you'll call me Jesper.'

'*Yesper?*' she repeated, uncertain. 'Is that like *Jasper*, but in Danish?'

He nodded. 'Delightful! Well, Jesper, you'd better go and look for that black cat in the coal hole, then when you come back down, perhaps Jane will make us all some lovely coffee.'

'Of course I will. Mr Olsen, would you follow me?'

As we began to mount the stairs, I heard Sylvia chuckle to herself, 'Obviously not there the night my wimple blew away.'

I paused and turned to look down at her, indulgently. Olsen and I exchanged a look, then he pivoted on the stairs and called out, 'Actually, I *was*. Hamlet caught it and *you* didn't miss a beat.'

Turning, Sylvia lifted her head and pressed a hand to her breast.

'O, Hamlet, speak no more.
Thou turn'st mine eyes into my very soul,
And there I see such black and grainèd spots
As will not leave their tinct.'

Jesper applauded. '*Marvellous Marlow* – isn't that what they used to say?'

'Oh, go on with you!' she called up, flapping a hand. 'Don't encourage me!'

'*Marvellous Marlow* is what *we* say,' I added, as I led the way upstairs. 'Almost every day.'

My favourite portraits were hanging on the wall in the Long Gallery and where there was room, I'd hung others. The remaining pictures – a motley collection rescued from the so-called Sale Room – were propped up on chairs. I'd arranged two more for us in the middle of the room.

'This is as bright as it gets without resorting to artificial light, which I thought you might not want.'

'Don't worry, I have my trusty torch. Do you have favourites?'

'I do, actually.'

'Don't tell me which. Not yet. I prefer to approach them with an open mind.' He paced the room, somehow looking elegant despite all the creases.

As he scanned the portraits, I said, 'I think if I knew more about the pictures, I might love them more, and I'd like to. At the moment all I see are the sitters, not the artist.'

He turned and said, 'With respect, Ms Summers, you don't even see that. Not yet.' He set off again, moving confidently, like a conjuror striding around the stage, inspecting his props. I almost expected him to produce a string of silk handkerchiefs from a capacious pocket. He approached Lady Edith Wyngrave and peered at her closely, shining his torch over the wooden panel. 'In some cases, we see only what the Victorian restorer wanted us to see. Your pictures are also masked by yellowing varnish and centuries of coal fire and tobacco smoke, so neither of us has much idea yet of what the artist actually painted.'

'But that could be revealed?'

'Oh, yes. It's there, underneath, but often what's there is very different from what you see on the surface. I can't show you or even tell you what will be revealed, but the painting will be worth more if all the surface rubbish is removed and if it can be authenticated. A date, if not a signature. Artists of this period rarely signed their work.' He turned to look at me, 'But you probably know all this. You're M J Somerville, aren't you?'

'I am, but I write commercial fiction. An author like me knows a lot about the period in a superficial way, but we're not academics. I can translate Latin inscriptions, but I don't always know what they mean.'

'Oh, I think that applies to the best of us. The Elizabethans loved their puzzles, didn't they?'

I remembered what Horatio had said about Queenie, then dismissed it instantly. Horatio was a *ghost*. A little flustered, I said, 'Shall I leave you to your examination?'

'Thank you,' he said removing an iPad from its case. 'But before you go, can I just check? You said in your email you're interested in two things, mainly: which paintings are important and which ones will sell. Are you aware the two don't necessarily go together?'

'Oh, yes. From bitter experience. My publisher rejected my last book because the Sales Director said it wasn't the sort of thing people wanted to be seen reading on the Tube. And he wasn't talking about a *Lady Chatterley* effect.'

Olsen smiled. '*Is this a book you would wish your wife or servants to read?*'

'He meant I'm not Instagram-worthy.'

'But very readable.'

'You know my work?'

'I've read some of *Time's Whirligig*.'

'Dropped.'

He looked surprised. 'I'm sorry to hear that.'

'Don't read it on the Tube. Your street cred will be zero.'

'I think being passionate about portraits of dead people painted by *anonymous* dead people means I have no street cred whatsoever.' He turned back and surveyed the paintings. 'Ms Summers—'

'Please, call me Jane.'

He smiled and nodded. 'Jane, if these are cleaned, you might not like what's revealed. Elizabethan and Jacobean portraiture is… *uncompromising*, so what you're considering is perhaps risky if you wish to keep the paintings.'

'I realise restoration is a flight into the unknown.'

'It *is*, and that's what I love about it. It's frequently surprising and never, ever dull. But would you say you were a gambling woman?'

I considered the question. 'I think I must be. I've ended up living in this ancient money-pit of a house, with a motley crew of women who didn't know each other beforehand. One's newly divorced, one's going blind, and we're all aged somewhere between forty and death.'

The blue eyes widened. 'What could possibly go wrong?'

'To answer your question – the *serious* one. Writing is hardly a steady profession, but it's what I've always done. I'm okay with uncertainty. I accepted the challenge of living here when I had little idea how I could make the place work because… well, because it just *felt* right.'

'There speaks a gambling woman.'

'It feels right to me to examine all the paintings now, to get to know them before deciding their fate. Some will have to go because I'll need the money, but I think I should make an informed decision.'

'Of course.'

'It also feels right to get back to what the artist actually painted. Authenticity is important to me.'

'Even less attractive authenticity?'

'I've lived with fake for years. I won't do it any more.' The fair brows rose in silent query. 'I'm not talking about art forgeries.'

Jesper Olsen regarded me seriously and for a moment I felt like one of the portraits. 'We can never see what the artists saw, nor even *how* they saw. The closest we can get is to discover exactly what they *painted*. And how. And when.'

'You mean, what they *saw* will remain a mystery.'

'Always. Well, until they invent time-travel. But that very mystery means these paintings aren't just about the sitters, even though the artist was rarely credited. Each portrait is about three people.'

'Three?'

He stepped away from the portrait of Lady Edith and came and stood beside me, facing the painting. 'The sitter… The artist… And the viewer.' He raised a hand and pointed. 'If you *are* a gambling woman, Jane, look at the gleam on her cheekbone… The eyes have been ruined, but fortunately the restorer didn't bother with the rest of her face. If it was my painting and I saw those very precise brush strokes on the ruff and noted the way her bone structure lights up the portrait, I'd have it on my easel and I'd be filling a bin with swabs of filthy cotton wool until I discovered what this nameless, but possibly gifted artist had actually painted.' He strode towards the portrait and bent so that his face was very close. 'Who is this?'

'Lady Edith Wyngrave.'

'She probably did have those cheekbones, but I don't believe those are her eyes, do you? I've seen livelier-looking dead salmon.'

I laughed and said, 'I'll leave you to it. I'll go and check on Sylvia, then make us all some coffee.'

Jesper Olsen was inspecting Lady Edith with his torch and didn't reply. I don't think he even heard. He was already at work.

As I walked down the uneven staircase, I held on to the wooden handrail. I feared my feet might miss their footing because I was writing in my head. An email to a friend. A long, newsy email to a friend who died in 2015. So I placed my feet carefully on the ancient wood, polished by centuries of use…

Hi Alison

How are you? I suppose I shouldn't ask, but I hope you're OK, or as well as can be expected.

Guess what? (But I expect you already know. I like to think you still know everything, the way you somehow always did when you were alive.) I've already met two new men! Both very different. One's dead, like you, but the other is very much alive. Neither has any interest in me personally and sadly, the dead guy is a lot younger. I know you'd say that doesn't matter, look at Maeve and Giacomo, but I think being dead makes a difference, don't you?

I arrived at the foot of the stairs without mishap and saw that Sylvia was asleep, soothed no doubt by the soft, repetitive *clunk* of the long-case clock. I picked up a throw from the back of a sofa and draped it gently over her. On my way to the kitchen, I resumed writing the email I could never send...

I'm trying to decide who will interest you most. Dead Guy probably, because – well, because he's dead. As I said, he's younger. Well, sort of. He's 30-something going on 430-something. It's tricky with ghosts.

You said if your illness was to have any meaning, we should all get on with living. Well, I'm trying! I think you always knew I didn't do a lot of "living" with Duncan, so perhaps I should tell you about Live Guy, who really is alive. He's older than Dead Guy, though not, I think, as old as me, but it doesn't really matter because you're dead and he's probably not even single, but he is alive, which gives him the edge over Dead Guy IMO. Anyway, I get to choose and sadly, you don't get to complain.

Standing in the kitchen, I stared at a row of canisters. I knew one of them contained coffee, but momentarily, I couldn't remember which. I'd let Duncan have the contents of our kitchen because I didn't want half. I thought half a kitchen was ridiculous and petty and I didn't want to be petty, I wanted a fresh start, so I bought three new canisters from *Next Home* that now contained tea bags and two kinds of coffee. I just didn't remember which was which. I pulled them towards me randomly, one after another, like the three-card trick, trying to find my favourite coffee. Did it matter? Wouldn't any coffee do? I bent and sniffed. Was *this* the coffee I liked? Would Sylvia still be alive by the time I'd made it? Was I descending into incoherence?

I found the special *Taylor's of Harrogate* coffee, then realised I should have put the kettle on first. While waiting for the water to boil, I stood at the window and watched the rain…

You'd like Live Guy. His clothes and hair are expensively rumpled and he looks Danish and arty, which is what you'd expect, because he is.

The kettle boiled. I turned and glared at it, wondering why I'd thought yellow would be a good idea when it showed every dirty mark. It must have looked nice in the shop, which matters when you're out shopping, post-divorce.

Now where did we keep the largest of our coffee pots?

Live Guy (who's called Jesper, but you say it "Yes-pair") has come to look at my portraits. (Not portraits of me, the ones I now own, which I hope will be worth £££.) I found Mr Olsen on the Internet, as you do, and watched all his little videos which made a very pleasant change from researching Tudor herbalism. He works in a London studio where they clean paintings and generally make them whole again. Isn't that a marvellous way to earn a living? I wish someone would do all that for me. (I mean _me_, not my paintings. And of course, you.)

There are lots of interesting things about Jesper, not least that he's actually alive, but the best thing is, he talks about my Edith (that's Lady Edith Wyngrave, who used to live here) as if she's important, and to me she is. Admittedly she looks a bit depressed, but Jesper thinks she'll look different when she's cleaned up. Maybe not better, but _real_.

I wish you could hear him. It's like being in the presence of a great detective. He makes me believe we will Solve A Mystery. Maybe not Queenie's, but I feel sure we'll solve something, or reveal something, even if it's just Lady Edith's eyes (which _are_ wrong, there's no getting away from it. It didn't occur to me someone would just paint over the top. What a nerve!)

No one knows what these paintings mean to me, how they seem almost like real people. But they _were_ real people and three of them lived in this very house. That's why I'm writing to you in my head, Alison, because I know you'll take me seriously, like Jesper. It doesn't matter if you don't believe in Dead Guy, (I'm not sure _I_ believe in Dead Guy), as long as you believe in Jesper and Lady Edith. I can't wait to see her new eyes!

Talking of eyes, I need to go and wake Sylvia and take her some coffee. Got to dash. Miss you so much.

Love always,
J
xxx

I placed the pot on a tray with jugs of warm and cold milk, sugar, sweetener, biscuits and three new mugs, then set off for the Great Hall.

The coffee smelled good.

Sylvia was still asleep in her chair, but I placed a mug beside her and coughed. She preferred not to sleep too long during the day. Like many elderly people, she struggled to stay asleep at night, so she'd instructed us to wake her if she slept too long.

She sat up at once, blinking and I knew she was struggling with the encroaching darkness, the ever-surprising fact of it. 'Coffee's on your right, Sylvia, and I remembered your sweetener.' I set down a side plate. 'And there's a couple of biscuits, in case you're peckish.'

'Oh, you're so good to me, Jane!' She lowered her voice quite unnecessarily. 'Rosamund doesn't remember things like that. Or perhaps she thinks I should lose weight. She's probably right, but I'm too old to care. Now go up and see to Mr Olsen. I expect he's gasping. I still can't quite believe he saw my Gertrude.'

'And *remembers* it.'

'It wasn't really my part, you know. Guilt-stricken and sex-crazed. Not me at all, but my Hamlet was awfully good. Tall and blond, like your young man.'

This time I lowered *my* voice. 'He's not mine and he's certainly not young. Mid-forties? And the blond is mostly grey.'

'Well, he seemed young to *me*,' Sylvia said and groped for her coffee. 'I always used to think of Queenie,' she added wistfully.

'I'm sorry?'

'When I was rehearsing Gertrude. It was a stretch for me, so I used to think of Queenie.'

'Guilt-stricken and sex-crazed?'

She nodded. 'Definitely more her part than mine. We'd done *Hamlet* together at drama school. Queenie wasn't yet twenty, but she was unforgettable as Gertrude! I played Ophelia. Very innocent and affecting, they said.' She sipped her coffee. 'I went mad very well.'

'I bet you did. Now, I must take coffee up to Mr Olsen before it gets cold.'

She waved me away. 'Yes, go and find out about your portraits, then come and tell me all the details.'

Jesper Olsen had removed his rumpled jacket to reveal an equally rumpled white linen shirt. He was now standing, arms folded, staring at Gervase de Vere, as if the portrait presented a particular challenge. At the sound of my footsteps, he spun round and bestowed on me such a bright-eyed smile, I found myself wanting to add a postscript to Alison.

'You look like a man who's happy in his work.'

'This has all been *very* interesting. I hope you don't mind, but I've photographed everything for research purposes, including the alarming Jacobean *mafiosi*.'

I laughed. 'The de Vere gang? Yes, if looks could kill...' I set the tray down on a side table and poured coffee.

He took a mug but was obviously eager to talk. 'I'll put everything into an email report, but I expect you'd like a preliminary assessment?'

'Please. I'm dying to hear what an expert thinks about my other family.'

'Is that how you think of them?'

'Well, I haven't had a family for a very long time. My mother died when I was twelve, my father and I didn't get on and I never had children. I'm divorced now, so when I moved in here – there were just two of us to begin with – these pictures did feel almost like family. I see them every day. They see me. I really like some of them. Others I prefer to avoid.'

'Just like a real family, in fact. Though I'm no expert. My wife died before we were able to have children, but I'm uncle and godfather to a great number of tiring young Danes.'

'I'm sorry about your wife.'

'It was a long time ago. Cancer.'

'I lost my best friend to cancer some years ago. Does one ever stop feeling angry?'

'I'll let you know,' he said and swallowed more coffee. A moment later he resumed his chatty tone. 'My mother and I live happily in different parts of London, but most of the family is in Copenhagen. Frankly, we're rather relieved about that, but we do have wonderful Christmases there and my mother enjoys going back for shopping trips.'

'Has this always been your line of work?'

'No, I used to paint.'

'Portraits?'

'Yes. I was good, but not good enough. I realised I could *see* better than I could paint and starving in a garret had never appealed. I love people and the good things in life, so I wasn't really cut out to be an artist. But I love portraiture with a painter's passion and I suppose I see with a painter's eye.' He set down his mug. 'You said you have your favourites?'

'Yes. There are a couple I'd really like to keep, but…' I hesitated.

'Trust your instincts. Something's made you doubt?'

I topped up our coffee. 'I suppose I was hoping you'd make a pronouncement first. Advise me what to do. You strike me as someone who would have decided opinions.'

'I do, but you live with these paintings. They're family.'

'Except that I prefer to keep some hidden away. I've only allowed them out today to meet you.'

'This is sounding more and more like the Copenhagen cousins,' he said shaking his head. 'Tell me about the pictures you keep on display all the time.'

'The two I'm happiest with – oh, that's not really the word. She doesn't make me feel *happy*.'

'The two you couldn't bear to part with, but you can't explain why?'

'That's it! A judgement based entirely on what I feel and what I think might be there if you cleaned them.'

His smile was beatific and not at all business-like. 'Music to

111

my ears! Tell me more. Or shall I tell you, so you don't suspect I'm agreeing with you to make money?'

'I would very much like to hear what you think. And I'd like to be advised, but I can't promise to take that advice. I'm sure you know best, but pictures are emotional things, aren't they?'

'They are for some people. Others buy them as they might buy good wine, as an investment. Pictures are laid down in the artistic cellar untasted, simply increasing in value. They aren't that family member who lights up the room when she walks in.'

'Like Sylvia.'

'*Just* like Sylvia.'

'My friend was like that too. Until she became ill.'

I listened to the profound silence of Wyngrave Hall, which seemed almost to wait for something, or maybe it was Olsen who was waiting. I took a deep breath and my words came out in a rush. 'The two I'd like you to restore first are mother and son: Lady Edith Wyngrave and her son, Samuel. They're both very dark, but I just have a feeling about them both.'

'The same feeling?'

'No, quite different. Samuel cheers me up and reassures me, but I feel rather sorry for Edith.' I looked away and stared at her portrait. 'Perhaps it's because she's a young woman, but the darkness that envelops her seems almost symbolic.'

'Of?'

'Powerlessness. Neglect, maybe. But I could be projecting on to her what I know about the life of Elizabethan wives.'

'There are no other pictures of her?

'No. And Samuel was an only child.'

'Only surviving child?'

'Only child, as far as I can tell.'

'So she probably didn't make old bones. Or *he* didn't,' Olsen said, indicating the portrait of Sir Walter Wyngrave.

'He outlived Edith by many years and Samuel was only an infant when she died. That's one of the reasons I'd like to hang them together. I found him wrapped up in a cupboard. I don't think the previous owner ever had him on display. The same goes for Edith. They're both very dark.'

'Black silk said *money*. It was the most expensive dye. It was also very difficult to paint. A challenge for the artist.'

'So when Sir Walter commissioned portraits of his wife and son, he was showing off?'

'Undoubtedly. Portraits were very much about how people wanted to be seen and remembered. Sir Walter wanted the world to know he had a young wife, a son and heir – *very* important – and pots of money. Sadly, not much of that would have gone to the artist, but you can tell from their clothes that they were rich.'

'Well, I have no time for Sir Walter, I'm afraid. Elizabethans believed *the apparel oft proclaims the man*, but in this case, I doubt he would have lived up to this image.'

'Which would in any case have been flattering.'

I looked at the portrait with distaste. 'Somehow his features don't seem to hang together as a face.'

'And why do we think that's the fault of the man himself and not the artist?'

It was a relief to laugh. 'I find my attention engaged more by his spectacular ruff than his eyes.'

'They *are* watery, aren't they? And vague. But that's how you know the picture is very good. Might be Robert Peake the Elder, if we're lucky. And the painting's in great condition – probably because no one wanted to hang it. But it's distinguished. It will fetch a good price.'

'But that would mean breaking up the Wyngrave family. And this *is* Wyngrave Hall.'

He shrugged. 'But you don't like him. You'll hang the picture somewhere you won't have to look at it. A guest room.'

'Oh, I wouldn't inflict Sir Walter on guests! He gives me the creeps.'

'So clean, restore and price to sell?' His finger hovered over his iPad.

'Yes, please. I don't think Edith will mind if she never sees him again, do you?'

'She might cheer up once he's out of the way. He must have cramped her style,' Olsen said, walking over to examine Edith closely again. 'She'll come back looking quite different once we've removed all that varnish and the nasty Victorian over-paint. I think there are indications something interesting lies underneath. Though sometimes I think I see what I want to see. What *could* be there.' He turned to face me and said, 'Which is a roundabout way of saying I could be wrong.'

'I suppose you have to say that, to cover yourself.'

'I do.'

'Are you often wrong?'

'Hardly ever.' He turned back to the portrait and switched on his torch. Peering at a brown ruff that must once have been ivory, he said, 'The brushwork here... You can just about see through the varnish... It's *meticulously* done. The painting of ruffs sorted out the wheat from the chaff, as did the depiction of hands. The preposterous elongation of fingers was a convention, but within that convention some men – and a few women – painted exquisite hands.'

I looked at Sir Walter, then his young wife. 'I think she'd want my roof to be watertight.'

'And I'm sure she'd far rather be displayed near her son. I see no family likeness, but they were done by different artists, a generation apart. And then there's the awful overpainting... May I make a suggestion?'

'Please do.'

'If you should wish me to proceed—'

'I do.'

'Excellent! Then I suggest we start with the two paintings you probably want to keep. I would take them to the studio, study them, then send you a report telling you what I think could be done. Then it's up to you.'

'I'm really keen to get that varnish off.'

'I'm *itching*,' Olsen said with feeling.

'Could you take them away today?'

'Certainly. I have packing materials in the car. Could you take the paintings off the wall while I'm gone?'

He left the Gallery and I heard him jog downstairs, then the front door groaned as it opened and shut. Neither portrait was large or heavy, so I lifted them down and propped them carefully against the wall, feeling slightly sad that I had to part with them. The door opened again and soon Olsen appeared, carrying a box of packing materials. He stood still and regarded me, his head on one side. 'Have you changed your mind? You look a little cast down. I won't do a thing until you've had my report which will tell you in detail what I propose.'

'I'm fine. I've just been saying my *adieux*.'

He set the box down, took out cloths and pieces of blanket and laid them on the floor, then he fetched Lady Edith and began to wrap her with a sort of reverence. 'It's when you actually handle them that you sense their great age. First you need to look very hard for a long time, then finally you get to touch… It's almost electric. And a great privilege.'

I watched as he set Edith aside and began to wrap the portrait of Samuel. 'Mr Olsen—'

'Jesper. As we're going to be working together.'

'You said you can see what isn't there—'

'I *believe* I can see what isn't there.'

'What's the difference between seeing something and *believing* you see something?'

He sat back on his heels, pondering the question. 'It's surely the difference between science and faith. Whether or not there's proof.'

'And in your work, you have to amalgamate the two?'

'I couldn't do the job unless I did.' He indicated the wrapped portraits. 'If you find you like what's underneath all the muck, if you actually prefer it—'

'My faith in your judgement will have been justified.'

He looked up at me and smiled. 'Which will mean a lot more to me than my popularity on Instagram.'

He carried the two parcels downstairs while I followed behind with the box and his iPad. There was no sign now of Sylvia. I put the box down and opened the front door, but Jesper set the pictures down, propping them against the jamb. Standing in the open doorway, he said, 'It's been a real pleasure to meet you, Jane, and see your beautiful home.'

'I wish you'd had better weather for your journey, but Bridget says we really needed the rain. She does all the gardening,' I explained.

He held up his hands in protest. 'Please don't apologise.' He pointed to the dense vegetation above his head. 'Listen to that sound... Rain dripping down through the wisteria... It's almost musical. And think how many others have listened to that sound over the years.' He looked over my shoulder, back into the Great Hall. 'You have something very special here. I sense it.'

'Do you?' I asked, alarmed. 'Are you referring to the building itself?'

'I wasn't, though it's notable of course, and contains what might turn out to be some important paintings.'

'What else do you sense then?'

'A real home. Support. Miss Marlow might be going blind, but she seems very happy here.'

'We haven't been here all that long, apart from Bridget, but it's working out quite well. On the whole,' I added, fearing to tempt fate. Or Horatio.

'Bridget has been here a long time?'

'Years. I inherited her with the house.'

'Maybe that's what I can feel. Continuity. The sense of history is palpable, isn't it? I hear the sound of feet on polished wood and stone... Theirs and now ours. And that huge stone fireplace...' He pointed. 'I can see some Elizabethan gentleman standing there, gazing into the flames.'

'Can you?' I asked in a strangled voice, turning quickly, dreading I would see the dark form of Horatio.

'Not really. I see what isn't there but could have been.' Perhaps Jesper noticed my obvious relief, because then he said, 'Do you have a resident ghost?'

Shocked by his apparent mind-reading, I said, 'Why do you ask?'

'The nature of my work means I visit a lot of very old buildings and stately homes. When you get chatting with the owners, they sometimes talk about the *other* residents.'

'Really?'

'It seems to go with the territory.'

'Ghosts?'

'Sometimes. Or just things that go bump in the night.'

'It sounds terrifying.'

'You'd think so, wouldn't you? But I've never come across anyone who seemed the least bit frightened. Annoyed, perhaps, but I remember a Duke who seemed almost proud of being haunted. He'd grown up with this apparition, as had his forefathers, and the ghost was apparently quite benign. He just thought of it as part of the family. He was a lovely old gentleman. Heartbroken to have to sell his paintings, but he badly needed the cash. When his wife died, I was relieved he wouldn't be holed up there on his own...' My face must have betrayed me, because he frowned and said, 'Sorry, Jane, I didn't mean to alarm you, but that's why I asked if you had a ghost. I walk into a place like this now and I almost assume—' He reached out and put his hand under my elbow, as if to steady me. 'Do you need to sit down?'

It was cowardly of me, but there was something about his kind and confiding manner that made me want to tell the truth, if not the whole truth.

'Sylvia says she sees something.'

'But... she's going blind, isn't she?'

'Yes.'

'Not just zig-zag patterns?'

'You know about AMD?'

'Some of my clients are afflicted. It's why they decide to sell.' He shook his head. 'Very sad.'

We were standing quite close now and I knew I could terminate the conversation with a word, a brisk movement, a step back. Instead, I said, 'Sylvia sees – or *thinks* she sees – a person. Someone from the sixteenth century.'

'Ah.' Jesper was thoughtful, then said, 'Is she in the habit of seeing things? Anything odd in her previous home?'

'No, but she says she's encountered ghosts before. In theatres.'

He nodded. 'A lot of actors say that. Well, far be it from me to cast doubts on the Marvellous Marlow. If she says she can see someone, she probably can.'

'You believe her?'

'I think I have to. We're in the same business, in a way. *Thou turn'st mine eyes into my very soul...* It's what artists, playwrights and the best actors do. Make us see things we didn't know were there.'

'But... *you* haven't seen anything here?' I asked.

'Only in the portraits.' His words were reassuring, but at the same

117

time I felt almost disappointed. I shivered, not with cold, but we were standing in the doorway and it was still raining, so Jesper drew the obvious conclusion.

'You're getting chilly, Jane. I must get going. I'll send you my report. Owners are understandably anxious, so I'll keep in touch, but you're very welcome to come to the studio if you'd like to see how work is progressing.'

'Thank you. I think I'd enjoy that.'

He bent to pick up his box, carried it out to the car, then came back for the portraits. 'Ring me if you're coming to town and we'll sort something out. Give my regards to Miss Marlow. It was a great pleasure to meet her.'

'I think you made her day.'

'Likewise. See you in London, perhaps?'

We shook hands, then he bent and gathered up the precious parcels. I stood and watched as he installed the portraits carefully in his car. When he turned back to wave, his cheerful smile was damp but undiminished.

Lamentation the Fifth

What was my sin but to love beneath my station?

Thy love was better than high birth to me and are not all men equal in Christ? For Saint Paul sayeth, "There is neither Jew nor Greek, there is neither bond nor free, there is neither male nor female: for ye are all one in Christ Jesus." Why then so harsh a punishment?

I brought shame on my family. Yet did I not also save my husband from gossip and calumny? He now has an heir – a son if he is yet living – without the trouble of lying with his wife, a wife not told her place in the marriage bed would be usurped by her husband's catamite.

In sooth, it was the Devil's own bargain and I was sold like a brood mare.

8

It is an honest ghost.

Hamlet

I closed the heavy door and turned back to face the Hall. The fire was in urgent need of attention. Normally I loved the sound of the rain beating against the windows, but today it seemed a dismal sound. I stood by the remains of the fire, longing for light and warmth, and wondered what on earth I was doing with the second half of my life. My career was stalled and I was living with very pleasant strangers. I was also seeing things. Roving chess pieces. Open books. A polite ghost. Was I going mad with grief and shame? How could I have been so wrong about my father? Despite an appearance of civilised acceptance, was I in fact raging silently about the end of my marriage?

Angry thoughts of Duncan's betrayal led to pleasanter thoughts of Jesper Olsen and I indulged in the vengeful luxury of comparison. I'd enjoyed chatting intelligently, knowledgeably, humorously about a subject close to my heart and apparently his. With so much in common, it was difficult to assess the exact nature of Jesper's impact. He was an attractive man and, even before I'd moved to the isolation of Wyngrave Hall, I didn't get out much, so I was perhaps easily impressed, but I was aware how Sylvia and I had basked in the warmth of his charm. No doubt this was a professional requisite. He was after all selling me his services and also hoped to sell some of my paintings on substantial commission. If the day appeared to have darkened since Jesper left, if I now felt restless and bored, it surely meant I'd fallen for the professional patter, lively blue eyes and a face creased by good humour – the fate of a sex-starved, embittered, middle-aged woman, struggling to rise above the ignominy of being left for a younger woman. I wondered what on earth Duncan and Sophie found to talk about, then it occurred to me, they probably didn't do much talking. Maeve and Susie would have understood my foul mood. Alison would have laughed me out of it.

A day out in London, to include a visit to the studio to see Jesper at work was an appealing idea. Sensible, really. I'd buried myself in the Essex countryside, settled into a dead woman's house, surrounded myself with portraits of the dead and discovered letters written by my dead mother. Now I was composing emails to the dead and believed I was seeing, even talking to the dead.

None of this was what Alison meant by *living*.

Chiding myself for mooning about like a teenager, I made a quick sandwich and went to sit in our little TV room. As I grabbed the remote and a blanket to put round myself, I thought of Jesper driving back to London with Edith and Samuel also wrapped in blankets in the back of his car. Cosy. Together. I hoped they'd be all right.

After Bridget and I had talked about the possibility of a poltergeist, I'd done some research and found there was a reality TV series dedicated to living with paranormal interference. Well, things had moved on since then. Now with a full-blown ghost to contend with, I selected *Haunted Homes* on Prime and sat down to watch.

It has to be said, I was not the target audience. I had no desire to be perplexed or frightened. I spent my working life steeped in plague, torture and executions, people burned alive because they believed in the right god, but not in the right way. My idea of a relaxing night in front of the TV involved Mary Berry or Prue Leith. Collapsed soufflés were all the small screen drama I sought at the end of a working day.

So I was braced for disappointment, but nothing had prepared me for hysterical mediums, shaky, hand-held camera-work and grainy, green-tinted footage of silhouettes sliding across ancient stone walls. There were even things that went bump in the night, duly recorded and played back to an astonished female presenter.

Despite the earnest input of local historians, the programmes failed to convince me because they lacked any intellectual rigour.

The medium would put his head on one side while attuning to information from "the other side" concerning historical death from fire, famine and flood – information he could easily have gleaned from Google or pamphlets produced by the local history society.

The only aspect that seemed even faintly convincing was the deadpan demeanour of the owners of these haunted homes. I thought of Jesper's aged Duke who really wasn't bothered whether anyone believed in his ghost. The spectre was just an annoying fact of life, something each generation had to grapple with, like death duties and dry rot.

These haunted homeowners told their stories with no attempt at sensationalism. In some cases I thought I detected a certain weary boredom as they recounted sleepless nights, blown fuses, stains on the wall that no amount of re-decorating could conceal. These people were tired, perhaps annoyed. What they weren't was frightened.

I noted an air of resignation, sometimes a tinge of pride in the exploits of "their" ghost. Their lack of fear carried conviction but was at odds with the ethos of the programme, which strove to generate terror of the unknown. The director had tried to create programmes that would alarm, miniature horror movies that would disturb the viewer, but prove nothing. Sensibly, he'd decided the owners of these haunted homes should be kept in the background. Their calm acceptance of the unexplained was no one's idea of entertainment.

But listening to the tales of the haunted, I was occasionally able to believe. I didn't recognise the nature of the hauntings, but I accepted the haunted. They had made their peace with the dead and knew to expect the unexpected.

I contemplated the speed with which I'd accepted that my new home was haunted. What else could one do when confronted – quite literally – with an ambassador from another world? When Captain Cook landed in Botany Bay and First Australians threw spears (not to kill, but to frighten him away), who or what did they think had arrived? What did the ten-year-old Pocahontas think of John Smith, a white man, when she first set eyes on him? Perhaps she thought he was a god. Or a ghost.

The credits rolled as one programme ended and another began. I switched off and sat staring at the blank screen, depressed.

I might have dismissed my own experience, but when Sylvia took me into her confidence, I had to decide whether, by some massive coincidence, we both shared a delusion that Wyngrave was haunted, or whether we'd both observed some inexplicable phenomenon. The fact that Sylvia couldn't *see* Horatio, but was nevertheless convinced of his presence, went a long way to persuading me he must exist. Her sixth sense seemed to me more convincing – and frightening – than any number of objects sailing across the room in *Haunted Homes*.

Why would I *invent* long conversations with a man who'd been dead for over four hundred years? To be fair, I did that all the time. I was paid to invent dialogues with imaginary people. I could see them. I heard them. When a book was going well, it felt like taking dictation.

But if Horatio *was* just a figment of my imagination, wouldn't he have spoken in the language of his time, with which I was familiar? Under what possible circumstances would I have conjured up an Elizabethan actor who was a regular viewer of *Coronation Street*, a programme I'd never even seen?

I decided to go upstairs and change into something warmer. Even on a fine day the heat of the sun failed to penetrate the thick walls of Wyngrave Hall with its chilly spots that radiators and open fires never seemed to reach. I was beginning to understand why Bridget spent every moment she could outdoors. Perhaps that's why Jesper Olsen had seemed like the ray of sunshine we lacked, breezing in with his wide-eyed, very un-British enthusiasm.

As I approached the top of the staircase, I heard a little cough, the unmistakable sound of someone clearing their throat to attract attention. It wasn't one of my housemates. They would have spoken.

I froze on the stairs, then closed my eyes. If I didn't open them, I wouldn't see anything. I stood still for what seemed a long time, clutching the banister rail. I thought of all the other hands that had touched that wood, people who had leaned on it and needed the smooth solidity of its support. I breathed again and felt slightly calmer.

He had coughed. Very quietly. He didn't want to alarm me. This was a *considerate* ghost. I thought of the haunted Duke and wished Jesper was here. Or the Duke.

I opened my eyes and saw the greyish, indistinct but unmistakeable form of Horatio Fortune, loitering in a gloomy alcove. I closed my eyes again, fighting the urge to run back downstairs, when the writer in me suddenly wondered what it must feel like to know your mere appearance inspired terror, like Stalin or Sadam Hussein. But this spirit had been no murdering dictator. Once, his performance might have been met with laughter or admiration. He might have lit up his world as Sylvia had lit up Jesper's in Elsinore.

I opened my eyes again and said in a preternaturally calm voice, 'Did you want to speak to me?'

'Madam, there is a matter I should like to discuss. I believe many things are disturbing you. Queenie warned me about your mother's letters.'

'You *know* about them?'

He nodded. 'I may be able to... *simplify* your life at the Hall. And I wish to do so.'

I swapped fear for irritation. 'Well, we can't stand here, gossiping on the landing. We'd better go into the library.'

'As you wish, madam.'

'And stop all this *madam* business!' I hissed. 'My name's Jane!'

He bowed slightly, then vanished. I hoped he'd gone off in a huff, but the library door opened to reveal Horatio, who stood aside to let me in. The door closed behind me – by itself – and I stood facing him. His colourless face looked almost transparent, and in the gloom of the library his eyes looked black and fathomless.

'What colour were your eyes?' I asked. 'When you lived?'

He didn't answer immediately and gazed into space, as if trying to remember. 'Brown, I believe.' He looked up. 'What colour are they now?'

'Black. What did you want to say to me?'

'I wished to explain my position.' He paused, as if gathering himself. 'I watched Queenie suffer for some years before I... made my presence felt. There had been many lovers, but as age and ill health encroached, she succumbed to fits of melancholy. She'd always been solitary, but she became lonely. I know because she started to talk to herself. I thought she might find talking to me more interesting, so I decided to show myself.'

'You mean, you began to haunt her?'

He winced. 'Haunting is a very negative concept. I merely let Queenie know, in various subtle ways, that she was not alone. I thought if I put in an appearance, it might give her a new interest in life. Or indeed death.'

'I think you did,' I conceded.

'It is an honour to serve.' Horatio bowed again and appeared to smile, but there was nothing of happiness in his expression. It was a mere re-arranging of facial muscles, a contortion that conveyed only resignation. 'She wished to return the compliment, as you know. She had plans for us. But there is a problem. You are distressed by my presence. Miss Marlow, too. Queenie didn't anticipate my general visibility.'

'I don't think it is general. Sylvia is rather special.'

'I believe Miss Marlow sees me because she can't really see anybody else.' There was a silence during which Horatio was very still. He broke it eventually, saying, 'Madam – *Jane*... I'm sorry to have to inform you, but I am unable to leave. Believe me—' The sad smile again. 'I *have* tried but, unlike Elvis, I cannot leave the building.'

'Horatio, I think I need to sit down. You can stand or sit, as you wish.' I sank into an armchair, but he continued to stand.

'Would you like me to explain my geographical limitations?'

'Perhaps you better had.'

'My territory appears to be bounded by Wyngrave Hall. I've never managed to leave it.'

'You're saying something *prevents* you?'

'A powerful force. It's as if I hit an invisible wall, a wall of what I can only describe as... nameless terror.'

'Do you mean the wall is within you? In your mind?' He looked down. Had I embarrassed a ghost? 'It's still real. Real for *you*. And your fear has a medical label. Post-traumatic stress.' He looked up, frowning. 'The brain can be affected by very bad experiences. Accidents. Witnessing violent death. Heaven knows what happens if you can remember your own murder! Instead of fading with the passage of time, memories can become intrusive, even crippling. Alternatively, the mind can forget bad experiences altogether. Well, they're not actually erased, they're buried deep in the unconscious. Do you know what it is you fear?'

'No. Not unless…'

'Unless?'

'Unless it's the fear of my memory returning.'

I gazed for a moment at Horatio's haunted and haunting face, speechless. Confronted with his fear, mine evaporated. 'You must feel as if you've been under house arrest for centuries.'

He shook his head. 'If you were under house arrest, you would be charged with a crime. From what little I can recall, I was a man more sinned against than sinning. But I do understand why you would wish me to leave. A household of ladies – and one a sceptic. One venerable, but also vulnerable. I'm hardly the ideal housemate.'

'Sylvia thought you were some sort of tradesman.'

He flinched. 'I have no desire to intimidate anyone, nor do I wish to conform to some Hallowe'en cliché,' he said firmly. 'I have had enough to do with fear.'

'The odd thing is, I'm *not* afraid of you. Not right now, this minute. It's just… well, the *idea* of you that's so alarming. You're a ghost. You're *dead*. But actually you're not nearly as scary as some of the weirdos I used to see on the Tube. Men who looked as if they might just whip out a knife and carve up commuters.'

'I thank you for the compliment, madam. I believe it *was* a compliment?' he said acidly.

'Don't mock me, Horatio. None of this is easy.'

'I do not mock, madam. I'm delighted to hear you do not fear me. Nevertheless, you would enjoy greater peace of mind if I were gone.' When I didn't reply, he stared at me, expressionless and unblinking. 'Would you not?'

'Yes, I would. Sorry, but I've never been a good liar and I really can't see the point of lying to a ghost.'

'And it's not as if you need to spare my feelings. I don't have any.'

'But you miss Queenie, don't you?' Eventually he nodded. 'I don't think you're completely dead, Horatio, even after four hundred years.'

'Thank you, madam. I beg your pardon. *Jane.*'

'You say you can't leave voluntarily but has anyone ever *tried* to— I'm not sure how to put this tactfully.'

'Evict me?' he said, with distaste. 'No. Perhaps that surprises you? But few have been aware of my existence. And I've never made a nuisance of myself, unlike some fictional ghosts I could mention – Banquo upsetting Lady Macbeth's seating plan for example. I know my place, you see, and it's not Wyngrave Hall. This is not and has never been my home. I merely died here.'

'You're certain of that?'

'My final memories are of a performance given here. I died waiting to make my entrance. And why else would I be spiritually shackled to this particular edifice, so far above my humble station in life?'

'I agree it makes some sort of sense. You don't haunt *people*, do you, you seem to haunt the *building*, like a phantom sitting tenant. You're not here to warn or inform the living… Are you?' I asked anxiously.

'On the contrary, I hope the living will one day inform *me*. Explain why I'm still here and how I arrived at my untimely end. Meanwhile, I'm aware I have no right to be here. In the absence of any sense of purpose, I've kept a low profile out of deference to the Hall's inhabitants, but children and animals have often detected my presence. And, of course Miss Marlow. Lately – for the last hundred years or so – I've felt a strong and surely not unnatural yearning for company. Three hundred years spent contemplating the enigma of my demise led me to conclude that, alone, I would come to no conclusions, so I decided it was time I came out of the closet. Literally. The reception has been mixed, but the last century has certainly been easier for me. Queenie was excellent company. An anarchic spirit, but she really wished to help. I suspect she wished to atone. She apparently had a lot to atone *for*. But I digress. Feel free to embark on some sort of exorcism if you wish. You might thereby render me a service.'

'How?'

'You would be putting me out of my misery – though I suppose I could be dispatched to Purgatory, or even Hell. The fact I no longer believe such places exist does not preclude their existence, unfortunately. But a change, as they say, is as good as a rest.'

'Has it just been… misery?'

'My *post mortem* life? No, not entirely, though I will own there have been many times when, had I not already been dead, I should have dispatched myself with a bare bodkin, or whatever came to hand. The first few years were the worst as I tried to come to terms with what I'd become. I endured periods of denial, followed by rage before I was able to accept my new status.'

'It sounds something like the grieving process.'

'I believe it was. But imagine if you will, trying to accept your *own* death. Not that you will die – we all know life is terminal – but the *fact* of your own sudden and, in my case, violent death. Imagine surviving – in another form – *the event itself.* Queenie grew old and then sick. She knew she lived on borrowed time. Then one day her physician informed her that her time had run out, so she made arrangements and put her house in order. I had no such luxury. I had no warning, no time to prepare. I made no confession, enjoyed no bedside vigil surrounded by loved ones. Queenie at least had me.

Cut off even in the blossoms of my sin,
No reckoning made, but sent to my account
With all my imperfections on my head…

Perhaps it's just as well I no longer recall the nature and number of those imperfections.'

'Might they have been the motive for your murder?'

He narrowed his dark eyes. 'The thought had occurred to me. You mean, did I deserve what happened to me?'

'No one deserves to be murdered.'

'I'm inclined to agree, but then I would, wouldn't I? To answer your original question: it has not been unalloyed misery. One day I realised I'd been dead for more years than I was alive. That was something of an epiphany and I decided I must make the best of my new rôle in life. Or rather death. There has been the sound of children's laughter and a good deal of music. Wyngrave has always been blessed with a good library. The invention of the radio and then the television made a huge difference to my life. My education began again as I watched and listened over the shoulders of the living. Whenever anyone acknowledged me, I found my blighted existence easier to bear, but relationships have been few. In the end everyone dies, so…' His chest rose and fell with a great sigh. 'I exist in a state of perpetual bereavement.'

'It sounds *appalling*. And no one ever… stayed on? After death?'

The wan smile. 'As a ghost? No. That has been disappointing, though to be frank, in four hundred years I've not met anyone with whom I thought I could spend eternity.'

'I did.'

Horatio looked surprised. 'Your husband?'

'No. Perhaps that's why my marriage failed, though he got bored before I did. No, it was a friend. A very dear friend. She was a life force, but she died. The eternity thing was never put to the test.'

He lowered his voice, so it was little more than a rasping whisper. 'My condolences, madam. Was she taken suddenly?'

'No. Cancer. We all knew what was going to happen, but it still came as a shock. I was prepared for her death, you see, but not her *absence*.' Horatio said nothing and I was grateful for his silence. 'I don't know how it's possible to live in a house full of people and still feel lonely.'

'Well, don't ask me. I've managed it for four hundred years,' he said in a discouraging tone.

'I would just like to *tell* someone. Someone who really cares. Cares about *me*. Tell them about my mother. My poor father. About Duncan and that wretched girl. And now about *you*. But the only person I want to tell, the only person who could possibly understand is Alison and she's dead. And here I am, *saying* all that, *confiding* in someone who is also dead! It's mad! I'm going mad!'

'Jane, you aren't going mad, but grief sometimes makes us fear that we will.'

'But how can you trust your mind when you're wrong about *everything*? Nothing is as I thought it was! I believed my mother was devoted to my father and I thought he was a shit. I thought cancer happened to people who led unhealthy lives. I assumed my husband was too lazy to have an affair. *And I didn't believe in ghosts!*'

I got up from my chair, snatched a tissue out of the box on my desk and blew my nose. I sat down again and tried to compose myself, aware that Horatio was watching me intently.

'Your friend. Alison. She died knowing that you loved her.'

'*Everybody* loved her. The wrong people die.'

'Undoubtedly. But it means a great deal to die knowing you are loved. I believe I did, but I've spent four hundred years trying to remember if that was indeed the case. Memory plays tricks, especially when you don't have one.'

I looked up at his pale, grey face. 'Oh, Horatio, it seems woefully inadequate, but I am so sorry for what happened to you.'

'Thank you, madam. It is not a small thing to lose a friend. Nor is it a small thing to die surrounded by those who love you. That was a service I was able to render Queenie.'

'You *did* love her, didn't you?' He didn't answer and I said, 'Does one ever get used to bereavement? Come on, Horatio. You're the expert.'

'I, madam?'

'You've lost every single person you ever cared for.'

I watched as his black, shining eyes clouded. He looked away, then said, 'After four hundred years, I think I can say I'm making *some* progress. But there are always setbacks. My years with Queenie were companionable, happy at times, but there was a price to pay. When death settled that account, I found I owed yet more grief and anger. I cherished hopes Queenie might reappear. She loved Wyngrave and wanted to live longer so she could solve the mystery of my demise. But she's gone. *She* had no unfinished business apparently.' His shoulders sagged and he stared at the floor. 'I envy you, Jane, for many reasons. You have friends. Housemates. Work. This splendid home… You have loved and been loved.' He raised his head. 'And you remember your love!'

'You mean, *you* can only remember that you've forgotten.'

The smile that was not a smile. 'A paradox! Yes, I remember *that* I have forgotten, not *what* I have forgotten. Or who.'

'What *do* you remember?'

'Love. I remember that I loved. And I think I remember that I was loved in return. Nothing more. Not in four hundred years. My beloved is dead – *obviously* – but I would endure the rack if it could furnish me with one glimpse of that woman's face. Or just her name.'

'I really wish I could help.'

'Thank you, but I shall not trouble you again with this or any other complaint. Send for a priest. Do whatever you can to be rid of me. *I* wish it. *You* wish it. You have my word, Jane. I shall co-operate as far as I am able.'

'But you have as much right to be here as I do. I'm sure Queenie didn't want me to evict you. This is your *home*.'

'No, this is merely where I was murdered. I remember my home.' His voice softened. 'A dark, smoky cottage… I shared a bed with a fidgety young brother, so I ran away to London to seek work. My family used to jest that Horatio had turned his back on a small Fortune, to seek a larger.'

'You remember your family?'

'I do. Those memories were old and well-worn on the day I died. As were all the plays I still remember.'

'But you don't remember your beloved?' He shook his head. 'So those memories must have been relatively new. They hadn't had long to embed themselves in your brain.' He frowned, evidently puzzled. 'That's how memory works. I think Sylvia knows the title of every play she's ever performed, the name of the author and the director, but she sometimes struggles to recall the name of the book she's listening to.'

'But eventually Miss Marlow *does* remember, or failing that, she can ask you. If parts of her long life go missing, they are retrievable. She can refer to her press cuttings.'

'Queenie wanted me to give you back some of your memories. That was the deal.'

'It wasn't a deal, it was a challenge, and a most unfair one in my opinion. You had no idea what living here might entail.'

'If she'd told me, I wouldn't be here, would I?'

'Precisely.' He clenched his fists. 'So much trouble over one paltry death! Why should *my* death matter, in the great scheme of things? Life is cheap and always has been. I lived with Plague and the great pox, which, like the poor, were always with us. Those that came after died in a bloody Civil War. Eat your royal heart out, Gloriana!' he snarled in a furious undertone. 'Then there was more plague, the *small* pox, the Napoleonic Wars, consumption, the Boer Wars, the War To End All Wars, the Spanish Influenza, *another* war and AIDS.' He looked up and said, 'So much for *This fortress built by*

Nature for herself against infection and the hand of war! When Nature isn't killing us, we like to kill each other, so why should I complain about my poor little death? It is the human condition to be dead. Yet I am not. Not quite.'

Horatio was silent, his expression bleak. Eventually he said, 'Madam, no exorcism will be necessary. I shall simply refrain from manifestation. I cannot prevent the sensitive from detecting my presence, but our conversations are entirely optional. Pure self-indulgence on my part. I was an actor. What worse fate could befall an actor than to be condemned to an eternity of invisibility and silence?' He placed a hand over his heart. 'I embrace voluntary redundancy. What could be more redundant than a *ghost*?' he asked scornfully. 'I wish you long life and continuing good health, Jane, but you are mortal. At best you have only a few decades to enjoy Wyngrave Hall. For all I know,' he said, with his travesty of a smile, 'I have *eternity*. You can rely on my discretion. Unless you wish it, you will never see me again.'

'But if I should *want* to see you?'

'I shall know. But for now, dear lady, I take my leave...

If we do meet again, why, we shall smile.

If not, why then this parting was well made.'

He bowed deeply. Upright once again, he said, 'Farewell!', then was gone. Like a light going out, he was completely and instantly gone.

And I felt completely and instantly bereft.

Lamentation the Sixth

This cruel inhumanity is but a thin disguise for murder.

When, as now seems certain, I shall sicken and die, a physician will at last be summoned. He will be my husband's man, bought with not near so much as thirty pieces of silver. At my death, it will be given out that I was delivered of a son but failed to thrive; that despite the ministrations of the best physicians and apothecaries, naught availed. It was not God's will that I should be saved.

That is how it will be managed.

I pray to God above that my son yet lives. He was a lusty babe, likely to live, and so I do fervently hope. My husband will ensure his heir flourishes. He will lack for naught but a mother.

My own sweet love, if ever thou shouldst read these lines that silent love hath writ, remember not the poor hand that wrote them. If thinking on me cause consternation in thy breast, I had rather be forgot.

Remember sweet meetings past and sad farewells, but O, if thou livest, remember not my fate!

PART THREE

9

Foul deeds will rise,
Though all the earth o'erwhelm them, to men's eyes.

Hamlet

That should have been the end of it. I should have felt better. Much better. I trusted Horatio to keep his word and I knew it was now unlikely I would ever see him again. I could get on with my new life without asking myself ten times a day if I was going mad. The passage of time would eventually reduce him to an anecdote, something I might recount in old age, like Sylvia... *"I saw a ghost once. Twice, actually. Or thought I did... No, he wasn't very frightening, just sad..."*

I should have felt better, so why did I feel worse? Why was I still pre-occupied with Horatio Fortune and his sudden, violent death?

I suppose if you're the kind of person who can just shrug your shoulders at unsolved crimes and live with the idea of people getting away with murder, it's unlikely you'd build a successful career writing mysteries where culprits are eventually identified and brought to justice. Queenie knew what she was doing. I sometimes asked myself whether she left Wyngrave to me to atone for the havoc she'd wreaked on my family, or because she thought I stood a chance of establishing the circumstances of Horatio's death. She might have heard from my mother about my youthful character: a highly developed sense of fairness, a tendency to champion the underdog and a passion for solving puzzles, all of which might have suggested to a dying and desperate Queenie that I would take up Horatio's lost cause.

Even as I tried to put his unexplained death out of my mind, I found myself pondering other unanswered questions. Duncan's infidelity. My mother's. My father's silence. Queenie's. A four-hundred-year-old murder offered a useful distraction from discoveries that had threatened to overwhelm me.

But that wasn't all. It took me a long time to admit it and by the time I did, I had to abandon the idea I still possessed some vestige of sanity. I *missed* Horatio. I missed that gaunt, grey, grumpy phantom. The thought that I would never see him again didn't bring me the expected relief, only an unexpected sadness.

But life went on. Bridget and I were fully engaged in restoring Wyngrave Hall. Occasional progress reports from Jesper dropped into my inbox to brighten my day and I wondered how soon I could descend on his London studio.

Digging our wildlife pond became Bridget's obsession. Her finds were intriguing, sometimes surprising, but not exciting until the day she appeared in the kitchen doorway, standing in her thick woollen socks, almost comically filthy. I was about to call out in protest that she should remain in the scullery, when I noticed her expression under the grime, then her hands.

Bridget was *excited*. Bridget rarely gets excited. Her calm, not to say phlegmatic personality has been a comfort to us all in these times of domestic upheaval. To see Bridget appear on the threshold of the kitchen without even washing her hands signified an event. I hoped it wasn't a crisis.

I searched her mud-stained face for a clue, but she'd already started to smile. She extended a hand which held what appeared to be a clod of soil. As I rose from the kitchen table, I was expecting to see more than the usual fragments of china and broken clay pipes. 'Have you found something interesting?'

'I don't know. I've never seen anything like this. It's a bit like a money box. But look... It isn't broken!'

She handed me a roughly spherical pottery object with a flat bottom and a little decorative knob on top. It looked something like a bishop's mitre and it fitted neatly into the palm of my hand. I took it over to the sink and ran the tap, gently washing off the encrusted mud and saw exactly what I was hoping to see. The sphere was completely closed, impenetrable apart from a small, thin vertical slit in the side. As I washed the soil away, a dark green glaze appeared. 'Tudor green,' I said, awestruck.

'*Is* it Tudor?' Bridget asked, standing at my side, excited. 'I haven't found any Victorian china for ages. The last significant find was a Georgian teaspoon. Have we hit the Tudors?'

'Well, I think this is an Elizabethan money box. It could be even older. But they were made to be *broken*. I've never seen one whole! People have only found pieces, mainly when they were excavating the sites of Elizabethan theatres in London. They found lots when they were re-building the Globe.' I shook it gently close to my ear.

'I already did that,' Bridget said. 'It's empty.'

'So it was never used, yet it was thrown away. That's odd.'

'Maybe someone dropped it by accident?'

I weighed the sphere in my hand. 'I think you'd notice if you dropped something as substantial as this, don't you? Or you'd hear it fall. And if it fell on most surfaces, it would smash. They weren't made to last.' I turned the pottery sphere over in my hands, examining it. 'This one is cracked on one side.' I looked up at Bridget. 'You know the term box office? Have you ever wondered where that comes from? What it actually means?'

'No. Now you come to mention it, it's an odd phrase.'

'It was the place at the theatre where they kept these – money boxes – and there would have been lots of them, containing the day's takings in the form of pennies. The gatherers, as they were called, stood in the theatre in various different locations, collecting thin little pennies from the audience as they came in. It was one penny to stand as a groundling. If you wanted to go upstairs and sit down, you paid another penny when you got there and another if you moved on to a better seat. The money was collected quickly and safely in these and they had to be smashed to get at the coins, so the gatherers couldn't pilfer. A *whole* one is so rare!'

'So it might be valuable?'

'I should think so. Certainly to a theatre museum. It's a lovely thing to have found.'

'Doesn't it confirm actors might have performed here?'

'No. An audience here wouldn't have been charged to watch. Not individually.'

'But perhaps the company had them in their baggage?'

'Oh, probably. But how did it end up in the stew pond?'

Bridget took the sphere and held it thoughtfully in her muddy hands. 'I can imagine *throwing* this. Like a cricket ball. It would make a lovely big splash in the water.' She examined the glaze. 'It's a bit rough and ready, I suppose, but now it's washed, the shiny green looks beautiful. Like a dragonfly's wing.'

'I've never seen a dragonfly. Not a real one.'

'You will when we've made our pond,' Bridget said proudly. 'I wonder how they made this lovely green?'

'They added powdered copper to a lead glaze.' Bridget looked up, impressed. 'I wrote a book where one of the characters was a potter, so I had to research what he made and how he made it.'

'The stuff you writers know!'

'Ah, but I've never seen a dragonfly. They say learning is never wasted, but I have to say, I didn't think Tudor pottery glazes would ever crop up in real life.'

Bridget handed the money box back. 'It would be nice to put it on display where we could all see it. Maybe not Sylvia,' she added apologetically.

'She will enjoy holding it. It's a nice tactile thing. And she'll love its history, won't she? I'm going to give it a good wash now. You look as if you could do with the same. Shall I get some coffee on for when you come out of the shower?'

'Thanks, but I want to carry on for a bit. This find has got me all fired up!' She retreated into the scullery and pulled on her wellingtons again. 'Who knows what else might have been chucked into that pond?'

Jesper emailed to say work on Lady Edith was going well and he would soon be starting on Samuel. He asked if I would like to come to the studio to watch some preliminary work. I needed no further encouragement and replied saying I would like to visit as soon as it was convenient. He suggested the following day.

After that I found it difficult to concentrate on work, so I cleaned the kitchen, then tidied away books, magazines and coffee mugs.

Sylvia was sitting by an open window with that alert look on her face that told me she was listening to the birds. As I passed, I collected her empty mug.

'Have you had some good news, Jane?' she asked.

I was surprised by the question. 'Not exactly. But quite exciting news. Well, for *me*. Jesper emailed to give me a progress report on Lady Edith. She can come home soon.'

'I do love the way you talk about the paintings as if they were people.'

'Well, they are to me. Almost. And I have every expectation now of her being a wonderful new addition to the family. Jesper warned me, I'll hardly recognise her now she's had "work done".'

'That reminds me of a friend of mine... Poor Jackie. Her career was in the doldrums and as she wouldn't see fifty again, she had some work done. Well, do you know, I cut her dead in the street. Didn't recognise her! She approached me, all smiles, and I thought she was collecting for something. I was in a hurry so I was a bit short with her. When I realised my mistake and apologised, she wasn't offended, she seemed terribly *pleased*. Must have thought she'd got her money's worth, I suppose.'

'I'm not going to tell you how much Lady Edith's makeover cost, but it entailed a lot of chemicals and many hours of highly skilled labour.'

'So did Jackie's. But Jesper is really more like a beautician, isn't he? Edith has just had a deep cleansing treatment, she won't have had her face *re-arranged*. I found it quite sad, seeing Jackie like that. It upset me for the rest of the day. I felt almost as if I'd lost a friend. She was still there, of course, *inside*, but you had to look past the shiny, smooth surface and a permanently startled expression to find her. Only the eyeballs were the same. It was as if I could see my old friend trapped inside somebody else's face. Horrible!'

'You sound like Jesper talking about his portraits. He thought the real Lady Edith was trapped inside a Victorian face that wasn't hers.'

Sylvia clasped her hands together, delighted. 'I can't wait! If the change is that radical, even *I* might be able to see the difference.'

'Did the rejuvenated Jackie get more work?'

'No. If your neck and hands don't match your face, it's a bit of a giveaway. She got a nice part in a sit-com playing someone's mother-in-law, but…' Sylvia lowered her voice, scandalised. 'They had to age her up! She was mortified, poor thing, but she needed the money.' Sylvia shook her head. 'You can't escape time, can you, however fast you run?'

'It holds us all prisoner and you just have to make the best of it.'

'Oh, *do* let's change the subject! Can we talk about lovely Jesper and your portraits?'

'Over a glass of sherry, perhaps?' Sylvia's face lit up. 'Sit tight and I'll bring you one.'

'You must join me, Jane. We'll celebrate your news.'

A thought suddenly struck me. 'How did you know, Sylvia?'

'Know what?'

'That I'd had some nice news.'

'You were humming. I could hear how happy and excited you were.'

I smiled and went off to fetch two sherries. Humming.

The next morning I took the train to Liverpool Street, then walked to Jesper's studio in Spitalfields, enjoying being in London again. After Wyngrave Hall, the city seemed so colourful, fast and noisy, I almost felt as if I was abroad. The day was a little holiday – a holiday from Wyngrave's past and from my own. I was making another new beginning: travelling to a fashionable part of east London to discuss portraits – *my* portraits – with a charming and knowledgeable craftsman. With miles between me and Wyngrave, it was almost possible to forget the existence of its ghost.

Almost.

I found the small gallery that was situated under the studio and pushed open the heavy glass door. As it swung shut behind me, I was enveloped by what seemed at first a complete hush, but as my ears adjusted, I detected the mournful sound of a lute – something melancholy by John Dowland – and there I was, back in the sixteenth century again.

There was no escape.

*

142

Jesper had said the young lady at reception was called Bella and had a degree in the History of Art. As she lifted her eyes from her computer, she looked professionally delighted to see me. When she'd discreetly checked her screen, she buzzed upstairs to say I'd arrived. Within a few moments I heard the whirr of a lift. 'There is a lift or there are stairs if you prefer,' Bella informed me, smiling.

'Thank you. I'm not a fan of lifts. I'll take the stairs.'

'It's only a couple of flights,' Bella informed me – unnecessarily, I thought, but she was half my age, so I let it go. Does one ever get used to being patronised by the young? Does one ever get used to the idea that one *isn't* young?

As the lift's double doors slid open, Jesper appeared. I had only a moment to dispel the memory of Horatio's first appearance before Bella was presenting me. Jesper, in a paint-stained over-shirt, came forward, extending his hand and took mine firmly. 'No introductions necessary, Bella. Ms Summers and I have met. She's come to check up on her portraits.'

The carefully painted eyes widened. 'Are they *yours?*' I'd clearly gone up in her estimation. 'Oh, you won't recognise them by the time Jesper has finished. Such wonderful work!'

'Mine or the artists'?' he asked.

'Both, of course,' was her adroit reply. 'Ms Summers said she'd prefer the stairs.'

'So would I. I've been sitting all morning. This way, Jane.'

He led the way to the back of the showroom and opened the door to an echoing staircase.

'I'm delighted you could come. I think you're going to be surprised by what you see and, I hope, pleased. What we've got is a lot more interesting than I thought, though I had my suspicions. Sometimes, of course, you get it wrong. You buy something that looks pretty awful at auction, and it turns out it is.'

'But it could be a lost masterpiece?'

'It happens, and that's the gamble. The artist struggles to speak through nasty nineteenth-century restoration, as well as a lot of dirt and discoloured varnish, and you have to try to see what isn't visible. I say *restoration*, but that's not really the word. The Victorians tried to "improve" old paintings. Make the women look prettier, or rather

143

more Victorian. But the originals are much more interesting, as I think you'll soon see. I'm sorry, am I going too fast? The stairs, I mean.'

'No, I'm fine.' I puffed. 'It makes a nice change to be walking up something that's level and doesn't groan beneath your feet.'

'The price of having a home that positively *creaks* with history. A privilege, but also a burden.'

I stopped climbing and stood still, struck by the truth of Jesper's words: how the weight of history oppressed me. Not just Horatio's history – my parents', Queenie's, Alison's and my own. How could I plan a future when I was obsessed with the past?

He turned and smiled encouragement. 'Not much further.'

'It's not the stairs, it's what you just said. About the burden. I hadn't realised till now.'

'Because you're already used to carrying that weight. Shall we…?'

I nodded and we continued up the stairs. 'Something else you've probably got used to is the darkness of your home. Very restful and atmospheric, but another reason why these paintings really needed to be cleaned. They weren't dark originally. The faces *glowed*, not least because they were painted at a time when light inside homes wasn't particularly valued, but pale skin *was*. Here we are.' He pulled open the door to his studio and I walked into the light.

It was a large, high room with tall windows on one side, many open, no doubt to keep the studio cool and to disperse the smell of chemicals. There were a few paintings on easels placed around the room. A young man wearing something like a helmet with, I assumed, magnifying lenses, sat hunched in front of a portrait, with a fine brush in his hand. He looked up briefly, then went back to studying his canvas.

I spotted Samuel's portrait on one of the easels, untouched I thought, though there was now a much lighter square at the top of the painting which stood out against the dark background. Beside him was another easel, covered with a cloth and I felt a frisson of excitement. Lady Edith, I presumed. I approved of Jesper's showmanship.

'Jane, come and have a look at Samuel first. All we've done so far is clean up a square, so you can see how much muck there is to come off and just how different the portrait looks now compared to the one the artist originally painted. I think you can assume, by the time it's cleaned and restored, he will look a new man. There's a lot of overpaint on his face that was added later for some reason.'

'How do you know?'

'It was applied by a different hand. You can tell from the brush strokes. The additions are left-handed.'

I stared at Jesper open-mouthed. 'It's like detective work!'

'It *is* detective work. Lives might not depend upon it, but livelihoods certainly do, which is why experts tend to be conservative. They have to be. They can't afford to be wrong.'

'So they *aren't* gambling men.'

'Far from it,' Jesper replied, with a look that implied he'd survived more than one bruising encounter with someone else's certitude. 'No one becomes an academic laughingstock because they won't accept something is by Holbein, but they'd look ridiculous if they claimed a picture *was* a Holbein and it later turned out it wasn't.'

'So they err on the side of caution.'

'They have to. It's not about what you feel, or even think, it's about what you can *prove*.'

'But if it weren't for the gambling men—'

'And women.'

'If it weren't for the gamblers, how would we ever find lost masterpieces?'

'A very good question. The gamblers have to know their stuff. They also need nerves of steel. In the heady atmosphere of the auction room, you might find yourself bidding a few hundred for a grubby canvas you believe to be a "sleeper" worth tens, even hundreds of thousands.'

'But you could be wrong.'

'That's not even the worst of it. That would just be an expensive human error and a gambler has to accept losses as part of the game. But suppose you're *right*? You know in your bones that you are, but you're unable to *prove* it. And the difference between a thousand pounds and a hundred thousand, Jane, is *proof*.'

'This is a really silly question, but I'd like to hear your answer.'

'Fire away. Silly questions make me think. And they usually aren't silly, not compared to the silliness of the art world.'

'Why does it matter if something is a fake?'

'It doesn't. Not until you want to sell it. If you believe your Monet is a Monet, but you can't get it accepted by the experts as a Monet, is your pleasure any the less when you look at it? Doubt will punish your pocket, but if you believe in your Monet, for you it *is* a Monet.'

'*There is nothing either good or bad, but thinking makes it so.*'

'Exactly. When he wasn't pretending to be mad, Hamlet talked a lot of sense.'

'I gave up academic research a long time ago when it seemed impossible to prove that some Elizabethan plays and poems were written by women. Or rather prove to the satisfaction of the establishment that they were written by women. If only it was just about authenticity! But you have to deal with tradition, vested interests and *so* much male ego. Sorry, but it was largely men then.'

'Don't apologise. The art world is the same. A new truth can wreck an old and established career.'

'Why wouldn't women have written plays? They wrote everything else. Poems. Letters. Translations. Literary studies. They read and wrote Latin and other languages and they went to the Playhouse in huge numbers. If women weren't allowed to appear on stage and had to watch men in drag speak words written by more men, what could be more likely than some of them writing their own plays, to tell their own truth?'

Jesper smiled. 'From the fervour of your speech, I'm guessing this might be the substance of an abandoned PhD?'

I laughed. 'Is it that obvious?'

'I'd love to read it. So would Bella. In her spare time she's researching women and the arts in the sixteenth century. I think you two would find lots to talk about. Now, would you like to see Lady Edith? Well, *half* of her? I've cleaned half so you can see *Before* and *After*, so it will be a bit of a tease, I'm afraid.'

'No, it will be fascinating.'

Edith's portrait was covered with two cloths, one on each half. Jesper pulled at one, whipped it away with a theatrical flourish, revealing half the portrait and then he stepped away, out of my eyeline.

I wasn't able to speak for some time. Jesper was also silent and neither of us moved. Eventually I said, 'I think if I speak, I might cry.'

'Don't worry, it happens,' he said softly. 'I stopped painting portraits because they *didn't* make people cry.'

'She looks so very young. Vulnerable. And yet such a serious young woman... Intelligent. Determined. You can see that, can't you?'

'She may be young, but I don't think she would suffer fools easily.'

I approached the portrait tentatively, almost as if I feared to invade Lady Edith's space. 'Her skin is *beautiful.*'

'Almost literally luminous. When the light fades in the studio, we've noticed Edith seems to glow against her dark background. She will literally light up your Long Gallery. Now, can you face seeing the other half? I warn you, it will be a shock.'

'Go ahead.'

He pulled the other cloth away and I found myself looking at some hybrid creation, both dark and light, where neither half resembled the other.

'Oh my God! Was she really *that* dirty?'

'You should have seen the state of the cottonwool swabs,' Jesper said with a grimace. 'In fact you will, because I'm going to do some more to demonstrate.'

He wheeled over a trolley laden with brushes, jars of chemicals and a container of cotton wool. He pulled out a piece and wrapped it deftly round a little stick, then dipped it into a colourless liquid. 'Just white spirit to begin with, to get rid of the surface dirt.' He rolled the swab back and forth over a yellow hand, held it out for me to see how it had turned dark brown in a matter of moments, then he discarded it and repeated the process several times.

He sat back and said, 'And that's just the surface dirt. Now we need to remove the nasty old varnish...' This time he dipped his swabs into a different liquid. As Jesper rolled the cotton wool gently across the surface of the picture, it became viscous and muddy. He wiped the stickiness away with yet more cotton wool.

'That looks so *satisfying,*' I said.

'One of the most therapeutic actions known to man,' Jesper murmured. As he wiped, Edith's yellow hand turned ivory and the fine details of a ring emerged. 'You get the idea,' he said, throwing away the last swab. 'Once she's quite clean and I've restored the few bits that are damaged, she'll get a protective layer of varnish which will also bring out the colours of the paint. Then she can go home and it will be my turn to miss her. Well,' Jesper said, removing his work shirt. 'That was all rather emotional, wasn't it? I could buzz down to Bella for some coffee, or… are you perhaps ready for some lunch?'

'I am. Breakfast was a long time ago.'

'Lunch then, and a glass of something to celebrate Lady Edith's transformation.'

We went to a wine bar a few doors away and were shown to a high-sided well-upholstered booth that obscured other diners. I sat on the bench and Jesper took a chair opposite me. Looking at the wine list, he said, 'Are you driving?'

'No. Train and then taxi.'

'Then shall we have a bottle to celebrate? How do you feel about Marlborough Sauvignon?'

'Very positive.'

We ordered wine and salads and I sat back, finally beginning to relax. 'You know, Sylvia is almost as excited as me. I shall have to give her a full account of my day when I get back.'

'Because you won't be able to show her a photo on your phone.'

'That's right.'

'Just as well you're a wordsmith by trade and Sylvia appreciates the power of words to paint pictures.'

'Not sure I'll be up to this,' I replied as the wine arrived.

'Of course you will. You write fiction. That's about conveying *feeling*, not information. And that's what Sylvia will want to know: how you felt when you met the new Lady Edith.' Jesper poured wine, then raised his glass. 'To Lady Edith Wyngrave.'

'To Edith.'

A waitress brought our salads and we ate for a while, then Jesper broke a companionable silence. 'Has Sylvia seen any more of her ghost?'

I was thrown but could see from his face that it was a serious question. 'If she has, she hasn't said anything to me and I doubt she'd mention it to Ros. That's her granddaughter. A very experienced nurse. She's also quite a tease, though Sylvia takes it all in good part.'

I sipped my wine. 'I was very surprised you took Sylvia's sighting in your stride. Most people would have laughed. Scoffed, even.'

'I try to keep an open mind. My work is heavily dependent on modern technology – chemical cocktails, infrared photography, dendrochronology – but science isn't enough. If you're any good, you also have that sixth sense. You have to be able to see what isn't there, or rather, what isn't visible to the naked eye. So I trust and respect the science that helps me do my job, but equally, I trust my own very un-scientific instincts. And other people's.'

'Even Sylvia's?'

'Why not? She's claiming to see what apparently isn't there, isn't she? So do I. How could I judge someone who says they can sense a ghost?'

'But you've never seen one?'

'I haven't, but I might not be all that surprised if I did. Maybe I have and just didn't realise.'

I stopped eating, my cutlery in mid-air. 'What do you mean?'

'Ghost sceptics like to point out that sightings are always of people in fancy dress. Grey ladies. Monks. Tudor nobility. Ghosts never appear as cleaning ladies. Or *do* they? If you walked round a stately home and saw someone who looked like a cleaning lady, you'd assume she *was* a cleaning lady. It wouldn't occur to you she might be the ghost of a recently deceased domestic who'd dedicated her life to polishing the family silver and found herself under-employed in the Hereafter.'

I blinked at him in astonishment. 'So you're saying, if the ghost had been wearing jeans and a hoodie, Sylvia might have thought he was a burglar?'

'That's *exactly* what I'm saying. I even wonder if some burglars caught in the act, the ones that don't actually steal anything and disappear while the homeowner's ringing the police or fetching a shotgun – might they actually be ghosts?'

I was stunned by the logic of Jesper's thinking. 'So you think we might pass ghosts in the street every day, oblivious to their true nature, because they're dressed in a familiar style. Because they look… normal.'

'As the boy in the movie said, "I see dead people." Do the rest of us fail to see dead people because they simply don't *look* like dead people?' Jesper laid down his knife and fork, leaned back and regarded me, a smile hovering at the corners of his mouth.

I could tell he was enjoying this. So, very nearly, was I, but I said, 'Are you taking this seriously? I'd rather not discuss it unless you are.'

His expression darkened. 'I promise, you, I take it *very* seriously. I've given death, grief, people who aren't there but should be, a great deal of thought. When I lost my wife, we were young and still in love. I'd have given an awful lot to be haunted. I'm no expert on ghosts, but I know a lot about grief.'

'Sorry I doubted you. It's because I'm a doubter myself.'

'But *you* see him too, don't you?'

I looked up, astonished. 'I never said—'

'No, you didn't, but it seemed obvious to me you had good reason to believe Sylvia.'

There was a long silence in which I felt as if I was teetering on the edge of a great chasm, looking down into the abyss. I was aware of the darkness beneath me, but also a source of light and warmth: Jesper and his patient silence. I didn't speak or move and neither did he until eventually he stretched out an arm across the table to lift the bottle and poured wine carefully into our glasses. Only after he'd set the bottle down again did he say, 'You don't have to talk about it, if you don't want to. I thought you might.'

'I do.'

'I told you I was rarely wrong.'

'We were talking about paintings then.'

'I think I'm also quite good at reading sensitive, intelligent women.'

'You're also conceited.'

'That too.'

'If I talk about it, you'll think I'm completely mad.'

'I doubt that very much. I might think you were delusional, but I'd never say so or think badly of you. Stones and glass houses.'

'Meaning?'

'My delusions earn me a living. Sylvia earned hers making us believe theatre fakery was real and *important*. Besides…' He leaned forward, his blue eyes intense and very bright. 'I want to hear the story! I know it's a lot to ask, but if you can bear it, I'd love to hear about your ghost. Does he have a name?'

I hesitated, then said, 'I'd only know that if he'd spoken to me.'

Jesper didn't reply but nodded slowly. His direct gaze didn't falter, so I looked away and said, '*You* might not think I was mad, but if I start talking about what I saw, as if it really happened—'

'Didn't it? Do you have any evidence apart from what you saw?'

'*Think* I saw... Chess pieces moved. So did books. And Bridget was the only other person in the house then and she denied all knowledge.'

'And you believe her?'

'I haven't known her long, but I already think I'd trust her with my life. She's rock-solid.'

'And she's lived at Wyngrave for many years, but never seen the ghost? Have her things ever moved about?'

'She says not.'

'So you're the chosen one, Jane.'

'But why me?'

'Because you're prepared to believe.'

'I don't think I do, even now, but I'm prepared to suspend my *disbelief.*' I sat up straight, stared at the ceiling and let out an enormous sigh. 'Oh, what does it matter if you think I'm mad! I'm *employing* you. And the customer is always right. Right?'

'Of course. And strictly between you and me, if you *were* mad, it wouldn't be the first time I'd been presented with that sort of a challenge, though in the trade we prefer to describe people as "eccentric". And *that*, Jane, you must surely concede. Making up stories for a living about imaginary people—'

'They aren't all imaginary. Some are historical figures.'

'And moving into a decaying sixteenth century manor house—'

'At my time of life.'

'At your time of life. And I'd venture to say you've even fallen in love. With a *portrait.*'

'Samuel Wyngrave? He's *very* appealing.'

'And you're not even in love with what he *is*, but what you think he might *become.*'

'I married my husband on much the same basis. But I'll love Samuel anyway, even if you don't find something better underneath.'

'Oh, I will.'

'I know you will.'

We sat in silence and I thought how little surprised Jesper. Perhaps it was just his professional manner, but I found his calm acceptance so reassuring, I let down my guard. 'If I do tell you about Horatio—'

'*Horatio?*'

'Horatio Fortune. He was an actor.'

'I'm sold already.'

'If I tell you his story, the worst you'll think of me is that I'm an eccentric client?'

'Absolutely, and that opinion would go no further.'

'Your fee buys your silence?'

'You don't need to buy it. I am a man of honour. I will never repeat your story, nor will I sell it to Netflix.'

Jesper's face was quite solemn, at odds with his flippant words, and my nerve threatened to fail me. 'Shouldn't you go back to the studio and do some more work, preferably for me? Bella will be wondering where you are.'

'Bella isn't paid to wonder, she's paid to be charming and unflappable. Tell *her* about Horatio and, I promise you, she wouldn't blink. I, on the other hand, am easily impressed and agog to hear more. What does he look like?'

I stared at him, weighing up the risk. What was the worst he could do? Laugh at me? No, laugh at Horatio.

'He looks like Hamlet. Dressed in black. Quite handsome in a mournful sort of way.'

'Is he young? I mean, *was* he when…'

'Hard to tell. He looks thirty-five-going-on-four hundred. But fit. He would have been an accomplished swordsman. So many fights in the plays of that period…' I shot another look at Jesper but saw no hint of a smirk. He was watching me in a quite disconcerting way – disconcerting, because he appeared to be taking me seriously. I swallowed and said, rather faintly. 'Apparently he died playing the ghost of Hamlet's father.'

'He died *during a performance?*'

'So he says.'

'Murdered?'

'He doesn't remember any details apart from a blow on the head. He was offstage and could have been anywhere. The ghost doesn't appear in Act Two.'

'Who administered the blow?'

'He doesn't know. Or rather he doesn't remember.'

Jesper sat back and a look of wonderment suffused his face. 'So you don't just have a ghost, Jane, you have an unsolved crime on your hands. The ultimate country house murder mystery.'

'Now you *are* teasing me.'

'No, I wasn't. Sorry, it's the Danish side of me. For us, nothing is so serious it's beyond laughter, and nothing is so funny that it doesn't give us pause.' He stared into space again, apparently reconstructing the crime. 'Did the blow to the head kill him?'

'He doesn't know. It's just the last thing he remembers. Look, I know this sounds completely crazy—'

'Eccentric.'

'Thank you. I do believe a murder took place. But there's no body and no evidence. We don't even have a motive.'

'Just the victim's testimony. From beyond the grave.'

'If he has a grave, he doesn't know where it is. The story goes – probably apocryphal – that the actor completely disappeared. I don't see how there could ever be proof now.'

'That's what they used to say about Old Masters until they invented X-rays.'

I regarded him with frank admiration. 'Do you ever give up?'

'What do you mean?'

'I'm curious to know if you ever give up. On anything.'

He shrugged. 'I gave up painting for a living, but I believed almost until the end that Freja would somehow recover. My wife. I didn't believe in God, but I believed in miracles. I fear that must have made it harder for her. The business of dying.'

'My friend Alison insisted we all accept it was terminal, but she didn't want to see our grief. She said, "You can do all that when I'm gone." She wanted to have a good time while she was still alive, but she wouldn't allow us the luxury of hope or pretence. That made it harder. For us, I mean.'

The silence that followed was protracted, then Jesper said, 'I suppose I should get back to work on Samuel. You didn't come to London for all this *sadness*.'

'Can't you stay a bit longer? I do enjoy talking to you.'

'When I'm not being conceited,' he said, straight-faced.

I laughed and he looked pleased. 'Is there any wine left? Fortify me with another glass and you can continue your interrogation.'

'Why do you think Horatio appeared to *you*?' he asked, emptying the bottle. 'I'm intrigued by the idea that ghosts are choosy. Children are often favoured – if that's the right word – and fey people like Sylvia.'

'Oh, don't be deceived. Sylvia is as tough as old boots.'

'But why you?'

'I've asked myself that many times. I have two theories, based on who he's appeared to in the past.'

'The previous owner?'

'Yes. Queenie Brooke-Bennet was an elderly recluse. Unconventional. Open-minded. She was also a novelist. She thought I might be able to solve the insoluble because I write Tudor whodunnits.'

'And?' Jesper's brows rose. 'You said there were two reasons.'

'Promise you won't laugh?'

He bowed his head. 'I am your humble servant. You've bought my loyalty and my silence.'

'I think Horatio appeared to me because he was lonely. And he'd been lonely for four hundred years. Don't you think that could be why ghosts appear? They want to fill centuries of emptiness. Or are they more altruistic? Do they sense loneliness in others? I have every reason to believe Queenie, who had no friends or family left, actually enjoyed being haunted.'

'You mean she thought of her ghost as a friend?'

'I think so. When you came to Wyngrave, you said something about ghosts that really cracked me up. It was about your old Duke. How when his wife died, you knew he wouldn't be alone, because he had his ghost…' My eyes begin to prickle. Dismayed, I couldn't remember whether the mascara I so rarely wore was waterproof. I stared at the table and willed the tears away. When I was able to speak again, I didn't recognise the querulous voice as mine. 'Perhaps Horatio targets vulnerable people. He thinks they might understand. His desperation. His loneliness.'

Jesper reached across the table and laid a hand on mine but didn't speak. I tried to remember the last time anyone had touched me who wasn't a doctor or a dentist. There was a big hug from Sylvia when she moved in, but before that? Air kisses with female friends and colleagues. When had a *man* last touched me? Apart from shaking hands with Queenie's solicitor, I couldn't remember. It must have been Duncan, before I found out about Sophie…

As the memories piled in, humiliating tears began to trickle down my cheeks. Furious, I snatched up my napkin and began to dab at my eyes.

'No, don't do that! Not starched linen near your eyes. Here…' Jesper produced a folded handkerchief, got up and came round to sit beside me, sliding along the bench. He said nothing more, but put an arm round my shoulders. When a waitress appeared, eager to clear the table, he waved her away with his other arm.

I buried my face in the soft folds of his handkerchief, then slumped against him. Still he said nothing, but his arm tightened slightly. We sat like that for some time. When the banished waitress re-appeared, Jesper asked for the bill.

Lamentation the Seventh

Thy name is known. They have it from one other than me. My love, we are betrayed! If they know thy name, then is it like that thou art dead, dead by their hand.

I know not if it be true, but my mind misgives, for they have abused my weakness and my melancholy and now doubtless hope I shall run mad.

Villains! Vipers! Damned without redemption!

If thou art dead – O, I pray it is not so! – if thou hast quit thy earthly body, wait for me patiently in Heaven. Or in that Other Place.

Gone, and without me? How do I yet live? The blood hammers in my head and my heart bleeds. Dead, and I knew not?

10

How long will a man lie i'th'earth ere he rot?

Hamlet

When I arrived home a delicious smell of roast lamb and garlic assailed my nostrils. I remembered Rosamund was cooking dinner and we were all eating together, which we tried to do at least once a week. It was a warm September evening and I found Sylvia sitting outside drinking sherry as Rosamund laid the big wooden table where we sometimes ate *al fresco*. Rosamund looked at her watch and grumbled that Bridget was going to be late.

'Where is she?' I asked.

'Still digging her blessed pond.'

'She must be through to Australia by now,' Sylvia laughed. 'She's been digging all day.'

'Well, I said dinner at seven so it's time she came in and washed off all that smelly mud. Jane, could you finish laying the table? I need to go and turn the potatoes. Red wine is open and there's white in the fridge.'

I decided I'd already had enough wine, so I poured myself a glass of iced water from the jug on the table, then went indoors to fetch cutlery. As usual, Bridget had left a jug of flowers on the kitchen table. I took them outside and set them near Sylvia so she could smell them.

Rosamund re-appeared looking grumpy and overheated and announced the potatoes were done to a turn. There was an anxious silence as we all looked down the garden at the gap in the hedge where Bridget would appear. When she finally came stumping up the path in her muddy wellingtons, Rosamund called out. 'At last! You're late and we're starving!'

'Sorry. I forgot the time. It smells delicious, whatever it is.'

'Fortunately for you, it's slow cooked lamb, but the potatoes won't wait, so I'm going to serve up now, whether you're clean or not.'

'Don't wait for me. I'll sit at the end of the table in disgrace.' As she approached, I could see she was holding what looked like a big stick.

'What on earth is that?' I asked.

'My biggest find yet, but on its way to the bin.'

'A *bone?*' I asked, horror-struck.

'A cow's. Or maybe a horse. Poor thing must have drowned when there was still a pond there.'

Rosamund stared at the bone, then at Bridget, apparently incredulous.

'Oh, Lord!' Sylvia shrieked. 'Bridget, we're about to *eat*! For Heaven's sake, get rid of it! Then give your hands a jolly good scrub.'

As Bridget walked off in the direction of the bins, Rosamund called after her, 'Get cleaned up as quick as you can. I'll put your plate in the oven.'

'Thanks. I won't be long.'

I fetched dishes of vegetables and set them on the table, then Rosamund brought out the joint to applause from Sylvia. The lamb fell off the bone and we all tucked in, appetites undiminished by Bridget's discovery. Rosamund seemed subdued and ate without speaking, but I assumed she was tired after preparing the meal.

Bridget soon joined us and Sylvia was avid to hear news about the portraits. She was delighted to hear I'd lunched with Jesper.

'He sends his best to you,' I said. 'You made quite an impression on him.'

'And *he* made quite an impression on *me*! I do hope he comes again. Such an elegant, cultivated man, don't you think? Lovely old-fashioned manners too. Oh, if I were thirty years younger!' Sylvia said with a mischievous chuckle. 'I can't really see him, but he *sounds* delicious.'

Seated beside her, I leaned over and said in an undertone, 'He looks pretty delicious too, if a bit dishevelled.'

'I knew it!' Sylvia exclaimed. She addressed herself to her lamb and said, 'Go for it, Jane.'

It wasn't so much encouragement, more of an order.

After dinner Rosamund and I cleared away leaving Sylvia and Bridget, tired and replete, to enjoy the last of the sunshine. As I finally switched the dishwasher on, I turned round to see Rosamund looking worried. Too tired to probe, I said, 'Fancy a cup of tea?' Without waiting for an answer, I began to fill the kettle.

'Jane, there's something I need to say. Out of Sylvia's earshot.'

I turned away from the sink, kettle in hand. 'Is something wrong?'

She looked round in the direction of the back door, then said, 'Sit down. I'll make the tea.'

By now I was really concerned and put the kettle down. 'Forget the tea, Ros, and tell me what's bugging you.'

'Don't repeat this to Sylvia. Not yet. Though she'll have to know eventually.'

'No, of course,' I replied, mystified.

'That bone Bridget found… It's not an animal bone,' she said, lowering her voice. 'It's human.'

My hand flew up to my mouth and for a moment I thought I might be sick. 'Are you *sure*?'

She nodded. 'I knew as soon as I saw it, but I just had a good look when I took the rubbish out. It's the right femur of a male. Thigh bone. And he broke it long before he died,' she added absently.

'Oh God.'

'So I'm afraid Bridget has to stop digging. Our pond could be a crime scene.' She looked at my face and laid a hand gently on my arm. 'Try not to get too upset. He probably died a very long time ago. Given the age of this place, it could be hundreds of years.'

I nodded, quite unable to speak.

I was in a state of shock. The resident ghost claimed he'd been murdered and now his earthly remains had been discovered in my garden.

But it might not be him. It might be the skeleton of a more recent murder. Or a suicide. Or the victim of an accident. Would an accident or suicide go unnoticed? Wouldn't the family search? And surely a drowned body would rise to the surface?

Not if it was weighted down.

Which ruled out accident.

Murder, accident or suicide, it made no difference. I should inform the police. That much was clear. What wasn't clear was whether I should inform Horatio. Or how. Would he know about our discovery? He said he was imprisoned at Wyngrave, but was he aware of what happened *outside*?

I decided to do nothing until the morning and went to bed. I lay awake, dreading Horatio might appear from the wardrobe, demanding answers and – like the ghost of Hamlet's father – revenge.

I woke to grey daylight and the sound of a gentle knock on my door. I sat up, confused, and checked the time. It was still early, just gone seven. My first thought was Sylvia. Had something happened to her? As I got out of bed, I said, 'Ros? Is that you?'

'No, it's Bridget. Can I come in?'

I opened the door to see a white-faced Bridget standing in her socks, dressed in her gardening clothes.

'What's the matter? Is it Sylvia?'

'No, she's still in bed. Ros is up, but I thought I should come and speak to you first. It's your house,' she added ominously.

I remembered then, the shock of the day before and I knew what Bridget had come to tell me. 'Have you been working outside already? Digging?'

Her smile was sheepish. 'I like to get out early when everything's fresh and peaceful. It's the best time of day…'

She faltered and I said, 'Have you found something, Bridget?'

She nodded. I thought she might be about to cry, but she said, very formally, 'I'm sorry to disturb you so early, Jane, but I *have* found something. I think you'd better come down and take a look. You'll need your wellies.'

We stood in silence at the edge of the muddy crater Bridget had dug. It was shallow at the edge, becoming much deeper in the centre.

There, lying on its side, half-buried but clearly visible, lay the skull, ribcage and one arm of a skeleton. It looked as if someone had lain down to go to sleep on his side. The sight was unutterably pathetic. I put an arm round Bridget's solid shoulders. I wasn't sure if I was comforting her or myself.

'It wasn't a cow,' she said miserably. 'Or a horse.'

'Oh, Bridget, I *know*. Ros told me last night. She recognised the bone as human. I should have told you to stop digging last night, but I couldn't face explaining and… well, it was such a shock.'

'We'll have to tell the police.'

'I know. I'll do that straight after breakfast.'

'Not sure I can face breakfast,' Bridget said, her face desolate. I'd never noticed how lined it was and how deep some of those lines were etched. I didn't know how old Bridget was. I'd assumed she was younger than me, but as she wiped away a tear with the back of her dirty hand, leaving a smear on her weathered cheek, I wasn't so sure.

'Bridget, are you okay?'

'Fine,' was the gruff response. 'It's just… upsetting.' She cleared her throat and said, 'I don't think I disturbed anything. I dropped the spade as soon as I saw the skull. I could tell it didn't belong to an animal.'

'Ros said it was a man.'

'Well, she would know. She studied anatomy.'

There was an awkward silence as we both contemplated the skeleton.

'You say you didn't move anything?'

'I scraped some soil away around the skull, just gently with my fingers. I wanted to be *sure*. Then it started to rain. Quite heavy. So I went and sat in the greenhouse for a bit. In a state of shock, I think. When I came back, the rain had washed away more soil. Exposed the bones.'

'I'm so sorry we didn't tell you. We could have spared you all this… Don't say anything to Sylvia, will you? I don't think we need to tell her until there are men in forensic suits tramping round the garden. She'll notice *that*. But obviously you have to stop digging.'

'The forecast for the week is rain so I was planning to work indoors anyway. Get those rotten floorboards up. To be honest, I'll be glad to get away from the pond for a while.' She regarded the skeleton for a moment, then said, 'When you're down there, close up…' She hesitated and her face looked grey. 'You can see the side of his skull. It's smashed in. He must have struck his head on something very hard, then fallen in the water. And drowned, I suppose.'

'What could you hit your head on out here that would fracture your skull? And if he fell face-down into the pond and drowned in shallow water, why did no one find his body?'

'Good question.'

'If he was still conscious after the blow, flailing around in the water, but ended up drowning in the middle of the pond, why didn't his gas-filled body eventually rise to the surface?' Bridget didn't reply, she just stared at the ground, looking uncomfortable. 'Sorry about all the gruesome detail, but I write this sort of stuff for a living.'

'It's not that, Jane.'

'What is it?'

'There were some heavy bits of stone.'

'Oh, *no.*'

'Not what you'd expect to find chucked into a pond. More the kind you might build with, which is why I set them aside when I found them.' She pointed to a small heap of masonry. 'I thought they might come in useful.'

'You found them near the skeleton?'

'I found them first. I realise now I shouldn't have moved them, but I didn't find the skeleton until after I'd moved the stones.'

'You weren't to know, Bridget. So an alternative scenario could be, a man was murdered and the killers disposed of his body in the pond, maybe in a sack weighted with stones.'

'*Killers?* It's a conspiracy now?'

'It would have taken two, maybe three people to lift, or drag a man, together with those stones.'

'If you're right,' Bridget said, brightening a little, 'that means it's not a recent crime. There was no pond here in Queenie's time.'

'I suppose they could have dug a hole and buried the body.'

'There's no sign of any digging. Just layer upon layer of undisturbed leaf mould and rotting vegetation, plus the kind of things kids might throw into a pond to make a big splash or frighten ducks.'

'*Oh…*'

'What?'

'Something you said.' I bent to pick up a thick dead twig, then stepped into the crater, moving towards the bones.

'Jane, should you be doing that if it's a crime scene?'

'Definitely not, but it's my land and you've already contaminated the scene with your DNA. I'm not going to touch it,' I said, bending down to peer at the skull. 'But if I just dislodge a bit more soil, we can get a better view.' I scraped gently with the twig. 'Bridget, come and look! The side of the skull where it's fractured… The damaged area is roughly circular.'

She approached cautiously and bent to examine the skull. 'So he was hit by something hard and round.'

'Looks like it. Not a cosh or a hammer. A blow like that would have felled him, even if it didn't kill him outright.' I looked up into Bridget's ashen face and said, 'I really *am* going to ring the police, but before I do, I want to test a theory.'

'Does it entail moving any bones?'

'No, it entails you going back to the house and fetching the pottery money box you dug up.'

Bridget looked puzzled, then realisation transformed her face. She nearly smiled. 'It's the same size and shape as the injury to the skull!'

'Possibly. In which case, Bridget Thompson, you found the murder weapon as well as the victim.'

Glad of a reason to get away, she hurried off to fetch the green pottery sphere she'd held in her hand and likened to a cricket ball. I stood looking down at the skeleton lying in the mud. Was that how it was done? A man with good aim and a strong arm had hurled the money box at Horatio's head from the cover of trees or shrubs, perhaps with no intent to kill, just injure him sufficiently, so he could be overpowered…

By whom?

And why?

Sylvia was the only one who didn't know why the site of our pond became a no-go area. Nor could she see it had become a crime scene, cordoned off with lurid tape, a tent erected to one side to house any evidence they found. But Sylvia had to be told and Rosamund volunteered.

She was shocked at first, but soon accepted the new situation and hoped the bones would prove to be of historical interest. 'You never know. They found the skeleton of Richard III under a car park, didn't they? Perhaps it will be that Elizabethan actor! The one who disappeared during the play.' Sylvia assumed my shocked silence meant I doubted her theory, so she elaborated. 'That would account for his disappearance, wouldn't it? If he'd ever turned up again – or if a *body* had turned up,' she added gleefully, 'people wouldn't have claimed he disappeared, would they?'

Grateful she couldn't see my face, I adopted a casual tone. 'It's probably the body of some poor old vagrant who fell into the pond, dead drunk. Someone nobody missed, so he was never found.'

'Oh, probably,' Sylvia conceded, disappointed. 'But if it *was* our actor, it would give the story a wonderful ending, wouldn't it? Oh, I really hope it's him!'

And for reasons I couldn't explain, even to myself, I really hoped it wasn't.

The police were on site for a week, taking photographs, collecting samples, lifting bones, putting everything into labelled plastic bags. I retreated to the library where I attempted to work, but found I was still preoccupied with the problem of Horatio: did he know what was happening outside? If so, would he have some understanding based on his television viewing? If he didn't, should I explain? Surely I need say nothing unless the bones were found to be over four hundred years old? In any case, Horatio had assured me he'd never appear again.

But that was before we found a body.

Seeking distraction, I was happy to join Bridget in the attic, lending a hand to lift crumbling elm floorboards, so an expert could inspect the oak joists beneath. It was hot working by torchlight under the roof and we had to wear special masks so we could breathe. Centuries of dust and debris filled the underfloor space. It lay in waves, the peak highest under the gaps between the boards. It was inches thick and lay on top of a layer of lime plaster. I wondered if the ancient dust contained any tiny objects that had fallen through the gaps. Donning cotton archivists' gloves that I used when handling old books and manuscripts, Bridget and I carried out a fingertip search.

We found pins, horn buttons, odd earrings, nests made by rats and mice, and a quantity of needles and pins where servants had sat with their mending. A section of one of the floorboards was unattached to the joist beneath and had apparently been lifted to provide a hiding place for, to our delighted astonishment, Bridget discovered a little leatherbound book, well nibbled by rodents, but largely intact.

She handed me the book. Despite the over-powering heat in the attic, I shivered as I took it in my gloved hands. I'd seen, even handled objects like these in museums and libraries, but I'd never *found* such an artifact, let alone in the place its owner had chosen to conceal it. Bridget must have sensed the importance of our find because she stood in reverent silence while I cautiously examined the book.

The contents were written in what I recognised as "secretary hand", a script used by most people in the sixteenth century, but the content was illegible, resembling rows of tiny, crushed spiders. The pages felt brittle and I turned them carefully, wondering why the book had been hidden under floorboards. Was it then forgotten, or had the author died before he or she could retrieve it? It seemed miraculous the paper should have survived several hundred years, but the enveloping dust was quite dry. No doubt any moisture in the air had been absorbed by that and the lime plaster the book had rested on.

'Can you read it?' Bridget asked eagerly, her eyes bright above her mask.

'Afraid not. Mostly I read transcriptions, not originals.'

'Is there a name? Or date?'

'Can't see any names.' I pointed to the first page. 'That could be a date. Looks like sixteen-something.'

'Amazing! I wonder what it says?'

'Something religious and subversive probably, as it was hidden.'

'What a find!'

I nodded, overwhelmed. 'This could be a *significant* find.'

For a moment we stood in awed silence, then, with a little laugh, Bridget said, 'This place!' She shook her head. 'Even the *dust* is special.'

I closed the book, but continued to stare at the cover, wondering who might have written in its pages.

'Shame we can't read it,' Bridget said. 'You'll have to show it to someone who's familiar with that funny writing.'

'Yes… Yes, I will.'

Someone like Horatio Fortune.

Using a soft toothbrush, I gently dusted the ornate leather cover of the book, then set it on my desk beside a dish holding our other, less exciting finds. The book presumably hadn't seen daylight for four hundred years and I half expected it to crumble before my eyes, so I drew the curtains to reduce any light damage.

I assumed the entries in the journal were written by someone who lived at Wyngrave Hall in the sixteenth century. Not a servant, though. The book might have been found in an attic where servants would have slept, but the hand was educated.

I sat and stared at the little book, wondering what I should do about Horatio. It was no longer just a question of what I should tell him. I realised there might be things he could tell *me* – about the author of the little book and its contents. He might also be able to enlighten me about the identity of the skeleton, though I wasn't convinced I wanted all the facts. Accidental death was looking un-likely, murder almost certain. Possibly Horatio's.

Overwhelmed, I folded my arms on the desk, making a pillow to rest my head. I closed my eyes and tried to think. There were only two people I could talk to honestly about Bridget's ghoulish discovery; only two who would understand the significance of that shattered skull to me. Sylvia and Jesper.

But I wasn't thinking of the living. I thought of Queenie and her challenge and how, despite the discovery of a damaged skeleton, I was no nearer to solving the mystery she'd bequeathed me with Wyngrave Hall.

I thought of Horatio, who could tell me if he broke his thigh bone years before he died; could tell me where exactly he received a blow on the head; could open the little book and just read it aloud…

It was with a sense of both dread and relief that I realised I was shivering. The temperature in the library was dropping. I sat up and laid a protective hand on the book. Clutching it to my chest, I swivelled round to find Horatio standing in a corner of the library.

'I gather I've been found.'

'I don't know if it's you. *Was* you.'

'There's a head injury.'

'You *saw* the skull?'

'I cannot leave the Hall.'

'So how do you know?'

'Miss Marlow is voluble on the subject. There have been telephone calls, conversations. I have been invisible, not absent.'

'The blow to your head… Where—' I couldn't go on and watched as Horatio pointed to his right temple.

'I don't think I died instantly. There might have been a struggle… After all this time, I really don't remember.'

'A massive blow to the head is why you don't remember.'

'So *is* it me? The fractured skull could be mere coincidence. I lived in unruly, violent times.'

'Did you break any bones?'

'I dare say my assailants broke a few for me.'

'I meant before you were attacked. Long before.'

'Ah, I see. You have additional information.' He looked away as he tried to remember. 'I broke my leg… Falling out of a pear tree. Faith, I had quite forgot! I was a boy, perhaps twelve years old, thieving pears and climbing too high, to prove I was a man.'

'Which leg?'

'My right.' He laid a hand on his thigh, remembering. 'Mother thought I would not recover. She bargained with God, promising Him anything, if He would let me live.' He gazed at me intently, his black eyes boring into mine. '*Is* it me?'

'I think so. The bones—'

'*My* bones.'

'They confirm your story.'

'Where are they?'

'They've been removed by the police. Taken away to be radiocarbon-dated.' He raised an eyebrow in query. 'We should hear soon how old they are.'

'So now we have a body – mine – but no murderer and no motive. The mystery still isn't solved.'

'How could it ever be?'

'A question I have asked myself for four hundred years.' He pointed to my hands. 'What is that book you clasp so tightly?'

'I don't know. We found it in the attic under the floorboards, but I can't read it. It's illegible to anyone but a Tudor expert.'

'Well, I'm a Tudor expert. Show me. Draw the curtains and set it down on your desk.'

I did as I was told, then stood back as Horatio approached. Moving towards the light, his form thinned until it was almost transparent and I could see through him to the bookshelves beyond.

He turned to me and said, irritably, 'This will look like showing off, but it's because I have no working parts.' I must have blinked in astonishment, so he waggled his long fingers in front of my face. 'Useless. For appearances only.'

'But the chess pieces. And my books?'

'I am able to channel energy contrary to the laws of physics as you understand them.'

'I don't understand them.'

'Neither do I, but I get by.'

He turned his attention to the book and after a moment it opened slowly, apparently of its own accord, and lay flat. I must have blinked because I didn't see Horatio seat himself at my desk, but suddenly, that's where he was, hunched over the pages.

'There's a date at the beginning. 1603... I take it you wish me to read aloud?'

'Please. It's not very long.'

His spine straightened, then he appeared to sit and wait. I remembered he'd been an actor. He was gathering himself, waiting for his audience to settle. I stood very still, looking over his shoulder, and eventually he began.

'Alas, I am condemned. No help, no hope doth remain, for I have made enemies, mighty and dreadful. I dare not say thy name, nor even write

it, for who might be listening at the door? Who might enter of a sudden and deprive me of the comforts of my poor candle, my precious paper and ink? My earthly life I prize at naught. It is but a trifle. I live to protect thee, my dearest love. I live in hope that we might meet once more; that I might see my son again...'

He paused and I said, 'Do you think this is a play?'

'I think not. I believe it is a chronicle of captivity.'

'That must be why the book was hidden.'

'Shall I go on?'

'Please.'

'Art thou yet living? And is thy name known to my tormentors? I have not uttered it, nor shall I, not even in the sanctuary of my narrow bed. I had rather dash out my brains on these walls that imprison me. But what if I should lose my wits, as I fear I am like to do? Or contract a fever and, raving, call out thy name, thus condemning thee to share my fate? Or a worse. In silence lies thy safety. So silent shall I be.'

'I think the author is a woman and she's protecting someone,' I said.

'Her lover, perhaps.' As Horatio looked down at the book, a draught appeared to lift and turn the page, then it lay still. *'What blessings have I now that I should fear to die? Better a thousand times to die than live thus tormented. I am barred, like one infected, from the crown and comfort of my life, first fruit of my womb: my infant son.'*

'They took her child?'

'I dwell in darkness, all cheerful light kept from me, but for my little candle.'

'The poor woman!' I exclaimed. Horatio looked up and gave me a withering look. 'Sorry. I'll try not to interrupt again.'

'Pale ghosts and frightful shades are all my acquaintance now, but even they cannot banish friendly sleep... Then there are some blots... The hand becomes more difficult to read.'

'Look ahead. Just read what you can.'

Another page turned. *'The serving woman is forbidden to speak to me. I address her and enquire if it is a fair day or a foul, or if she has word of my son, but she delivers my meagre victuals and empties the slop pail in silence, her head bent in fear. No eye looks into mine. No voice answers. If I did not write this journal, certain, I should go mad. Yet is this prison full of noises. I hear sounds outside my door. Whisperings at the keyhole. Footsteps. The shift of waiting bodies, bent on revenge. They listen. Listen for a name. Thy name...* The writing becomes erratic. Then... *In sooth, I fear I am not in my perfect mind.'*

Horatio paused – out of respect, I think – and I said, 'An educated woman, imprisoned and deprived of her baby son... She's writing to the father of her child, isn't she? With little hope he'll ever read her words... Who *are* these people?'

Horatio continued, his voice softer now, the detached tone gone. *'Oftentimes I yield to the sin of despair and consider whether I might hasten mine own end. Yet what need is there? I know it will come ere long. The cords that tether me to this earthly life are thin now and frayed. Soon, yea, very soon I shall be free. When last I walked in the sun it was almost harvest time. Now I feel the approach of winter in my weary bones, yet have I no fire. I starve for lack of nourishment. I have no water with which to wash, scarce enough to drink. Why does my husband not kill me?'*

'She's being held prisoner by her *husband*?'

'Who is presumably not the father of her child.' He shook his head slowly. 'I'm afraid I can read only the odd phrase on this page. The hand seems... agitated.'

'Move on. Can we find out any more about her?'

Another page turned. Horatio read on silently for a moment, then said, 'The picture is becoming clearer... *What was my sin but to love beneath my station? Thy love was better than high birth to me and are not all men equal in Christ?'* He looked up and said, 'She must have been very young. Spirited. Devout. But not obedient.'

'It doesn't sound as if she was seduced. Or raped. She loved him. She chose to endure all this rather than name him.'

'*I brought shame on my family, yet did I not also save my husband from gossip and calumny? He now has an heir – a son if he is yet living – without the trouble of lying with his wife, a wife not told her place in the marriage bed would be usurped by her husband's catamite. In sooth, it was the Devil's own bargain and I was sold like a brood mare...* Matters are becoming clearer. Someone influential—'

'And homosexual.'

'—wanted an heir, but not, apparently, the encumbrance of a wife. Nor did he want some lowly individual claiming paternity.'

'Or threatening blackmail.'

'Indeed. While they lived, these lovers were… inconvenient.'

'Please read on.'

'*This cruel inhumanity is but a thin disguise for murder. When, as now seems certain, I shall sicken and die, a physician will at last be summoned. He will be my husband's man, bought with not near so much as thirty pieces of silver. At my death it will be given out that I was delivered of a son but failed to thrive; that despite the ministrations of the best physicians and apothecaries, naught availed. It was not God's will I should be saved. That is how it will be managed…*' His chest rose and fell. 'Astute… And doomed.'

'Is it possible she escaped and never retrieved her journal? Perhaps she caved and gave them his name? She's starving to death!'

'I don't think she escaped. The writing deteriorates still further. Her mind is now much affected by what she has endured… *Thy name is known. They have it from one other than me. My love, we are betrayed! If they know thy name, then is it like that thou art dead, dead by their hand. I know not if it be true, but my mind misgives for they have abused my weakness and my melancholy and now doubtless hope I shall run mad.*' He paused, then said, 'I cannot discern what follows, but the page ends, *Dead, and I knew not?*'

'She's broken.'

'I fear so.'

'Is there more?'

'A little, but difficult to decipher.' He read haltingly, '*The serving woman comes no more. The pail is not emptied. Sometimes the door is opened and a bowl of bread and cup of water are left inside the door. I have not the strength to crawl and fetch them… There will be no more ink and this is my last candle…* Should I continue, madam? You weep.'

I wiped my eyes, embarrassed. 'I don't know why I should care so much,' I muttered.

He looked up at me with a faint smile. 'You have a tender heart.'

'Please read to the end and just ignore me.'

Another page turned. Horatio scanned what appeared to be the last entry in the journal. He made an indeterminate noise, of shock or perhaps pain, then threw his head back and moaned. His thin, grey form appeared to convulse, then break up. As bits of his body dissolved and drifted, he uttered an unearthly noise, a deep groan that seemed to emanate from the floor beneath us. It grew louder until it became an agonised roar, a single desperate word: '*No!*'

Unable to bear the noise, I clapped my hands over my ears and shut my eyes. The hideous sound stopped abruptly and I knew even before I opened my eyes that Horatio would be gone.

The book lay open at the last entry. Shaken, I sat down and peered at the black scrawl. I still couldn't read it, but Horatio had, and what he'd read had shattered him, literally torn him apart.

And I had no idea why.

The Final Lamentation

The serving woman comes no more. The pail is not emptied. Sometimes the door is opened and a bowl of bread and cup of water are left inside the door. I have not the strength to crawl and fetch them.

There will be no more ink and this is my last candle. The time has come to hide my secret testimony. My gaolers will search my cell, find and destroy the pious journal their prisoner kept. This one they shall not find. This one might never be read, least of all by thee, dearest love, but I pray that one day others will read and choose to pity me and my sufferings.

And if they do not? If in time this paper rots beneath the floorboards, long after I have rotted in my grave? No matter. I know – as doth my God – what I have suffered and how truly I have loved.

I die dishonoured, wedded to my woes, bedded in this tomb. Yet shall I be raised in glory. For as in Adam all die, even so in Christ shall all be made alive. It is written. One short sleep and I shall wake eternally.

My journal too is written and now it will be hid. I die, but the word liveth. May the word live for ever and ever. Amen.

My soul is heavy now. Fain would I sleep. It is winter, dark, and I am bitter cold.

Signed, I know not which day nor month

Edith, Lady Wyngrave

II

For murder, though it have no tongue, will speak.

Hamlet

I was still shaking when my mobile rang. The screen told me it was Jesper and I hesitated. I really wanted to hear his voice, but I wasn't sure I'd be able to speak coherently. Then it occurred to me, my priority was transcribing that last page. I doubted Jesper would be able to read the handwriting, but he might know someone who could. I answered my phone in as casual a tone as I could muster.

'Jesper, how nice to hear from you. How are you getting on with Samuel?'

'Finished. That's partly why I was ringing, to say the portraits are both ready now.'

'Oh, that's good news. I shall be pleased to have them home again. I've missed them.'

I thought I'd done a good job of disguising the fact a ghost had just made his exit in a manner that would have gratified the makers of *Haunted Homes*, but Jesper wasn't deceived. 'Jane, are you all right? Is this a bad time?'

'No. The others are out for the day. I'm on my own,' I said, glancing quickly over my shoulder to make sure.

'Has something happened? You sound a bit... odd.'

'Do I? Well, a lot *has* been happening, I suppose. Some of it upsetting.'

'Do you want to talk about it?'

'Well, yes, I do. I want to pick your brains about one of the things we've found. You're also the only person I can talk to frankly and know there's a chance you might take me seriously.'

'I'm all ears.'

'There's a rough piece of ground, some distance from the house. It was once the stew pond, but it's been dry for I don't know how long and the hollow has filled up with layers of dead vegetation and rubbish. Bridget offered to dig it out and re-create a pond there. She's very keen on encouraging wildlife.'

'And she found something?'

'Lots of things, including a large bone. Rosamund – she's a nurse – recognised it as human. A man's.'

'Good God!'

'Unfortunately we didn't tell Bridget. She carried on digging and she found… the rest.'

'Poor Bridget. That must have been a horrible shock.'

'It gets worse. The skull was fractured where he'd been hit on the head, so our wildlife pond is now a crime scene.'

'How old are the bones?'

'We don't know. We're waiting for the results of carbon dating.'

Jesper was silent a moment, then said, 'Given the skull fracture, do you think this could be Horatio?'

'I know it's Horatio.'

'Does *he*?'

Surprised and relieved, I gasped. 'Oh, it's good to talk to you, Jesper! I really wasn't coping.'

'But are you sure you *do* want to talk about this, Jane? First you inherit a ghost and now you've acquired a corpse. It's a hell of a lot to deal with.'

'I so wanted this to be a happy place, about the *living*. So far I've managed to resurrect my father, my mother and Queenie, as well as Horatio. Wyngrave Hall doesn't seem to have a future, only a past.'

'Should I just get off the phone?'

'No, I'd really like you to keep talking to me. About anything. It helps to hear your voice.'

'Well… There was some shocking overpainting on Samuel's portrait, but we got rid of all that and the fellow underneath looks quite different. Much better. I think you'll be pleased.'

'That's exciting,' I replied, without much enthusiasm.

There was another awkward pause, then Jesper said, 'There's something else, isn't there? You said you needed to ask me about one of your finds. Presumably not the skeleton.'

'I do want to hear about Samuel, but yes, there was another horrible discovery.'

'And you think I can help?'

'Possibly.'

'Then try me.'

'We were lifting floorboards in the attic and we found all sorts of things underneath, including what appears to be a journal. It's pretty much intact and my guess is, it's sixteenth-century, or early seventeenth, which means I can't read it.'

'Secretary hand?'

'Yes, but it was also written under appalling circumstances. The author was a woman being held prisoner by her husband. *Here*.'

'So *someone* has been able to read it?'

I hesitated, my mind racing, then said, 'Yes.'

'That pause suggests to me you didn't go to the British Library and ask to speak to their seventeenth-century manuscripts expert.'

'No, I didn't.'

'Because *you* have your own. Resident.'

'Please don't be facetious, Jesper. It's been very distressing.'

'I wasn't being facetious and I'm sorry if my feeble attempt at humour was out of place. I'm still not sure what tone to adopt when discussing your ghost and when I'm nervous, I fall back on humour.'

'Horatio makes you nervous?'

'No, you do.'

'*I* do? Why?'

It was Jesper's turn to hesitate. 'I just don't want to get things wrong.'

'You're not getting anything wrong, I'm just over-reacting.'

'I'm not sure you *can* over-react to a ghost.'

'The content of the journal upset me, even though the poor woman has been dead for four hundred years. She'd recently given birth, but they took her baby away.'

'And you know this because... Horatio read the journal?'

'Jesper, do you actually *believe* that?'

'Why would you lie? And I'm pretty good at spotting fakes. Fakes of all kinds. I bet you're an awful liar, Jane.'

'I am, actually.'

'So you're either a deluded fantasist or you're telling the truth. I don't think there are any other options are there? If you were deluded, wouldn't you be making more effort to convince me? But you're clearly struggling to believe *yourself* – which oddly enough makes you all the more convincing.'

'But why on earth would you believe me?'

'Two reasons. My mother has been chatting to my late father for the last ten years. The conversations, though necessarily one-sided, sound so natural, I've pretty much come to accept that – as she's always claimed – Dad never really left her. You see, she's just not the type to see ghosts. She's an academic and taught Viking and Old Norse Studies for thirty years. But she had an exceptionally happy marriage and refused to believe death was the end. And for her it wasn't. So I'm comfortable with the idea that *there are more things in Heaven and Earth* and I've come to wonder whether one of those things is the presence of the dead among the living, in various forms. Journals and portraits, for example. And ghosts.' He paused, then said, 'Are you still there?'

'Yes, I'm here. Sitting in stunned silence. I'd really like to meet your mother.'

'She'd really like to meet *you*. It was she who recommended your novels to me.'

'You said there were two reasons why you believed me.'

'Well, I'm afraid my other reason is quite irrational.'

'Because of course your first was *so* scientific.'

'Now who's being facetious?'

'*Touché.* I'm desperate, Jesper, so I think I can handle your irrationality.'

'I believe you, Jane, because I *like* you. I like you a lot, so I *want* to believe you. I've seen how important the past and your dead are to you and I'd rather believe in a dead madwoman in your attic than think *you're* the madwoman in the attic.' I didn't reply and there was an audible sigh at the other end of the phone. 'Have I got it wrong again?'

'No. No, you really haven't. I was just trying to think how to respond. Right now I can't think of any response other than I wish you were here.'

'That could be arranged. Say the word and I can come down today. I'll bring Samuel and Lady Edith. We could throw an impromptu homecoming party.'

'It seems a lot to ask, but I do feel in need of moral support right now. I don't just mean you. I really want the portraits to come home.'

'So do I. Look, I can come tonight, but I've got a few things to do first at the gallery, so it could be quite late. Or I can come first thing tomorrow if you prefer.'

'Whatever suits you best.'

'Could you feed me if I come tonight?'

'Yes, and you can of course stay over. Not sure there's any wine, though. Sylvia does get through it.'

'The Marvellous Marlow! I can't wait to see the dear lady again. I shall bring wine. Copious amounts. We can't have a party without wine.'

'You'll bring the portraits?'

'Of course! I can't wait to show off.'

'Because you saw what wasn't there.'

'I saw what *was* there, but invisible to the naked eye.'

There was another silence, then I said, 'He's gone, Jesper. Vanished.'

'Horatio?'

'He went to pieces. Literally. In front of me.'

'Something he read in that journal?'

'The very last page. I don't know what it says, but Horatio does. When he read it, he sort of *broke up*, then vanished. I need to find someone who can read that journal.'

'Bella.'

'*Bella?* Your receptionist?'

'She fancies herself as a bit of an archivist and if she can't read it, she'll know a man who can. Bella knows lots of men.'

'I don't think I could bear to part with it, even for a short time.'

'No need. Email me a photo of the relevant page, as big and clear as you can get it and I'll show it to Bella.'

'Oh, why didn't *I* think of that?'

'Because you've got a lot on your mind.'

'She'll find it a challenge. The last page is the worst. The poor woman was dying of cold and starvation.'

'It sounds like a Jacobean revenge tragedy.'

'It's *exactly* like a Jacobean revenge tragedy.'

'No wonder you're upset. Look, send me a couple of the better pages as well. They might help Bella with letter recognition.'

'Thank you, Jesper. You've been such a help.'

'My pleasure.'

'Come soon.'

'I'm on my way.'

He rang off abruptly and, in the silence, I sat clutching my phone, afraid to move, almost afraid to breathe, and I remembered the prisoner's words...

I fear I am not in my perfect mind.

I was still sitting at my desk, staring at the open journal, when my phone rang again. I jumped as if an electric current had run through me and looked at the screen. Relieved to see it wasn't Jesper ringing back to cancel, I answered.

It was someone who described herself as an osteoarchaeologist, phoning, she said, to reassure me. Radiocarbon dating had revealed that our skeleton was over four hundred years old.

'The blunt force trauma to the skull was unlikely to have killed the victim immediately,' she went on, matter-of-fact. 'There were no bone splinters around the edge of the injury, which suggests the object that caused the fracture was ball-shaped.'

'The pottery money box,' I said, feeling nauseous.

'Almost certainly. There were other fractured bones, indicating signs of a struggle. As they showed no sign of starting to heal, the victim must have died soon after they were broken.'

'Murder, then,' I said.

'Probably, but not a crime that can ever be solved now, or punished, so the police won't be taking the matter any further.'

'I see. What will happen to the bones now?'

'That's up to you. Obviously there's no way they can be identified.'

'Nevertheless, I'd like to give the man some sort of burial, as a mark of respect. Could you see that the bones are returned to me? And the money box? It's rare and of historical importance, so it should be packed carefully.'

'Of course.'

'Thank you. And thank you for... all the information.'

'Not at all. It's been an unusual and interesting case.'

After she'd rung off, I sat thinking about Horatio's ambition to be a footnote in history. Had he finally achieved it? Hardly. He was merely an interesting and forever anonymous cold case.

I took photos of some journal pages on my phone and sent them to Jesper, then sat at my desk, gazing out the window. As long shadows advanced slowly across the garden, I realised I was watching the passage of time...

Horatio had been struck on the head, then beaten up pretty thoroughly. He was probably bundled into a sack with some heavy stones, then dragged into the stew pond where, if he was still alive, he drowned.

He wanted answers. He'd wanted them for four hundred years. Now so did I.

When the others arrived home after their day out, Sylvia looked tired and said she'd like to go to bed and rest. She declined to eat a meal so I offered to take her a tray of tea and toast. Rosamund helped her along to her room and into bed while I made tea for everyone and Bridget rooted around in the freezer for something for dinner.

'I've taken out the *cassoulet*, Bridget. The big one I was saving. Jesper is coming later. He's bringing the portraits back and I said I'd feed him. I don't know when he'll get here. It could be late, so don't hold dinner. He's going to consult someone about our journal. Find out what it says.'

'What a useful guy.'

'Isn't he?' I busied myself making toast for Sylvia. 'While you were out, I got a call about the skeleton.'

'Any news?'

'It's very old. Over four hundred years.'

'So our pond isn't a crime scene any more? I can carry on digging?'

'Yes, if you can face it.'

'What will happen to the bones?'

Avoiding Bridget's eye, I gave the toaster my full attention. 'I've asked for them to be returned. I'd like to bury them in the grounds. Somewhere secluded.'

'That's a nice idea. Did they think it was murder?'

'Yes. Other bones were fractured. He must have put up a fight before—' The toast popped up and I didn't complete the sentence.

'Are you *sure* you want them buried on your land, Jane?'

'Oh, yes,' I said, buttering toast. 'I feel very strongly they belong here. And I'd like to treat the remains with respect.'

'Well, let me know where you want him buried and I'll dig the hole.'

'Grave, Bridget. I'd like to think of it as his grave. I'll mark it somehow. Something very simple.'

'It will have to be as we don't know anything about him.'

I spilled some tea as I was filling the mugs and mopped up quickly. I put two mugs on a tray, together with the toast and a jar of honey. As Rosamund came back into the kitchen, I said, 'How's Sylvia feeling now?'

'Better, but she's dehydrated. It's hard to get her to drink enough. Unless it's wine.'

'Your tea's on the table, Ros. I'll take some into Sylvia and stay and chat to her for a while. Bridget will fill you in on the news.

'Good, I hope?'

'Oh, yes, all good,' I said breezily and hurried away with the tray.

I tapped on Sylvia's door, but there was no answer. I assumed she was already asleep, but as there was always a worse possibility, I set the tray down outside and opened the door quietly.

Sylvia lay in bed asleep, as white as her pillowcase. I stood watching her chest until I saw it rise slightly, then I went back for the tray, set it down silently and sat in her armchair. I drank my tea, then began to nibble the toast. I could hear distant laughter in the kitchen and the murmur of lively conversation. They would be relieved. Bridget could start digging again and we'd all get our lives back.

But Horatio wouldn't. Neither would I, really.

Sylvia made a little whimpering noise, then settled again. The toast was finished and the tea was cold, but I continued to sit, thinking of another bedside vigil…

Hi Alison

Me again. Thinking of you as I sit at the bedside of a wonderful old lady. You'd have loved her. Everyone does. She's alive, but asleep and I'm sitting here willing her to stay alive. It didn't work with you, but apart from being tired and quite old, Sylvia isn't likely to leave us. Not yet.

Dead Guy has gone. Remember him? I'm not sure he'll ever come back now. I suppose I ought to be pleased about that. It was all getting so complicated. Long story, but I wish it could have ended better. I feel as if I've let him down, which is ridiculous, because he's been dead for over four hundred years. There must surely be a statute of limitations on feeling guilty.

We now know how he died. Bridget found his remains. I'll spare you the grim details and focus on the positives. That's what you used to say, isn't it?

Sylvia is right here beside me, breathing.

I can hear Bridget and Ros laughing in the kitchen. (They get on really well, so well that I sometimes wonder…)

Remember Live Guy? Jesper. We had lunch in London and I spoiled it by cracking up on him. I literally cried on his shoulder. So embarrassing. I wasn't even wearing waterproof mascara. I haven't seen him since, but he's coming later and the timing couldn't be worse – or better, depending on how you look at it. Its been an awful day, I'm very tired and I think all I want to do is cry on his shoulder again. Actually, that's not all I want, but if I allow myself to think about what I might want, I'll feel embarrassed again.

So I've stopped thinking about my needs. There doesn't seem much point. I wanted to move on. I wanted to stop thinking about the past because thinking about it just makes me angry – even the four-hundred-year-old past of Wyngrave Hall and its inhabitants. Obviously I'm angry (raging!) with Duncan for not being straight with me, but now I'm also angry with my parents for not being straight with me either. Sometimes I'm even angry with old Queenie Brooke-Bennet for not being straight with me and dumping Dead Guy on me along with Wyngrave Hall. If she'd said there was a resident ghost, do you think I would have taken this place on? Exactly.

To be absolutely frank, Alison, I think sometimes I'm even angry with you, which is totally unreasonable. I'm angry that you're dead, angry they couldn't save you, angry that you never reply. (I know you can't, and I don't even expect you to. I just wish you could.)

Sorry, I've gone on and on, and if you were alive, you'd be asleep by now, like Sylvia, who's lying here, perfectly still. Peaceful, and somehow regal, like an effigy on a tomb. But she's asleep. Definitely not dead.

Are you there, Alison? There, but invisible? Or are you absent? If you've gone I suppose I should stop talking to you, but I don't know if I can. It's so much easier talking to the dead. They always understand and they never interrupt.

Sylvia is stirring now, so I have to go. When she opens her eyes, she'll sense that someone's in the room, but she won't know who. We're all ghosts now to poor Sylvia.

Thanks for listening. If you did. (Wouldn't it be wonderful if you did interrupt, just like you used to!)

Love always.
J
xxx

Sylvia opened her unseeing eyes and I saw the confusion, almost panic on her face as she adjusted once again to her dark new world.

'Someone's there... And I can smell toast! Is that you, Rosamund?'

'It's me. Jane. I brought you some tea and toast a while ago, but you'd dropped off, so I didn't disturb you. Would you like some fresh tea? This is cold now.'

'No, don't go to all that trouble. Re-heat it in the microwave. In the corner, by the kettle. Rosamund got it for me. Wasn't that thoughtful? I often forget to drink my tea, you see. Sometimes I put it down and then I just can't find it! She said, if I could re-heat my tea, I might drink more. I *should*, apparently. She says it's one of the reasons I get confused now and again. I'm dehydrated.'

'Well, I'm sure Ros knows what she's talking about,' I replied, closing the microwave door on Sylvia's mug of cold tea.

'One minute should do it.' As the machine began to whir, Sylvia said, 'Now tell me all about your day! Did you get lots of work done? How's the new book coming along?'

'I didn't get much done. Too many distractions.'

'Nice or nasty?'

'Both.' I took the mug from the microwave and set it down on Sylvia's bedside table with the handle towards her. 'Jesper rang to say he's finished work on the portraits.'

'Hooray! Is he bringing them back soon?'

'Tonight. I'm not sure how late, but he's staying over.'

'Excellent! I'm looking forward to seeing him again. Oh, hark at me! I'm still talking in that senseless way. I shan't *see* him, shall I? Not properly. But you can't say, "I can't wait to *hear* him again", can you?' As Sylvia reached for her mug, I watched anxiously, but she soon found it. 'You know, losing one sense has made me think about all the others. I realise now just how unimportant looks are compared with a comforting word or touch.'

I remembered Jesper placing his hand silently over mine in the restaurant. If it hadn't quite calmed me, it did at least seem to *contain* me. 'I know what you mean, Sylvia. We spend most of our lives fretting about our appearance, but what do we actually remember about the women in our lives?'

'Coty's *L'Aimant*,' Sylvia announced. 'The perfume my mother always wore.'

'I don't remember much about my mother, but I remember her hands. They were always very soft. Regular applications of hand cream, I suppose. My father always gave her some for Christmas. She used to lay a hand on my forehead when I was ill. I thought she must have magical powers and was healing me with her hands, like Jesus, but of course she was just checking me for fever.'

Sylvia sipped her tea, apparently staring into space, then suddenly her face became animated. 'Is there any news about our skeleton?'

'Yes, and you'll be interested to hear that according to the carbon dating, he died more than four hundred years ago.'

'*No!*' She gaped in astonishment. 'It's the disappearing actor! I *knew* it. Was he murdered, then?'

'It seems likely.'

'Poor man. I wonder why?' She drank more tea and smiled in my direction. 'I suppose we'll never know now, not after all this time.'

'I suppose not... Let me make you some toast, Sylvia. I'm afraid I ate yours.'

Without waiting for an answer, I hurried out of the room.

While the others ate their *cassoulet*, I made up a bed for Jesper, then hoovered and dusted in the Long Gallery, feeling, despite everything, excited about the return of Lady Edith and Samuel. And Jesper. The prospect of his invoice was daunting, but the value of the two restored portraits had much increased. The flaw in this argument was, I had no intention of selling Samuel or Edith. But there were other portraits. *All* the others could go, provided Edith and Samuel remained.

I rummaged in our "Sale Room" for something like an easel to display the portraits. I drew a blank but found several old candelabra, some candlesticks and boxes of candles, put by, I imagined, for power cuts. There were a few church candles around the fireplace in the Great Hall and I had some scented tea-lights in my bedroom. I decided to move them all to the Long Gallery to create an authentic atmosphere for the homecoming of the portraits.

When I'd arranged all the candles, I fetched my portable speaker and placed it on a windowsill, then set about finding some suitable mood music. I recalled the melancholy lute music Bella had been playing at the gallery and I searched for a similar playlist. *Julian Bream Plays Dowland* sounded perfect.

I went to my bedroom to change and stood in front of the open wardrobe, gazing at the contents. I sensed nothing odd. The room temperature was normal. Relieved, but still irked that I didn't know what had driven Horatio away, I selected a pair of black velvet trousers and a loose, vivid shirt that moved beautifully. It was a flattering outfit that I enjoyed wearing on festive occasions and I thought the shirt fabric would look vibrant by candlelight.

I changed, brushed my hair and went downstairs. The kitchen was empty but tidy. Rosamund and Bridget were in the TV room. Sylvia had eaten a little *cassoulet* when it was offered on a tray and was now asleep again. Bridget had piled logs on the perpetual fire in the Great Hall, so there was little for me to do but wait.

I put the remains of the cassoulet in a low oven, together with two part-cooked jacket potatoes, then checked the time. Nine o'clock. I poured the last of the wine and went back upstairs to sit and wait. As I stared at the soon-to-be-occupied spaces on the wall a text came through. It was from Jesper.

We'll be with you in 20 mins.

I checked that it said *We'll* and not *Will.* It did. I could have hugged him for that.

Slowly, enjoying the ritual, I lit all the candles. I switched off the lights but the Gallery still seemed to be ablaze. I turned on the music, sat down again and sipped my wine, listening to the mournful, but achingly beautiful sounds of Dowland's *Lachrimae.*

Why was I happy? It had been a difficult, at times depressing day. Now I sat alone in a candlelit Gallery with sombre portraits of the long dead for company. My marriage and quite possibly my writing career were over. I was halfway (at least) through my life and had no idea what I would do with the remainder. The *Darby and Joan* scenario had never appealed, but now it was no longer an option. I had no plans for the future other than to survive – perhaps because my mother hadn't.

Yet I felt happy.

Well, content. I was alive. Unlike Alison, Nigel, Felicity, Queenie, Edith, Samuel and Horatio. I was alive. Waiting. Ready.

For what?

Anything, including ghosts.

I heard the crunch of car wheels as they advanced slowly over gravel. I stood up, hesitated for a moment, then moved through the Gallery so quickly, the candle flames danced. I hurried downstairs, my heart unaccountably light.

12

Night and silence!

A Midsummer Night's Dream

By the time I'd got the door open Jesper was already unloading his car. He approached carrying a cardboard wine carrier, reassuringly full, and a bunch of flowers.

'Welcome!' I called.

'Good evening, Jane. I come bearing emergency supplies,' he said depositing the wine carrier on the doorstep. 'And these,' he said, looking at the flowers, 'are for Sylvia. I got freesias and carnations which she'll be able to smell even if she can't see them clearly.'

'How very thoughtful. Thank you, Jesper.'

'I would have liked to bring some for you too, but it seemed rather unprofessional.'

'Oh, I quite agree. After all, I still owe you a huge amount of money.'

'I trust when you see the portraits, you'll think I was worth every penny.'

I took the flowers from him. 'Sylvia will love these, but she's in bed already, I'm afraid. A busy day. Do you want to bring the portraits in now? I think it's starting to rain.' I took the wine and flowers into the hall, then went back to the car.

Jesper had arrived dressed for a weekend in the country and looked as dishevelled as ever. He wore a collarless white shirt over navy cords and a brown tweed waistcoat with the buttons undone. His thick, silvered hair was even more anarchic than the last time I saw him, standing up from his broad, tanned forehead as if he'd run his fingers through it in exasperation. Driving out of London on a Friday night at the behest of a hysterical client, perhaps he *had*.

I picked up his holdall while he took charge of the wrapped portraits. He put one under each arm, pointed his key fob at the car and locked it.

'Jane, wait a moment, let's do a swap. You take Lady Edith – that's this one – and I'll take my bag. I think you should carry her back into her home.'

'Thank you. Another lovely thought.'

I set down the bag and he passed me one of the portraits. I gripped it firmly with both hands and led the way into the house. As we entered Jesper exclaimed as he saw the log fire. 'And I can smell something very delicious coming from the kitchen. This is a hero's welcome.'

'You're a hero for coming at such short notice. I'm very grateful.'

He set down his holdall and the portrait of Samuel, then regarded me for a moment. Subjected to that frank blue gaze, I felt like a painting – possibly one in need of restoration.

'I haven't said how marvellous you look, Jane. The rainbow hues,' he said, indicating my shirt. 'They're sparkling like jewels in the firelight. You know, every so often I miss painting. Doing it myself, I mean. This,' he said with a gesture of his hand that included me, the fire and the Great Hall, 'is one of them. Shall we open the champagne? It should still be chilled.'

'Yes, let's.' As we headed for the kitchen, I said, 'The others have eaten already. Ros and Bridget are watching TV. Well, they were. They might have dozed off by now.' I turned the oven up, then took a vase out of a cupboard and filled it with water while Jesper set about opening a bottle of champagne, something he did with such nonchalant dexterity, I concluded they must be in the habit of celebrating at his gallery.

As I arranged flowers, he told me how excited Bella was to be involved in my historical detective work.

Alarmed, I said, 'You didn't tell her about—?'

'No, I just said you were anxious to find out what the journal said and who it was written by. Bless her, she was very keen to help.'

If Jesper was tired after a long and tedious drive, it didn't show.

His eyes were bright with good-natured mischief at Bella's expense and occasionally mine, and he strode round the big kitchen looking for glasses and a tray with the same spring in his long-legged step that I remembered from his first visit.

Finally he said, 'Champagne is poured. Now, shall I go up to the Gallery and set up the portraits, or would you like a drink first?'

'Why don't you go upstairs and set up? I'll bring the drinks up in a few minutes. Check my candles. If any have gone out, feel free to re-light them. You'll find matches on the windowsill... What is it?' Jesper was staring at me with a look I couldn't fathom.

He shook his head and smiled. 'Nothing. I've been in this business a long time, but I've never shown paintings by candlelight before. *Real* candles.'

'I know it won't be the best light to see your work—'

'It will be brilliant light, not to mention authentic.'

'I've lit rather a lot, so I think we'll be able to see pretty well. And I remembered what you'd said.' He looked a query. 'About pale faces lighting up a dark room. Not that Edith's face *was* pale then.'

'It is now. Give me five minutes. That's all I need.'

'Go on up. Do you remember the way? You'll see there are two gaps on the wall, side by side. That's where I'd like you to hang them.'

Jesper left the kitchen and a moment later I heard his quick footsteps ascending the wooden stairs.

I laid the table, placing Sylvia's flowers in the centre and was about to light more candles, then hesitated. This wasn't Date Night – not that I knew anything about Date Nights as I hadn't experienced one this century. But Alison used to light a candle at every shared meal, even before she was dying, and I seemed to remember Scandinavians are a bit more relaxed about candlelight. Irritated by my inhibitions and dying for a glass of champagne, I fetched two candlesticks from the dresser and lit candles either side of the flowers. The effect was fabulous.

Jesper had placed full glasses and the bottle on a tray, so I lifted it carefully and set off upstairs – hungry, tired, but very excited.

As I mounted the stairs, I could smell beeswax and heard the plaintive sound of the lute. Entering the Gallery, I met a wall of hot air and I stood in the doorway for a moment, admiring the effect of the flickering light. Evidently too warm, Jesper had slung his waistcoat over a chair and rolled up his shirtsleeves and was now sitting, arms folded, with an expectant smile on his face. He sprang up as I moved into the room and took the tray from me.

'You are to be congratulated, Jane. The candlelight, the music, the Gallery... It's all just *perfect*.'

'Thank you. I'm sure the heat won't do the paintings any good, but it's not for long.' Jesper had hung the portraits on the wall, but they were each covered with a cloth which he'd draped over the frames. 'I see I'm not the only one indulging in showmanship.'

'If you're a conservator, you know all about delayed gratification.' He handed me a glass, then picked up the other. 'Ladies first?'

'Oh, yes, I think so.'

'Well, then,' he said, raising his glass. 'To Lady Edith Wyngrave. It has been a privilege and a delight to work with her. With you too, Jane,' he added.

'Thank you. To Lady Edith.' We clinked glasses and drank.

'Now, are you ready for the grand unveiling?' Jesper asked eagerly.

'Can't wait.'

He approached one of the portraits and I followed, taking up a viewing position at a slight distance. He tugged at a corner of the cloth, it slithered to the floor and Lady Edith's eyes met mine.

With her arched brows, she looked a little surprised, as if she found herself somewhere she hadn't expected to be. Her skin was now a dazzling ivory, with just a faint rosiness in her cheeks. The direct gaze, the unnaturally pale skin, the unadorned lips didn't conform to any modern idea of beauty. Nevertheless, Edith's was a remarkable and unforgettable face, one I knew I could gaze at – and love – for the rest of my life.

When I felt able to speak, I turned to Jesper and said, 'It's as if there's a third person in the room.' His eyes flickered and he nodded. I found I couldn't say any more as emotion threatened to overwhelm me. Embarrassed, I managed, 'Sorry, I'm—' before he rescued me.

'It's quite all right, Jane. Stunned silence is what I expected and I'm pretty well used to it. Clients often feel overwhelmed, especially when the painting that comes home is very different from the one they sent away. As this one is.'

I pointed to the portrait. 'Her mouth… She looks as if she might actually speak at any moment. And you were right about her eyes.'

'Wasn't I? You see, my conceit is not entirely without foundation,' he said with mock seriousness. 'Now, shall we charge our glasses for Samuel Wyngrave?'

As he returned to the tray, a text came through on his phone. He put his glass down and reached into his trouser pocket. 'It's late for texts. Would you excuse me while I check? Could be my aged mother.' Sipping my wine, I watched the candlelight play on his face and saw his eyes widen with surprise. 'It's from Bella. I told you she was keen. She says she's sent me an email. Shall I…?'

'Of course.' I waited while he read it.

It was hard to tell in the candlelight, but as he looked at his phone, it seemed to me that all the colour drained from Jesper's face. He didn't speak, but I could see he'd stopped reading and was just holding his phone.

'What is it?' He didn't reply but looked up. Alarmed by his expression, I said, 'Tell me, Jesper.'

He looked down at the screen again and said in an oddly expressionless voice, 'Bella says she hasn't deciphered much of the final page yet, but she's confident she will be able to in time. The name of the author is almost legible…' He paused and, without looking up, said, 'I'm so sorry, Jane.'

'Tell me.'

'Bella says the first name is clearly *Edith* and the surname looks as if it could be *Wyndham* or *Wyngarde*.' He swallowed and muttered, 'Then she asks if any of those names mean anything to you.'

I turned away and stared at a guttering candle. As I watched, it went out and a little plume of smoke drifted up into the warm air. After a moment I found the breath to say, 'Would you text her back and ask if she thinks the name could be *Wyngrave*?'

He quickly typed a text into his phone, then sent it. The music had stopped and we stood in silence. Neither of us looked at Edith's portrait.

Another text came through and I watched Jesper's face, quite impassive now, as he read it. 'Yes. The signature might say *Edith, Lady Wyngrave*.' I was unable to reply. Jesper said, almost apologetically, 'I'll just text her back. To say thanks.'

I nodded, still unable to speak.

He sent the text, then put his phone back in his pocket. He stood quite still, his hands folded in front of him. I heard his intake of breath, then he said, 'If there's *anything* I can do, Jane—'.

Finally I found my voice. 'You can pour more champagne, come downstairs and distract me while we eat my delicious *cassoulet*. I intend to honour your brilliant work and Edith's life – short and terrible though it must have been. I'm absolutely gutted, but I'm going to behave as if I'm not, for as long as I can. It's just a painting, isn't it? I didn't *know* this woman – though the brilliance of the artist has made me feel as if I did. And hearing the journal read—' As my voice broke, Jesper moved towards me, but I glared at him, repelling any approach, knowing it would wreck what remained of my composure. 'I'm *not* going to let this piece of the historical jigsaw ruin everything.' I pointed to the portrait, but still couldn't bring myself to look at it. 'It's a brilliant painting of a woman I now know to have been quite remarkable. Discovering she wrote that journal makes me all the more determined to celebrate her tragic life and my very good fortune in becoming the custodian of both her portrait and her written testament.' I raised my glass. 'To Lady Edith Wyngrave!'

'To Edith,' Jesper echoed. 'And you, Jane. *Skål!*'

'To the three of us, Jesper.' We drained our glasses. 'Apologies for the speech', I said, trembling now with hunger and shock. 'But I thought the occasion called for it.'

'It did.' He refilled our glasses and said, 'I think he'd probably cheer you up a little, but shall we postpone Samuel until later? Maybe even tomorrow?'

'Yes. We need food. Leave the candles,' I said, glancing round the room, but still avoiding the challenge of Edith's solemn grey eyes. 'Let's eat. You must be famished.'

As I led the way into the kitchen, I glanced at Sylvia's flowers and the two candles either side. They looked quite different now. Gaudy. The bright colours seemed to assault my eyes. I looked away and concentrated on feeding Jesper.

Determined to celebrate, I told him to open some wine, then sit at the table. I took the *cassoulet* and potatoes out of the oven and set them on the table beside the salad bowl. When I lifted the lid, a cloud of delicious-smelling steam emerged. I stared at the contents of the pot for a moment, then replaced the lid. Sinking into my chair, I said, 'Jesper, do you think you could serve? I'm sorry, but I don't think I can find the energy.'

'Of course.' He poured us both a glass of wine, then addressed himself to the *cassoulet*. 'This looks wonderful, Jane. Have you been slaving all day?'

'No, it came out of the freezer. I *did* slave over it, but not today.'

When he'd served us, he sat down again and said, 'Would you mind if I moved the flowers and candles? I'd like to see you.'

'Oh, of course. Silly of me to put them in the middle. I'm not used to eating with people I want to look at.'

'Or people who want to look at you.' He forked some meat into his mouth, closed his eyes, swallowed, then said something guttural that I took to be Danish.

'I hope that was complimentary.'

'*Never has food tasted better,* roughly speaking. It's quite true. And somehow only Danish would do.'

'Are you fluent?'

'Fluent, but far from eloquent. We moved to England for my mother's work when I was about nine, so I remember it all and practise when I go back, but I speak it with the simplicity and restricted vocabulary of a child. My wife was Danish, but bi-lingual and we mostly spoke English, so my command of Danish is certainly not one of the things I'm conceited about.' He raised his head from his food and looked at me. 'Oh, Jane, not even a smile? And you're not eating.'

'I'm finding it hard to swallow.'

'Mash some potato into the delicious sauce.'

'You're good at nagging, Jesper. Nagging nicely.'

'I had a lot of practice with Freja. She was ill for a long time and she was a lousy invalid. Couldn't bear feeling powerless. Neither could I, but at least there was the nursing to do. And the nagging… Eat up, Jane. It's good.'

Dutifully, I picked up my fork and mashed potato into the sauce. 'I think it's feeling powerless about Edith that's upsetting me.'

'Perhaps because of Alison? It's hard to accept we can't save people.'

'Even when we're four hundred years too late?'

'Apparently.'

'If Edith had been a friend in trouble, I would have rescued her somehow. Offered my home as a refuge. Lent her money. Called the police. But she's dead, so I can do absolutely nothing.'

'But you've already done a great deal.'

'I have?'

Jesper laid his cutlery down. 'Edith wrote a secret journal and concealed it. She hoped someone would find it one day after she was dead, but she must have thought that anyone who found it would be quite likely to destroy it. But *you* found it. And you will preserve it, along with Edith's portrait and a portrait of the son she never knew. You'll display those portraits side by side in the house where he was born and she was imprisoned and died. One day, you'll probably tell Edith's story in some form or other, because you're a writer.' He picked up his knife and fork again and said, 'Damned if I know how you could have done any *more* for Edith. If she knew, she would be very, very grateful. You feel powerless, but you're not. Sadly, Edith *was*. But you've brought her tragic story to light. In her final days, she can't have hoped for any more than that: for the truth to be known. And now it is. Thanks to *you*.'

'And Horatio.'

'You'd have found someone to translate the journal for you. It was only a matter of time.'

'The discovery of Edith's true face is thanks to you.'

'Partly. You bought my time and skills. It was your choice to find the real Edith. Her face could have remained hidden – like her journal – for further centuries, perhaps for ever. But you're a gambling woman, Jane. You gambled on Edith and took a chance on me.'

'And I hit the jackpot. But poor Edith...'

'There's nothing more you can do for her. Grieve. Honour her memory. Tell her story. What more can we do for our dead?'

I looked up directly into Jesper's eyes for the first time since he'd read me Bella's email. He was watching me intently, willing me, I thought, to hold it all together, not because he minded if I fell apart – I'm sure he didn't – but because *I* did.

I looked down at my plate, blinking ferociously. 'I know you're right. I just wish I'd never found that bloody journal.'

He paused for a moment, then said, 'The hope that it might be found one day gave Edith strength. Kept her alive for a bit longer, perhaps.'

'Right again. Oh, I should stop being so pathetic.'

'And I should stop being so insufferably wise. Shall I be trivial instead?'

'Please.'

'You might have noticed my tweed waistcoat.'

'I did.'

'Technically, it's an antique. It's also a family heirloom.'

'I love it. In fact, I want to try it on. How old is it?'

'My great-grandfather had a three-piece suit made after the First World War. He bought the cloth on the Isle of Harris from a man who wove it in his shed, so the fabric is even older than the suit, which has been passed down from father to son – with alterations, of course. It eventually came to me looking, as tweed will, as good as new. Sadly, the trousers don't fit – my legs are too long – but the jacket and waistcoat do. I don't know Harris, but my father did. He said the colours of traditional tweed are inspired by the landscape: the dull browns, greys and soft greens of the land and the brilliant blues of the sea and sky. You only notice the bright threads in certain lights and he said Harris is like that. On a misty day, the sun will suddenly appear and reveal all the dazzling, hidden colours of rocks, seaweed and wild flowers. I've always wanted to go and see for myself what he saw and perhaps paint it.'

As Jesper re-filled our glasses, I said, 'That was a lovely story. I think I'd like to visit Harris. And I certainly want to see you in the waistcoat again. There's a bright blue thread in it that matches your eyes.'

'So I'm told.'

'And the red? It's a sort of burgundy colour.'

'Seaweed, apparently. It's worth looking at the cloth close up with a magnifying glass. There might be twenty colours in one tweed. The Harris weavers paint with woollen threads.'

I smiled. 'You weren't being trivial at all, were you? You were talking shop.'

'Guilty as charged. That's the trouble with art. It encompasses everything. My father said the fishing was excellent on Harris. Fishing was his great passion, but I only enjoyed eating it, so I was something of a disappointment to him.'

'But you fit two-thirds of the family suit *and* you wear it.'

'There are many ways to honour our dead, Jane. We aren't *quite* powerless.'

'I feel a bit better now.'

He put down his cutlery and gestured towards his empty plate. 'It's your wonderful food.'

'And the talk. Would you like some more?'

'It was delicious, but no, thanks. "Eat less, chew more", as my grandmother used to say.'

'In Danish, I imagine. It doesn't sound like an English sentiment.'

'She was an object lesson in nagging nicely. And thin.' He pushed his plate away and leaned on the table, his arms folded. 'So... are you up for Samuel tonight?'

'Are you?'

'Me? After that meal, I'm up for anything.'

'I feel nervous about viewing him. I *was* really excited. Now I'm fearful for some reason.'

'It's Bella's news. It has rather blighted the evening, but I'm confident Samuel is bomb-proof. He *does* look very different, but he looks better. Not just cleaner, but more handsome, more sensitive and more intelligent. How can you resist?'

I narrowed my eyes and tried to look severe. 'You're very good at selling things, Jesper.'

'I am, which is why I make it a principle to sell people only the things I'm pretty sure they want. Especially as they don't always know what they want.'

'Do I want to see Samuel tonight?'

'You do. And I'm sure he wants to see you.'

'Right, you've sold him to me.' I stood up and bent to blow out the candles. Jesper was halfway to the door when I said, 'But I warn you, I might just burst into tears.'

He turned and spread his hands. 'The ultimate compliment. For the artist, for Samuel and for me.'

The Long Gallery seemed darker now. It wasn't just the sobering effect of Edith's portrait. Candles had gone out and, without a word, Jesper set about re-lighting them. Averting my eyes from Edith, I chose some more cheerful music and I set it to play quietly while I sat and watched Jesper light candles. There was something reassuring about his energy and confidence. I allowed myself the tentative hope that between them, he and Samuel Wyngrave would somehow salvage the evening.

Jesper turned to me with a broad, excited smile. 'Are you ready?'

'Yes, I am.'

He stood to one side of Samuel's portrait and pulled the cloth away.

I don't know what I'd been expecting, but I thought I'd prepared myself for whatever Jesper's chemical magic might reveal.

I was wrong.

I rose to my feet, took a step towards the portrait, then turned away. I looked down at the dark polished floorboards, thinking very fast.

Jesper was at my side, laying a hand on my arm. 'What's wrong? Are you disappointed?'

'Jesper, would you follow me outside please?'

'*Now?* It's raining.' He glanced at the window. 'It's also pitch black out there.' When he looked back, I saw confusion fighting with concern. 'What *is* it, Jane?'

'I've got a big umbrella. Did you bring a jacket? It doesn't matter, you won't be cold. Put your waistcoat back on. Tweed's warm, isn't it?' I turned my back on Jesper and the portraits, marched out of the Gallery and started down the stairs. As he followed me, I said over my shoulder, 'If I switch the downstairs lights on, we'll be able to see our way.'

'Where are we going?'

I wheeled round to face him and we almost collided.

'*Please*, Jesper. I'll explain when we get outside. I know it must look as if I've finally lost it, but I haven't. Trust me.'

Not waiting for an answer, I continued down the stairs and made for the light switches. Pressing the outside light, I discovered it wasn't working. 'Damn. The bulb must have gone.' I picked up a raincoat and looked at Jesper who had put his waistcoat back on. 'Where *is* your jacket?'

'I don't remember. I might have left it in the car.'

'Never mind. Button up.' As he did so, I took a long woollen scarf from the coat stand and wrapped it several times round his neck.

'I feel like Bob Cratchit now. I hope we don't meet any ghosts. Past, Present or Future.'

'We won't,' I said firmly and picked up the largest umbrella from the stand. As Jesper pulled the big door open, rain blew into the doorway.

'Give me the umbrella, Jane. I'm taller. You can take my arm.'

'Sorry, it's colder than I expected,' I said, pulling the door shut behind us.

'The candles deceived you. They do raise the temperature of a room. We really should have blown them out. Shall I go back up?'

'This won't take long.'

'What won't?' he asked, opening the umbrella.

'We have to get away from the house,' I said, ignoring the question. 'Well away.'

We set off smartly along the path, with Jesper clutching the umbrella and me clutching Jesper. As we left the Hall behind, we were plunged into almost total darkness. Clouds obliterated the moon and the lighted windows soon became vague yellow shapes, barely penetrating the blackness.

'Now turn left… There's a gate in the hedge. *Here…*' I fumbled with the rusted latch. 'Stay on the path. I know you can't see it, but you can feel the gravel under your feet.' I tugged on Jesper's arm and pulled him forward in the darkness. 'It should be here… Yes, here we are.'

He laughed. '*Where?*'

'The old summerhouse. It's the nearest shelter, but I think it's far enough.' I leaned on the warped wooden door and shoved while Jesper wrestled with the umbrella. The door creaked and we stepped inside.

'What's the wonderful smell?'

'Fruit. Bridget stores apples and pears in here. From our orchard. Last year's are all gone now, but the smell lingers. Nice, isn't it?'

'Nice to be out of the rain too.'

'Are you *very* wet?'

'Very damp,' he admitted.

'Sorry, but we had to get away from the house. I don't know if he's still there, but I couldn't risk it. He isn't able to leave the Hall, so I know he won't hear us here.'

'Horatio?'

'Yes.'

'What mustn't he hear?'

'Me talking about the portrait.'

'Samuel's?

'Yes. It's all so obvious now you've restored it. The likeness is staggering.'

'Jane, slow down. You're not making sense.'

'Samuel's portrait. It's Horatio. To the life. Oh, what a stupid thing to say! He's *dead*.'

'But… if Samuel Wyngrave looks just like Horatio, that means—'

'He was Edith's lover and father of her only child.'

'And he doesn't *know*?'

'I think he does now. He read the journal, saw her name and his memory came flooding back.'

'But surely Horatio heard her name in four hundred years?'

'I don't see why he would. She was effectively murdered by her family. They wouldn't have talked about it. Apart from her portrait, she was probably forgotten. Regardless of whether it was a good likeness, Horatio had no memory of Edith or anything to do with her after the blow on the head. I think it could have been a combination of things: her name, her handwriting perhaps and the way she wrote about her devotion to her lover. I think Horatio suddenly realised who had written the journal and… everything came back.'

'Imagine discovering the woman you loved had been kept prisoner and starved to death.'

'I can't imagine it, but I saw what imagining it did to Horatio.'

'But Samuel's portrait was the image of him, you say. Surely that was a big clue? And Horatio must have seen it – certainly while old Wyngrave was alive.'

'Samuel's portrait was painted long after Horatio's death – Samuel was only a baby when he was murdered – and in any case, Horatio remembered nothing about the end of his life. Would he notice his resemblance to a portrait if he never saw himself reflected in a mirror? And he wouldn't. It's scientifically impossible. There's nothing for light to bounce off. You can actually see *through* him sometimes... Jesper, your teeth are chattering. Are you very cold?'

'Spooked, mainly, but I'm keeping up. Bear with me because there's something else. After a number of years, the portrait *didn't* resemble Horatio, because of all the overpainting... Ah!'

'What?'

'Most of it was seventeenth century. And that *did* surprise me.'

'How could you tell?'

'Paint analysis. You have to do that, so you know how best to remove it. I was expecting the additions to be much later, maybe Victorian. They usually are. But perhaps Wyngrave Senior had the painting altered to look more like *him*.'

'Samuel died as a young man, so the overpainting could have been done after his death, when no one was alive to object.'

'So you think Horatio now remembers Edith?'

'It's worse than that. He's learned what happened to her. He must also know he fathered a son he didn't live to see, who was raised as the Wyngrave heir.'

'All supposition, Jane.'

'I know, but it adds up, doesn't it? And it explains why Horatio *disintegrated*. And if his memory suddenly returned when he saw Edith's name at the end of the journal—'

'He now knows why he was murdered.'

'But, do you see, I didn't want him to hear any of this because I don't know how much he knows, or rather understands. He must have known that she married to have recognised her name in the journal. He knew her as Edith de Vere.'

'Did he ever know she was pregnant? And if he did, would he have known he was the father?'

'Even if he did, marriage was out of the question. He was an actor, a vagabond, little better than a criminal in some people's eyes. Edith must have agreed to marry Sir Walter to give her child a name. And a future.'

'Well, she seems to have achieved that, but at huge personal cost.'

'When Bella's transcribed it, you must read Edith's journal. It's heartbreaking.'

'So is her son's portrait, when you *know*. Nevertheless, it's a fine picture of a handsome young man. Such lively and intelligent eyes. I always tackle the eyes last, after I've done everything else, as a reward for my labours... Oh, Jane, I can hear that you're weeping.' His arm went round my shoulders. 'Come on, let's go back. It's very late.'

I looked up to where I thought Jesper's face would be, but could see nothing, only an area of darkness that was slightly paler, but I could feel the warmth radiating from his body as he stood close. I reached up, searching for his face, and laid a hand on his cheek. 'I need to know you're there,' I said faintly. '*Really* there.'

He leaned into my palm. 'Oh, yes. I'm here.' He pulled me towards him with the arm that circled my shoulders. With the other he folded me against his long, damp body, holding me there with a hand pressed firmly into the small of my back. My head fitted under his chin, so I lay my head on his chest and breathed in his scent. An astringent herbal smell mingled with the sweet aroma of the fruit.

Neither of us moved for a while. The rain drummed gently on the summerhouse roof and I felt the steady rise and fall of Jesper's chest against my cold cheek.

'I'm sorry,' I mumbled.

'For?'

'For getting so emotional about dead people.'

'Don't apologise. I get emotional about dead people too.'

'Your wife is different.'

'I didn't mean Freja, though of course I do get emotional about her. I meant the portraits. The sitters. And if I'm not careful, I can get emotional about the people who bring them to me, together with their stories. Some are just curious. Others are bereaved. Going blind. Fallen on hard times.'

'Your impecunious Duke.'

'Yes, my dear old Duke. Caring about people, alive or dead, can be draining.'

'Still, I'm sorry I had to drag you out here. And in the rain.'

'I wouldn't have missed all this *for the world*. But I do think we should go back and get warm.'

As he released me, I caught hold of one of his hands.

'I'm so glad we found you.'

'We?'

'Edith… Samuel… Me.'

He squeezed my hand. 'Glad I was found. I wonder, Jane… Even though you owe me a lot of money and it goes against my professional code of ethics – yours too, I'm sure – would it be all right if I kissed you? I mean, *ethically* speaking, the damage is already done because I've asked… And you're still holding my hand,' he added.

I didn't reply. Nor did I let go.

'Afterwards,' Jesper continued reasonably, 'after I've kissed you, I mean, we could simply forget it ever happened.'

'I don't think *I* could.'

He laughed softly in the darkness. 'Would that be a yes?'

'Yes. It's a yes.'

Jesper must have bent his head as I lifted mine. His chin, rough with stubble now, grazed my nose and I laughed, then his mouth found mine and I clung to him while he held me. After a while he lifted his head and whispered, 'Not for the *world*…'

The rain had stopped and we walked back to the hall in silence, holding hands. As we approached the front door, I said, 'Would you mind dealing with the candles in the Gallery? I don't think I can face going in there again tonight.'

'Not at all.'

I pushed the front door open. 'Would you like another drink? A brandy to warm up? Herbal tea?'

'No, thanks, Jane. I'm ready for bed.'

As the light from the interior fell on Jesper's face, it struck me he looked even livelier than when he arrived. I wondered whether his answer had been deliberately ambiguous.

As we entered, the warmth was blissful. I took off my raincoat and hung it up while Jesper unwound his scarf.

'I'm just going to clear the table and get the dishwasher on, so people can eat in the morning.' I attempted a casual smile but got distracted by the way Jesper's damp shirt clung to his chest and arms. 'You need to get those wet clothes off,' I said without thinking.

'I'll check the gallery.' He bent to pick up the holdall he'd left by the door when he arrived. 'Which room am I in?' I opened my mouth to speak, then closed it again. I stared at him helplessly. 'No pressure, Jane. It's been a hell of a day for you.'

'You too. You must be exhausted.'

'Me? No, I'm wired. Ready to party like it's 1599. But what do *you* want?'

I thought fleetingly of Alison, then said, 'My room is opposite the Long Gallery. There are candles... Beside the bed. Would you light them? I shan't be long, but I can't just leave things—'

Jesper dropped the holdall, took my face in both hands and kissed me again, then without a word, he picked up his bag and headed for the stairs.

I watched until he turned at the top of the staircase, then went to the kitchen and tidied up as quickly and quietly as I could. I switched the dishwasher on, locked the front door, turned out the lights, then ran upstairs before I could change my mind.

The sight of Jesper half-naked by candlelight strengthened my resolve. I fear my sharp intake of breath was audible. He smiled as I came into the room, then with an easy grace, reached into the open wardrobe for a hanger. I watched as he hung his shirt and waistcoat over the back of a chair, then unzipped his cords. My expression must have changed, because he frowned and said, 'Second thoughts?'

'Good heavens, no! But there's something I must do first.'

I approached and lay a hand on his naked chest, partly to reassure him, but mostly to reassure myself that he was real. With my other hand I reached behind him and pulled the sliding wardrobe door until it was shut. 'That's better. I have to keep them closed.'

He looked puzzled. 'Why?'

'I had a very disturbing experience,' I said, running appreciative hands over the curves of his arms. 'With those doors.'

'Seriously?'

'Long story. I'll explain tomorrow. Now, do you need any help with the rest of your clothes?'

13

A most lovely gentleman-like man.

A Midsummer Night's Dream

I woke first. It was light and we'd neglected to draw the curtains the night before, so I was able to observe Jesper as he slept, lying on his front, his head pillowed in his arms. The duvet had ended up on my side of the bed, so he lay there mostly exposed. I'd spent decades with a man so darkly hirsute, he never looked quite naked. Jesper's sleeping body, frosted with golden hair, looked pale and vulnerable in comparison. I sat up and dragged the duvet carefully over him, then lay down again.

There's something to be said for having sex with a man you hardly know. Well, there is if most of the sex you've had was with someone whose next utterance you could have predicted with mind-numbing accuracy. As I stared at Jesper's sleeping face, I had no idea what he would say when he woke, but I knew it was likely to be considerate, probably amusing, possibly surprising.

His face looked different now, shaded with unexpectedly auburn stubble. His eyelashes flickered, then he rolled onto his side, facing me. I lay with my face close to his, willing him to wake because I didn't know how long he could stay and I wanted to see whether his eyes were as blue as I remembered.

He opened them and I saw that they were. I watched him blink and struggle to remember where he was, then when he did, his face folded into deep creases as he smiled. 'Good morning, Jane. So it wasn't a dream, then.'

'Unless you're still asleep.'

'No, I'm wide awake.' He propped himself up on one elbow and regarded me intently.

Disconcerted, I said, 'You look as if you're studying my face for a portrait.'

'No, sheer pleasure. But perhaps you *should* sit for a portrait. One to join your collection.'

My smile must have faltered. I could tell Jesper wished he hadn't mentioned the portraits, so I quickly changed the subject. 'Do you realise, this is only the third time we've met? I feel as if we've known each other for ages, but I don't actually know much about you.'

'Yes, you do. Well, you know everything about me that matters.'

'Things your grandmother said?'

'Exactly.'

'How old are you?'

He looked surprised. 'Does age matter?'

'Not really. Well, not if you're a man. I was just curious.'

'Forty-six.'

'Really? Well, that's a relief. I thought you might be younger. Time spent at the gym is never wasted.'

'Especially at my age.'

'Is that why you go? Because you obviously go a *lot*.'

'I spend my days hunched over canvases. The gym irons out the creases, mental and physical. And I cycle round London. But it's also a Danish thing. *Friluftsliv*.'

'Meaning?'

'*Open air living*, I suppose. We like exercise and fresh air. We see it as fun, not a chore.'

'Difficult to do in London?'

'Not really. There are parks, the river, canal paths. I have a balcony where I sit out in all weathers, to the amusement of my neighbours. I tell them, there's no such thing as bad weather, only bad clothing.'

'Your grandmother again?'

'Correct. When we were kids, my sisters and I used to roll our eyes at her sayings, then gradually we discovered they were all true. I hear myself repeating them now, sounding quite elderly. So then I get on my bike and go to the gym.'

'You haven't asked how old I am.'

He looked shocked. 'I wouldn't dream of being so rude.'

'Don't you want to know?'

'No. But if I did, I'd look it up on Wikipedia. I'm more interested in where you went to university and what you studied.'

'St Anne's, Oxford. History.'

'First Class?'

'Yes, actually.'

'Time spent in the Bodleian is never wasted.'

'Oh, but I think it *was*. I should have spent more time consorting with young men. I must say, I find it refreshing that you're more interested in my *alma mater* than my age.'

'Age evidently matters to *you*, but the way I see it, we're either alive or dead and as long as what happens is consensual and legal, what does age matter? The mind is what attracts me. You're interesting. And seriously brainy.'

'And you're not?'

'No, I'm just a dumb blond who cleans for a living.'

I laughed. 'Not even very blond any more.'

'*Sic transit gloria mundi.*'

'Do you have clients throwing themselves at you?'

He laughed. 'Occasionally. But desperation is easy to resist.'

'Did I seem desperate?'

'Not at all. In fact, I thought you were in love with your ghost: younger, and to judge from Samuel's portrait, better-looking than me. And he had the ultimate *cachet*. He was dead.' Jesper rolled onto his back and locked his hands behind his head. 'But that was okay, because I don't get involved with clients, however tempting.'

'Yet here we are.'

'Yes. Here we are…' He sighed. 'The circumstances have been *unusual*, to say the least.'

'Exceptional,' I conceded, moving closer and laying a hand on his chest. 'And I suppose technically you finished working for me when you delivered the portraits.'

'Sadly, no. I haven't been paid yet, so you're still my client, which means I've behaved unprofessionally. By my own standards.'

'By *any* standards,' I said severely.

He turned his head to face me, his expression grave. 'Would you prefer me to leave?'

I slid my hand downwards under the duvet. 'Not yet...'

I showered and dressed, then left Jesper doing the same and went downstairs to join the others. As I walked into the kitchen I affected a studied casualness, but Rosamund gave me an appraising look, then smiled in what seemed a rather knowing way.

Sylvia was holding court. I told her the flowers on the table were a gift from Jesper who was going to bring the two restored portraits downstairs. We all knew Sylvia would be able to see very little, but I hoped she'd get an impression. If nothing else, she'd want to be included in the excitement and would enjoy hearing Jesper holding forth on the technical aspects of the job, which, to the uninitiated, did sound pretty much like magic.

He appeared in the doorway, beaming and studiously avoiding my eye – a detail that probably didn't escape Rosamund's. He was wearing jeans and a pale, close-fitting cashmere sweater, which could have been unforgiving if Jesper had anything to forgive, but he didn't. I introduced him to Bridget and Rosamund whom he hadn't met, then poured coffee, while Sylvia thanked him effusively for his flowers.

'I'm afraid I can't really see them, but the scent is gorgeous. *So* thoughtful of you, Jesper.'

He bent and took her hand in both of his. 'It's a pleasure and a privilege to bring you flowers, Sylvia.' He turned and said, 'Now, ladies, whenever you're ready, Edith Wyngrave and her son Samuel await your pleasure in the Great Hall.'

Sylvia squealed and actually clapped her hands together. Jesper caught sight of a jug of orange juice on the table and said, 'I believe I left a bottle of champagne in the fridge last night. Buck's Fizz, anyone?'

Bridget fetched glasses while Jesper opened the champagne. He didn't meet my eyes until he handed me a glass. It was only a conspiratorial smile, but it was enough. It hadn't been the wine last night, or the shock of Horatio's real identity, or Edith's. As Jesper breezed round the kitchen dispensing drinks and charm, my insides turned over and I longed to touch him.

Clutching our glasses, we trooped into the Great Hall where he'd arranged the portraits on chairs near the windows so the meagre light would fall on them. As we approached, the sun must have broken through the clouds, because Lady Edith's face seemed to light up, almost as if she was pleased with all the attention. Chiding myself for being fanciful, I turned to examine Samuel in daylight and was shaken once again by his resemblance to Horatio.

While Jesper explained his work process and Sylvia asked intelligent questions, Rosamund sidled up to me with the jug of Buck's Fizz and asked in an undertone, 'You okay?'

'Yes, I'm fine. Silly of me, but for some reason he makes me feel very emotional.'

'Samuel or Jesper?' she whispered, sipping her drink. She spared me the trouble of answering by saying, 'He's very handsome.'

'Samuel or Jesper?' I asked.

She grinned. 'I was referring to the portrait.' She moved over to Sylvia who was nursing an empty glass which Rosamund duly refilled.

I turned from Samuel's portrait to Edith's, trying not to dwell on what I knew about her final weeks. It was then that I realised... It wasn't a guess, or even a hope. I *knew* where Horatio was. It was so obvious, I couldn't imagine how it had taken me so long to think of it.

When I could focus once again on my housemates, I heard Bridget offering bacon and eggs to Jesper who was explaining to a captivated Sylvia how Danes manage to consume so much coffee and cake without putting on weight. I didn't think I would be missed, but I moved over to him and said softly, 'I've just had an idea. About our Missing Person.' His eyebrows rose. 'Can you hold the fort while I'm upstairs? You're not in a hurry to get away, are you?'

'Far from it, especially if someone's cooking me breakfast. But where are you off to?'

'The attic.'

*

Moving away from the laughter and bright chatter, I began to feel apprehensive. As I climbed the stairs to the attic, I told myself I could be wrong, but the closer I got to the room that must have been Edith's prison, the colder the air felt and I knew the reverse should be true. Warm air rises and it would collect beneath the roof. When Bridget and I had searched under the floorboards, the heat had been stifling. Now as I stood outside the small door, I shivered with cold as well as fear and wished I'd thought to grab another layer on my way up.

I picked up the big flashlight we left outside the attic, which had neither window nor electric light. I switched it on, lifted the door latch and pushed. Ducking as I entered, I shone the light quickly round the little room.

It was freezing, but cold wasn't all I felt. The air seemed heavy, thick with misery, something I hadn't noticed when Bridget and I were sifting through the ancient dust. A pall of suffering now hung over the room. I placed each foot carefully on one of the oak joists and said softly, 'Horatio? I know you're here. Will you show yourself to me?' There was no response. As my eyes began to adjust to the darkness, I said, 'I think we're close to finding out who killed you.'

I felt some sort of vibration in the air but saw and heard nothing.

'I want you to know that Edith lives on in her portrait. It's mine now and I shall never part with it. It will live in this house as long as I do.' The vibration again. I shivered violently. 'I really want to hear your story, Horatio. If we can fit all the pieces together, I think you'll be free. Free to leave. To find some sort of peace.'

Silence.

I was now so cold, I was about to give up and go downstairs, when the beam of my flashlight caught something in the far corner of the room. It looked like a large black stain on the plaster, but it was spreading, and rapidly.

Alarmed, I almost lost my balance, but I stood firm, pointing the beam, raising it as the stain expanded until it was the height of a man. The blackness gradually assumed the shape and size of

Horatio, but it clung to the corner, cowering against the wall. I could now see a lighter patch in the black: his face, though it took me a moment to work out he was covering his face with his hands.

Feeling like an intruder, I lowered the torch beam and stepped across the joists to perch on a pile of lifted floorboards at the edge of the room. I waited.

Horatio slowly lowered his hands. He looked different. Skeletal, his eyes huge black pits in a face that hadn't just aged, but decayed. He opened his mouth, then seemed to abandon the effort to speak. He tried again. 'She died in this room... I can feel it. She died here. For me. Her silence condemned her.' He shook his head hopelessly. 'The scrabble of rats was the last sound she heard. These walls were the last thing she saw... And they killed me anyway,' he added bitterly.

'Her last thoughts would have been of you. Of your child. And her God. All that would have been some comfort to her.' He looked at me then for the first time and I felt myself thrust back against the wall, as if I'd been struck. Terrified, I said, 'I have to believe it, Horatio, because that's all there is!'

'Still the tender heart, Jane?' The pressure stopped suddenly. I lurched forward, gasping, as if I'd been released from a powerful grip. 'So many times,' he went on, 'I have cursed the loss of my memory and prayed for its return. Now I see it was a kind of mercy: if I needs must die, I should be allowed to forget why. But now, God save me, I have remembered and I've been trying to piece our story together, separate the truth from what I was told.'

'You fathered a son. He was raised as Samuel Wyngrave and he lived. Both his parents were killed, but Samuel lived.'

'Edith was imprisoned by her husband, but who killed *me*, Jane? God's blood, it is something to look into the eyes of men who have but one thought – the extinction of a human life – but to look into those eyes and know not who, nor why... The pain of the blows was great, but the agony of incomprehension was greater.'

'You saw their faces?'

'Not the man who administered the blow to the head, but I saw the faces of the men who approached me, beforehand. And I saw their faces as they broke my bones and stifled my cries with a filthy rag.' His hands were shaking but he steadied himself by clasping them together. 'I drowned, tied up in a sack, like a litter of pups, and I died in ignorance. I didn't know I had a son. I didn't know Edith still loved me. And what has tethered me here for centuries is that very ignorance.'

'You didn't recognise the men, but do you remember anything about them?'

'Fine clothing. Hands as white as their lace. Those men were killers, but they were not for hire.'

'Can you bear to know who they were when you can do absolutely nothing about it?'

'At first I wanted vengeance, but as the years went by, I realised the best I could hope for was... certainty.'

'Knowledge is surely the only thing that could bring you a kind of peace. Knowledge, and telling your story. You were an actor, Horatio. You should tell your story. And Edith's.'

'She would have told it better.'

'What makes you say that?'

'She was a poet. I spoke other men's words. Edith wrote words for others to read and speak.' His voice softened. 'Her desire to tell stories is what drew us together.'

'Then surely she would want her story to be heard – and told by you.' He said nothing, but I persisted. 'The portrait of Edith downstairs... It was covered in dirt and old varnish and bits of her had been painted over. You couldn't *see* Edith, but now you can. I asked a man to clean it and what you see now is what was painted. It must really be her. I never knew Edith, but I love her, as a sort of friend, a friend I never met. The portrait will always live with me and so will her journal, but I don't know Edith's story. Or yours. It might help you to tell it. I know it would help *me*. Queenie wanted me to solve your mystery. I think I very nearly have, but I still need your help.'

'Queenie! Fie, I had quite forgot that dear lady and the message she gave me for you.'

'For *me*? What was it?'

'I must not say – not yet – nor do I understand the message, but I was to give it to you when— *if* all was known... What do you think will happen to me then, Jane?'

'I think you will leave.'

'Though all that matters to me – Edith's portrait, her journal, perhaps her very *dust* – lie within these walls.'

'In 1603 you would have had no trouble memorising the journal.'

'Faith, that is true! I carried thirty-odd rôles in my head. Like any actor, I was a quick study.'

'Her journal is on my desk, but I can leave it anywhere it will be safe.'

'Thank you, Jane. There are words in that little book that I shall treasure—' He broke off and covered his eyes again.

'Never doubt that you were loved, Horatio.'

Still shielding his eyes, he let out an anguished cry. 'But what's to become of me, Jane? After four centuries, where shall I go?'

From somewhere, the words came to me, words he had once quoted to me. '*The undiscovered country, from whose bourn no traveller returns.*'

Horatio lowered his hands and seemed to grow taller. 'I wish to see Lady Edith. Her likeness. And I shall tell you our story. Tonight.'

'We should meet in the Long Gallery, when the others will be in bed. Midnight?'

'*The very witching time of night,*
When churchyards yawn, and hell itself breathes out
Contagion to the world.'

'You will come?'

'I shall come.'

As I watched, he shrank back into the wall, dwindling until there was nothing to see but an ugly black stain that might have been mould. I rose from the stack of floorboards, picked my way across the joists, then lifted the latch on the door. Turning, I looked back over my shoulder, saw nothing and stumbled downstairs.

At the foot of the steep, narrow staircase, I opened another door onto the first floor, daylight and warmth. Animated female chatter drifted up from the Great Hall. Jesper murmured something, Sylvia replied, then everyone laughed. It all sounded so very normal, I could have wept with relief.

As I made my way down, I looked over the banister into the Hall. Catching sight of me on the stairs, Jesper pointed discreetly towards the kitchen, then picked up the almost empty jug of Buck's Fizz and announced he was off to re-fill it.

He got to the kitchen first and I found him waiting. As I shut the door behind me, he said, 'No need to ask if your mission was successful. You look as if you've seen a ghost. Was it grim?'

'Yes. I'm chilled, drained and very much in need of a hug.'

'And coffee?'

'*And* coffee.'

Jesper filled the kettle and switched it on, then turned back to me and took me in his arms. I pressed myself against him, relieved to feel human warmth and solidity. 'Keep your eye on the door,' I murmured. 'I haven't got the strength to go public yet.'

'Oh, I think Ros already knows. I wonder which of us came downstairs looking smug?'

'That would be me.'

'Could have been me. Despite physical exhaustion, I find I can't stop smiling.'

The kettle boiled and he released me. 'I'll make coffee,' I said. 'Are you doing more Fizz?'

'That was my excuse for leaving the room – and Sylvia does appear to have hollow legs.'

I opened the fridge and took out milk and the remains of the champagne. I handed the bottle to Jesper who stood looking at me, his gaze serious, but sympathetic.

'You found him then?'

'I sensed he was there as soon as I went into the attic. He was huddled in a corner of the room, like some faithful dog who won't leave his owner's grave. It was pitiful, Jesper. We agreed I'm going show him the portraits and he's going to tell me his life story. Or rather death story. At midnight. In the Long Gallery.'

'You don't do things by halves, do you? It will be like the end of an Agatha Christie, minus Hercule Poirot.'

'Horatio saw the faces of the men who killed him. There were two of them, but he didn't recognise them.'

'Rent-a-thug?'

'He says not. I think they could have been members of Edith's family, or even ghastly Sir Walter. So I'm going to set up an identity parade. Of portraits. If he *can* positively ID someone, think what that would mean to him!'

'Will you manage on your own?'

'I'll have to. Horatio may have been an actor, but he doesn't want an audience for this.'

'I'm afraid I'll have to leave later today anyway. I'm booked for Sunday lunch tomorrow with my mother. We eat out together once a month and she'll be disappointed if I cancel now.'

'No, you must go. I'll be fine. I just need to dig out my thermal underwear.'

Jesper laid both hands on my hips and pulled me towards him. 'I shall be sorry to miss that.'

'Horatio's story?'

He pulled me closer and breathed in my ear. 'You in thermals.'

Before he left, Jesper helped me set up in the Long Gallery. He was thrilled to be allowed to trawl through the Sale Room, examining portraits I'd consigned to oblivion. Edith and Samuel were joined by her husband, the rest of her family and various other men who might have been connected in some way to Wyngrave Hall or the two families. Jesper said, if there was to be an identity parade, we should have a good selection of potential villains for Horatio to inspect.

As usual, I wasn't entirely convinced Jesper was taking things seriously, but he fetched and carried and took endless trouble to arrange the portraits. He suggested a better place for Edith's, as far away from her husband's as was possible within the confines of the Long Gallery. He retrieved cloths from the back of his car to cover each portrait so they could be revealed one at a time, though I had a suspicion that if Horatio could read thoughts and walk through walls, he'd be able to see through Jesper's tactful veils, but covering the paintings would at least show respect for Horatio's feelings.

I contemplated the vacuous face of Sir Walter Wyngrave, the monster who had married Edith, imprisoned her and starved her to death. Jesper came and stood beside me. He regarded the portrait and said in a low voice, 'The banality of evil.'

'I hated it even when I didn't know.'

'Maybe at some level you *did* know, Jane. The artist has perhaps conveyed the essence of that appalling man. It's technically brilliant. Sir Walter hired one of the best.'

'I really appreciate your professional advice, Jesper, but if I discover any of these men are responsible for Horatio's death, I shall sell their paintings or even donate them to charity, regardless of their artistic merit or worth. I won't have them in the Hall for one minute longer than necessary. I only hope I won't be tempted to destroy them.'

'Don't do that,' he said gently. 'I understand why you feel that way and I admire you for it, but you're sitting on a lot of money here and in some cases you have portraits of considerable importance. They say revenge is a dish best served cold. Why not sell and donate the proceeds to a struggling theatre company? Or set up a scholarship so some hard-up youngster can study acting? Edith might have wanted you to donate to a women's refuge. You could do so much *good* with the money! God knows, destruction would be emotionally satisfying, but I think you might regret it. You'll come to realise you destroyed only an innocent artist's work, not the men who murdered Edith and Horatio.'

'As always, the voice of reason.'

'And sound business sense. Maddening, aren't I?'

'Yes, but I think I'll keep you on. I might even pay you.'

'Good to know… Look, if necessary, I can drive back on Sunday night and remove any portraits you want taken off the premises. I can store them at the studio while you decide their fate.'

I looked at him gratefully and said, 'Am I crazy, Jesper? Can this possibly work?'

'No idea, but I think it's what you've got to do. And all this will make a terrific book one day, won't it? Fiction, of course.'

I surveyed the Gallery which looked crowded now, full of dark faces against even darker backgrounds. Edith and Samuel, side by side, seemed to illuminate the room with their pale skin and candid expressions.

I turned back to Jesper. 'I think everything's ready now. I just have to wait.'

'You think he'll show?'

'Oh, I think so. *It is an honest ghost.*'

'Hamlet?'

'I think about that play all the time now. Horatio's farewell performance, playing a man who was murdered in the prime of life, taken from his beloved wife and son.'

I began to cover the portraits, starting with Edith. Without a word, Jesper followed suit and in a few minutes, all the faces were gone and he and I were alone again.

'You should leave now, Jesper. You've been a wonderful support, but you're also a distraction and I don't want to be distracted, I want to concentrate on Horatio and Edith.'

'You'll ring me if there's anything I can do? *Anything.* Any time. I doubt I shall sleep for worrying about you all. And you'll let me know if...' His voice trailed off.

'I'll let you know.'

'Then I'll get my things together, say goodbye to the ladies and go.' He looked at me doubtfully. 'May I kiss you goodbye?'

'If you do, I don't think I'll be able to hold it all together,' I replied, my voice unsteady. Unable to meet his eyes, I laid a hand on his arm and said, 'Just leave, Jesper. Go now and come back when it's all over.'

'If you need to get away, come to London.'

'Thank you, but my place is here.'

'Take care then, Jane. I'll be thinking of you.'

'Thanks.'

He left me staring at the covered portrait of Horatio's son.

14

But were some child of yours alive at that time,
You should live twice, in it and in my rhyme.

Sonnet 17

That night, seeking solitude, I went up to bed early and set my alarm for just before midnight. I was very tired. Jesper and I had retired late the night before and then we hadn't got a lot of sleep. I lay on my bed, dozing fitfully for an hour or so, but woke before the alarm went off. I sat up, changed into warmer clothes, including my thermals, brushed my hair and left my bedroom, shutting the door silently behind me.

I crept downstairs, made a flask of coffee and collected a blanket from the Great Hall. I doubted I would need the caffeine but knew I would be cold.

Outside the Gallery, I hesitated, then grasped the doorhandle and entered. The temperature seemed normal, but the central heating had gone off, so it wasn't warm. I switched on a lamp so I could find matches and start lighting candles. I would need their warmth even if Horatio didn't, and I wanted him to be reunited with Edith by their light, the only light apart from firelight that would ever have illuminated the lovers' faces after dark.

By three minutes to midnight all the candles were lit. I sat on one of the chairs I'd set out earlier and waited, nervous, but not frightened. I hoped I wouldn't have to witness Horatio's disintegration again, but if I did, I would know what it signified. I also knew we might be about to meet for the last time. It was hard to know how I felt about that, preoccupied as I was with Horatio's hope that he would identify his murderers, then quit Wyngrave Hall for ever. I would get my life back, I supposed, and Horatio would get his death back – and surely this was one death I need not mourn?

I felt a sudden icy chill at the back of my neck. Turning quickly, I saw Horatio towering over me. Despite all my mental preparation, I sat rigid in my seat.

He raised a hand, palm towards me and said, 'Fear not, madam. My heart is full of gratitude. Queenie chose her successor well.'

Horatio vanished, then appeared in front of me, taking up a position in front of Edith's and Samuel's covered portraits. Some of the candle flames shone *through* him and it looked almost as if he himself was alight.

'I shall not keep you long from your bed,' he continued. 'You are tired and anxious, so I shall be as brief as my tale allows.'

Calmer now, I said, 'Do you want to see Edith first?'

'Not yet. Her portrait is likely to un-man me. I think it best I tell you my story, then we can examine the *Dramatis Personae.*'

'Whatever you wish. This is all for you, Horatio. And we have all night.'

'Thank you. You have been kind and understanding, Jane. In another world we might have been friends. The actor and the word-smith… If you are ready, you shall hear now of *The Brief Life and Ignominious Death of Horatio Fortune, Actor.*' He bowed deeply, then began. 'My family lived as tenants on the de Vere estate, in this same county of Essex. My mother was a widow and my sister, Agnes, was servant to Edith de Vere – they were much of an age – and one of my brothers was a stable boy. To avoid a life of servitude, I ran away to London to become an actor. There I rose from lowly beginnings to share lodgings with other members of the company. Edith's older brother, Oliver came often to the Playhouse. De Vere was tolerated for his generosity in the alehouse where he liked to read aloud the plays and poems he'd written, but they were of little merit. What merit they had belonged to another, for he had stolen their words.'

Horatio paused and looked down. He appeared to steel himself before saying, 'Oliver de Vere brought his sister to the Playhouse one day and we all met backstage after the performance, as was his custom. Oliver wished to talk about the play he had seen and the one he was currently writing. As humble actors, we were required only to listen, and so I observed Edith, not simply because she was fair, but because her eyes moved constantly, taking in everything about her, delighting in all she saw, like a child. She made an impression upon me, but not as a woman. She was far above me in station and members of my family served hers. I thought no more of Edith de Vere, but thereafter I sometimes noticed her in the audience, chaperoned by her brother or my sister.

'One day Agnes presented me with a playscript: *A Fair Maid's Vengeance* by Oliver de Vere, according to the title page. I said I would pass it on to be read by an actor-manager, but Agnes insisted I should read it first. She claimed no one esteemed de Vere's plays and this one would likely moulder with the others, or be used to light fires, but *this* play, Agnes assured me, was different and someone should read it. Now Agnes could read, but she was by no means educated, nor was she clever.' Horatio's voice softened as he recalled his sister, dead for centuries. 'I surmised she had been taught what to say. Indeed, she looked relieved when she'd finished her little speech. I own, I was intrigued and promised Agnes I would cast an eye over the play. I did... and burned candles all night until I'd finished reading it. It was not a play by Oliver de Vere. It was written by a poet, but one who understood how the stage worked and had perhaps studied the classical dramas of Ancient Greece. When Agnes returned to hear my judgement, I told her the manuscript was clearly the work of another man. Were it anonymous, I would happily share it with the company, but the playwright should come forward in his own right, since he was a man of far greater talent than de Vere.

'Unable to depart from her script, Agnes was at a loss. I sent her away, saying I wished to meet the author. I asked her to convey my congratulations to him and promised I would read anything else he had written. A few days later I was visited at my lodgings by a young man, scarce more than a boy. He was of good family to judge from his speech and attire. He would not give his name, but said he was the author of *A Fair Maid's Vengeance* and other plays, but wished, for his own reasons, to give the credit to his good friend, Oliver de Vere. He handed me another manuscript and told me messages could be conveyed using Agnes.

'By the time he turned his back and fled, I knew of course.' Horatio smiled with a warmth I didn't recall having seen before. 'Edith de Vere had worn her cap pulled down over her eyes and she'd disguised her voice and manner well – apeing her brother, I supposed – but I knew I had been speaking to a woman. I have watched too many boy actors struggle to portray the essence of womanhood to be mistaken. This talented young man was a woman in disguise, much like one of her own heroines, or Will Shakespeare's.

'I read the second play and we met again at "his" request in the courtyard of an inn. Edith did not touch the ale I purchased and was barely able to conceal her astonishment at the coarse language she heard from ostlers and pot boys, but we discussed her plays. I said they needed more work but should be performed. However, I would do nothing more until I knew the author's identity.

'She left abruptly and I heard no more until I received a message from Agnes to say I should walk in a secluded churchyard at midday. Edith came. As Edith... That was the first of our trysts, chaperoned by Agnes, who didn't understand that we might want to meet in quiet, uncongenial places to discuss poetry. I would recite Edith's lines and make suggestions. Sometimes she noted them down on the manuscript, sometimes I did. That was a fatal mistake.'

'Why?' I asked.

Horatio looked affronted at the interruption. 'Patience, Jane. You shall hear in good time. I struggled to disguise my admiration for Edith's person and she, being so young, was unable to conceal her feelings for me. I believe my foolish sister thought marriage was a possibility, that she might one day be related to a noble family, so she did everything in her power to help us. She carried letters back and forth – anonymous, but it was another grievous error.

'Agnes should not have left her mistress alone with me, but doubt-less that's what Edith ordered her to do. Perhaps in her youthful ignorance, even she thought we might marry. Edith knew nothing of the world or of men, other than what she'd read and heard at the Playhouse. Her head was full of fancies and romantic stratagems. I was entirely to blame, and some would say justly punished.'

Horatio paused and regarded me, then the blanket and flask on the floor beside my chair. 'You are chilled, Jane. Come, fortify yourself with your beverage and wrap that blanket round you. You are but mortal.'

I realised I *was* very cold and did as he said. When I unscrewed the top of the flask, fragrant steam rose into the icy air. I swallowed a welcome mouthful and said, 'I wish I could share this with you, Horatio.'

'Nay, do not concern yourself. I do not feel the cold. Neither do I feel any warmth,' he added. 'Sometimes I wonder if I sense anything other than absence. What I was. What I had. Who I knew.'

'You have your memories now.'

'They serve only to remind me what I lack,' was his sharp reply.

'But you remember now that you were *loved*. You know it as a fact. When you died, you didn't. You thought you'd been dumped in favour of wealth and position, but now you know Edith loved you until she died. You were probably her last thought. Surely that's something?'

'It is perhaps everything,' he conceded. 'I am justly rebuked.'

I swallowed more coffee, screwed the top back on the flask and set it on the floor again. 'Please continue, Horatio.'

'Edith came to my lodgings unannounced one day, unaccompanied and in her manly disguise.' He paused. His substance seemed to thin and the candle flames behind him looked brighter. 'When I think of what happened then and on two subsequent occasions, I am ashamed, but in my defence – *can* there be any defence? – I did nothing to instigate the intimacy we enjoyed. But… I responded. Then I was a man of flesh and blood. Passionate. Weak. Whatever sins I committed, I surely paid for them. But so did Edith. Now I know the consequences of my selfish lust, I believe I did not suffer *enough*, except that to discover Edith died alone, in darkness, cold and starved, is a torment beyond anything my murderers could devise.

'Our messages and meetings ceased. Agnes would not or could not explain. She said only that her mistress was unwell. There was no final letter from Edith, only word from Agnes that her mistress was to make a splendid marriage to Sir Walter Wyngrave, a wealthy and much older man. And so Edith de Vere put away her poetry and became Lady Edith Wyngrave.'

'I think a marriage was arranged in a hurry because she was pregnant. She might not have had much say in the matter.'

'I fear you are right.'

'And Sir Walter was complicit for his own reasons.'

'But he knew the child wasn't his. While the father lived, he would always be a threat to the Wyngraves.'

'But if Edith refused to betray you, how were you identified? Surely it must have been Agnes? If your letters were found, it would have been obvious Agnes carried them. Perhaps they threatened her. Or worse.'

'I comfort myself, that would not have been necessary. To protect Edith, I destroyed her letters and told her to destroy mine. She said she did, but now I doubt it. I believe she concealed them merely, and they were found.'

'But you said they were unsigned.'

'Yes, so I could not be identified. That was the foolish assumption I made. But as well as Edith, two others knew my hand. I'm sure Agnes would not have betrayed me wittingly. She might have had nothing to do with my exposure. If Edith's annotated manuscripts were seen by Oliver de Vere, he would have recognised my hand from the copious notes I made on *his*. Or if my letters were found, it would be a simple matter to compare them with his manuscripts and Edith's. They did not need my name.'

'But even if Oliver was instrumental in identifying you, would he have murdered you for seducing his sister?'

'Men killed for less. But Oliver didn't. I knew neither of the men who assaulted me.'

Horatio fell silent and I noticed the Gallery had grown darker. Some candles had burned out and the temperature had dropped still further. Hesitant, and very cold, I said, 'What happened in the end? How was it… arranged?'

'Our company was invited by Sir Walter to perform at Wyngrave Hall. *Hamlet* was requested and I was to play the Ghost of Hamlet's father. I hoped I might see Edith in the invited audience, but it was given out that the lady of the house was too ill to attend. I was disappointed, but I suspected no danger, to her or myself. Despite the apparent strength of her feelings, I assumed she'd abandoned her dalliance with plays and her social inferiors in favour of an advantageous marriage. Remember, I knew nothing of my child. But before the performance, Agnes gave me a verbal message that I should meet Edith in the grounds of Wyngrave, a quiet and distant spot, near the stew pond. I was concerned about the risk, but Agnes insisted it was a matter of life and death. As indeed it was…

'I now assume Oliver gave Agnes that message – perhaps a sealed note, purporting to be from Edith. Agnes was too witless to realise it might not have come from Edith and I was too witless to ask Agnes who had given it to her. After many months Edith had asked to see me! She'd cried off the performance so we could meet. I could think of nothing else. It so happened I had a long period offstage—'

'The whole of Act Two.'

Horatio nodded. 'Normally a tedious interval, but I was thus able to tell Agnes when I could meet her mistress. Instead of playing cards as I waited for my next entrance, I took myself off for some "fresh air" and went to wait by the pond. Eventually I heard footsteps approach through the undergrowth. Not a woman's. Immediately I suspected a trap. Two men appeared and walked towards me purposefully. Without thinking, I reached for my sword, but I was of course unarmed. Another mistake.'

'Had you seen either of the men before?'

'Never. One was young, the other much older. I had time to register they were both big men, as tall as me, but broader. I was afraid then, not for myself, but for Edith, also for Agnes who had been duped. The older man called out, "Horatio Fortune?" As I was about to run, I received a massive blow to the temple. It seemed to come from nowhere.

'Then there were *three* men. They belaboured me with blows. One had a cudgel. I lost consciousness. When I opened my eyes, I could see nothing but darkness. I was imprisoned in what I now assume was a sack and dragged into the pond. As I sank, I tried to move, thinking I could kick my way to the surface or tear the sack open. That was when I realised my hands and feet were tied and I was going to drown.'

Another candle guttered and went out. I stared at Horatio who was very still, his face quite impassive.

'My dying thoughts should have been of God and repentance, or at least my poor family, but they were of Edith. Knowing nothing of the child, I saw no reason why I should be killed, other than I had taken the maidenhead of Sir Walter Wyngrave's young wife. If he knew that, then I feared for Edith too. When I could hold my breath no longer, I inhaled muddy water and for a few moments endured the worst pain I had ever known. And so I drowned. Damned.'

Horatio bowed his head and was silent for what seemed a long time, but I didn't dare speak. He looked up suddenly and said, 'After a time – I know not whether it was minutes or months – I became aware again, conscious that I was dead, but not *absent*. I remembered the last words I'd heard – my name – but could remember nothing else, apart from a blow to the head. I appeared to be in some dark, windowless room, with walls but no door. I don't know how long I remained in that unearthly place, but after a time, there came some light and the walls seemed to recede, then gradually dissolve. I found myself in a house I didn't recognise, but later when I explored, I realised it was Wyngrave Hall. I observed a large household, but no one observed me. I assumed I was both invisible and inaudible. A terrible fate for an actor,' he added, with the slightest curl of his lips. 'Bored to distraction, I tried to leave, but found I could not. Hurling myself at internal walls and doors, I discovered I could pass through them at will, but could not leave the Hall. I never saw Edith, nor the men who killed me. Occasionally I heard the pitiful cries of an infant. My son, I now assume. Then the household went into mourning and Wyngrave was shut up. Fires were extinguished, tapestries taken down, silver plate packed away and all the doors were locked. I became the sole inhabitant. I don't know how long the house remained empty. It might have been years. Decades.'

'And you could remember nothing of how you came to be… in your position?'

'I remembered I had been an actor. I recalled every play I had performed. I remembered my family and my childhood home, but I didn't remember Edith, nor the manner of my death, only the fearful blow that evidently caused great injury to my mind as well as my skull.'

'And you knew no more until you read Edith's journal.'

'Then I remembered *everything*. It was as if I'd died all over again, but this time was worse, far worse, for I knew what had happened to Edith and I knew I was to blame.'

'Your feelings do you credit, Horatio, but Edith had choices. She chose to protect you rather than be reunited with her baby son. You must know she would never have wanted you to blame yourself for what happened.'

'*If thinking on me cause consternation in thy breast, I had rather be forgot.*'

'Her words?'

'Yes.'

'You've memorised them?'

'I have the little book by heart. *Remember sweet meetings past and sad farewells, but O, if thou livest, remember not my fate.*'

'She was very clear, Horatio.'

'Edith always knew what she wanted.'

'And she wanted you, so you must try not to blame yourself.'

'But I shall. For all eternity.' He gestured towards the Gallery walls. 'You wish to show me all these portraits?'

'It's a long shot, but you might recognise your killers. And I want to introduce you to your son. Shall we start with him?'

Horatio bowed slightly but didn't reply. Glad to move at last, I walked over to the portraits of Edith and Samuel and lit some more candles, then I took hold of a corner of one of Jesper's cloths and said, 'Horatio, I'd like to introduce you to your son, Samuel.'

I pulled at the cloth and let it fall to the floor. I stepped aside, but otherwise I didn't move or speak.

After some time Horatio said, 'Does he resemble me?'

'You look much older, but otherwise, he could be your twin.'

'I have no memory of my appearance. The last time I saw myself was in our tiring room here, where I dressed to play the part of the Ghost.' He approached the portrait and stood very close, almost as if he studied his reflection in a mirror. 'A fine-looking young man, is he not?'

'I loved this portrait at once, long before I knew who he was. Now I love it even more. My friend Jesper thought there was a different face underneath and he was right. This is the original work.'

'You have brought my son into the light, Jane.'

'Jesper has. He was buried under the grime of centuries.'

'As were my bones.' Horatio looked away from the portrait and said, 'What will happen to them, Jane? My earthly remains?'

I tried to keep my voice level as I answered. 'The police said they will return them. Then it's up to me.'

'Forgive the macabre interest, but I should like to know where my *bones* will rest, even if I do not enjoy the same luxury.'

'I'd like to bury them here in the grounds, though I'd understand if you didn't want to be buried where you were murdered.'

'My son must have lived here. It was Queenie's home. Now yours. I have dwelt at Wyngrave for centuries, so I should like my mortal remains to rest here.'

'I shall choose a site in the grounds, nowhere near the pond. I'll mark the grave with a headstone and flowers. Is there anything you'd like especially?' He shook his head. 'Bridget will know what to plant. I shall make it a special part of the garden, with a bench. For quiet contemplation.'

'Jane... You have bereft me of all words.'

Suddenly very tired, I said, 'Would you like to see Edith now?'

'I wish to see her and yet I *fear* to see her.' He seemed to struggle with himself. I walked over to the portrait and said, 'Whenever you're ready, Horatio. Take your time.' I thought my legs might soon give way, but I focused on Horatio's face which seemed to move in and out of focus in the candlelight. I was about to ask if I might sit down again, when he said, 'I am ready, Jane. I have not seen my dearest love for four hundred and sixteen years and I shall not see her now, only her likeness. But I am ready.' He stood very tall and straight with his arms hanging loosely at his sides. I thought what an impressive Ghost he must have made, appearing at midnight on the battlements of Elsinore, and pulled the cloth away.

Horatio's face did not change, but his eyes did. Eventually his mouth opened and I feared I was about to hear another agonised howl, but he was silent, his eyes and mouth wide open in a rictus of shock and pain. He approached, lifting his arms as if to embrace the portrait, until his face was level with Edith's, their mouths almost touching. He moved closer still, then *into* the picture, until his form had disappeared and the portrait hung unobscured.

I quickly examined the painting and checked it was unharmed. I bent to pick up the cloth and when I straightened up, Horatio was there again, staring fixedly at the portrait.

'It is Edith. To the life. I believe the artist must have been a little in love with her too.' He extended an arm towards the picture and said, 'Behold, the mother of my son,' then he bowed deeply. 'I am reunited with my family.' He turned away from the portraits and surveyed the rest of the Gallery. 'Now to find the killers who separated us.'

I gasped as all the cloths fell from the portraits at once. Horatio began to move round the room looking closely at each painting. Jesper and I had managed to find ten male portraits of the period and we'd displayed them randomly.

When Horatio arrived in front of Sir Walter Wyngrave, he paused and said sharply, 'Who is this?'

'Edith's husband, Sir Walter.'

'He was not one of the men who killed me, but I have seen him before.'

'Perhaps you saw him here on the day you died. He was your host.'

'And the monster who imprisoned Edith in the attic and deprived a mother of her child.'

He studied the portrait for a long time. I wondered whether the destructive urge Jesper had curbed in me would triumph over Horatio's unnerving self-control. Then the picture began to move of its own accord and seemed to fling itself away from the wall and into the air, where it was directed by Horatio to the floor. As it landed soundlessly, he flicked his hand and the portrait spun round so it faced the wall. Horatio glared at it for a moment, then turned to me. In an icy whisper that seemed to lower the temperature still further, he said, 'You will never let that fiend set eyes on Edith again.'

'I won't. That portrait doesn't normally hang in the Gallery. I only brought it in for you. But I'm getting rid of it,' I said firmly. 'When Jesper returns, he's taking it away. And any others that shouldn't be here.'

Horatio turned away to inspect portraits of Tudor and Jacobean merchants, scholars and minor aristocracy, some of whom I'd identified, some not. He paused in front of one I did know. So apparently did Horatio. 'Oliver de Vere... The portrait is flattering. His eyes were smaller and his nose larger. A vain and stupid man,' Horatio said with a snort of disgust, 'but not a killer. At any rate, he did not kill *me*. Nor did he save his poor sister.' The portrait leaped from the wall, hovered a moment, then turned and settled on the floor, facing the wall.

Horatio moved along the Gallery, continuing his examination of the remaining portraits. 'This man,' he said without turning to me. 'Who is he?'

'Oliver's older brother, Ferdinand.'

'A good likeness. I saw him for a few moments only, but I recognise his face after four centuries. This brother *was* a killer.'

The portrait sprang into the air, turned a somersault and landed facing the wall like the others. Horatio turned to me, his eyes huge and black. 'Forgive what must look to you like vulgar showmanship. Were I able, I still would not deign to handle the image of that miserable coward, one who needed the assistance of two others to despatch an unarmed man.'

I continued to watch in dumbfounded silence, holding my breath as Horatio paused before a ruthless-looking Duke, long past his prime, but clearly still clinging on to waning power. Horatio moved on. Arriving at the last portrait, he said nothing but examined it closely before saying, 'Who is this?'

'Gervase de Vere. Edith's father.'

'The man who arranged her marriage. Who must have known she was imprisoned. Who was prepared to kill me and let his only daughter die in order to preserve an alliance with Wyngrave. God's blood, de Vere had two sons! Why should he care about the fate of a *daughter*?'

'They died without issue.'

Horatio turned to face me. 'What?'

'Ferdinand and Oliver. They had no surviving children. Oliver produced none and Ferdinand's all died in infancy. Edith was the only one to produce a child who reached adulthood. And he was yours.'

'Oh, Jane… My dear Jane! Those words are balm for my tortured soul. You have studied the records then?'

'I wanted to know who all these people were, if they were related, what connection they had with Wyngrave.'

'So the de Vere name died?'

'That branch did. But Sir Walter lived on and so did Samuel.'

'And Sir Walter lived on knowing Samuel was not his child and his wife had loved another.'

'*And thus the whirligig of time brings in his revenges…* You had your revenge, Horatio. Not personally, but the worst thing for those men would have been to watch their male heirs sicken and die while yours thrived.'

He turned back to face the portrait of Gervase de Vere. It moved away from the wall, turned through the air several times, then sank onto the floor where it lay face-down at Horatio's feet. He stood in silent contemplation, then turned to me, suddenly alarmed. 'Jane, it has begun! I feel it! I must be brief.'

'What is it?' I asked, but I could see already that he'd begun to fade, his substance becoming thinner, his features indistinct.

'I believe this is the end. I am no longer to be a prisoner at Wyngrave. Whether I will or no, I must leave you.' He stared over my shoulder. 'And Edith… And my son.' He drifted past me, back to the portraits that hung side by side. More candles had gone out, but I could see that Horatio's form was now quite transparent. Some parts had disappeared altogether.

'Queenie's message!' I exclaimed. 'Don't leave without telling me what it was! She wanted me to solve the mystery of your death and we have. You said there would be a message for me. What was it? Quickly!'

'Some lines from *Hamlet*.'

'*Hamlet?*'

'Queenie said I was to recite the lines to you and then you must—'

He began to fade away and I shrieked, 'Come back! You mustn't go yet!'

His head reappeared like the Cheshire Cat's, followed by some of his body. 'The man of law,' he said faintly.

'*What?*'

'Queenie said you were to inform the man of law that matters were concluded.'

'And then?'

'She didn't say. Perhaps she doubted they ever would be.'

'The *words*, Horatio! What were they? Quickly! They might be your last!'

'If thou didst ever hold me in thy heart,
Absent thee from felicity awhile,
And in this harsh world draw thy breath in pain,
To tell my story.'

Tears sprang into my eyes, tears of grief, exhaustion and recognition… Hamlet has only moments left to live and he's speaking to his dearest friend. A man called Horatio.

'Jane, I must take my leave.' It was just a disembodied voice now, a whisper in my ear. 'It is not in my power to stay.'

I spun round, searching for him, but saw nothing. 'I shall remember you, Horatio,' I said, addressing the air. 'Always!' But by then I knew I was alone.

I switched on a light. The Gallery looked as if it had been ransacked. With shaking hands, I extinguished every remaining candle, but left the portraits and Jesper's cloths where they had fallen.

Stumbling across the hall in the dark, blind with tears, I groped for the handle of my bedroom door. Clutching it with relief, I entered, kicked off my shoes and fell onto the bed. I rolled myself in the duvet and slept.

When I woke, I assumed I was still asleep. Jesper was sitting in a chair, watching me intently. I shut my eyes again and became aware I was drenched in sweat. I wondered if it was all part of an erotic dream featuring Jesper. I groaned and tried to push the duvet away, then realised I was rolled up in it. As I struggled to free myself, a blissfully cool and cultivated voice said, 'Can I be of any assistance?' I opened my eyes again, wider this time, and said, *'Jesper?'*

'Good morning, Jane. I didn't like to wake you, but I admit I've been concerned. You didn't answer your phone last night or this morning.' He tugged at the duvet, unwinding me from its folds to reveal my sweaty layers of wool and fleece. 'Ah, I see. I thought you'd succumbed to a raging fever, but you were simply over-heated. You dressed for arctic conditions last night, didn't you?'

I sat up, pulled a fleece top over my head and tossed it onto the floor. 'Jesper, you're supposed to be in London having lunch with your mother.' As I swung my fleece-clad legs out of bed and removed thick woollen socks, a thought struck me. 'Sorry to sound like Ebenezer Scrooge, but is it still Sunday? Have I slept through a whole day?'

Jesper sat down on the bed beside me. 'It's still Sunday and my mother cancelled late last night. She's gone down with a nasty cold, poor thing. I rang straight away, but you didn't answer. I assume your phone is dead.'

'Oh, yes, it will be. I forgot to charge it last night. So you drove *back*?'

'This morning. Mainly because you didn't answer your phone, but I also wondered how you'd coped last night. Bridget let me in and asked no questions, bless her. I looked in and saw the Gallery was a mess, so when you didn't respond to my knock, I came in. You looked as if you'd just fallen into bed. Afterwards.'

'Jesper, it was *awful*.'

'Horatio showed up, I take it.'

'And identified his killers. De Vere, father and son.'

'The *mafiosi*?'

'Yes.'

'Damn good portraits, those. For all their glad rags, those fellows actually looked like killers.'

'I want you to take them away. All three de Veres and Sir Walter. I won't have them under my roof a minute longer than is necessary. Take them and sell them. I'm going to use the money to fix the roof and renovate the old cottage. The rest I'll donate to good causes.'

'So Horatio is gone? For good?'

'I think so. He started to fade as soon as he recognised the de Veres. But there was something else very strange. A message from Queenie.'

'Good grief, did you hold a séance?'

'Before she died, Queenie gave Horatio a message to pass on

to me if ever he was released. He didn't know what it signified and it meant nothing to me. Apparently, I have to give it to Queenie's solicitor.'

'What was the message?'

'A quotation from *Hamlet*.'

'But why do you have to tell the solicitor?'

'I don't know. I shall ring him first thing tomorrow. Right now, I need a shower and some breakfast.'

'Why don't I go down and make you some while you shower? I'll bring it up on a tray, then you can tell me all about your midnight exorcism. I imagine you don't want to discuss it in front of the girls.'

'Not yet. Maybe never.' I got out of bed and peeled off my fleece trousers.

Jesper exclaimed. 'At last, the thermals! This striptease is most unorthodox, Jane, but... stimulating.'

'Jesper, shouldn't you be visiting your ailing mother?'

'She wouldn't hear of it. I said if she didn't feel up to our usual restaurant, we could get a takeaway and I would sit and entertain her. She said that sounded exhausting and she preferred to stay in bed, feeling sorry for herself. She'll binge-watch Netflix.'

'So you're here for the day then?'

'And the night, if I'm invited.' His voice was casual, the blue eyes were not.

'You're invited,' I said. 'But don't expect too much. I know it sounds silly, but I feel as if I've suffered a family bereavement.'

'That's why I'm offering to stay. I'm the only one who knows what you're dealing with. I might also be the only one who'll believe you.'

'What about work tomorrow?'

'I'll set off at the crack of dawn.'

'Jesper, you're a hero. If you bring me breakfast on a tray, I shall bow down and worship.'

'Steady on...'

I flung my arms round his neck, kissed him and said, 'Tea, please, pints of it. I'm so dehydrated. I must have been sweating all night. Bring me breakfast and I'll tell you all about *The Brief Life and Ignominious Death of Horatio Fortune, Actor*.'

'Cracking title for a play.'

'One Edith de Vere might have written.'

'*Edith*?'

'Tea first, then I shall reveal all.'

He regarded me speculatively, his head on one side. 'The thermals are coming off then?'

'Tea, Jesper. *Now!*'

15

I will make my very house reel tonight. A letter for me?

Coriolanus

At nine o'clock on Monday morning I was waiting anxiously for someone to pick up the phone in Laurence Putnam's office. I got the answerphone, so I left my number and a message saying it concerned Queenie Brooke-Bennet's bequest and the matter was urgent. Then I sat down in a window seat to wait, gazing out at the golds and yellows of the autumn garden, fighting an irrational sense of loss. I told myself I was missing Jesper. I knew I was mourning Horatio.

When Putnam finally rang, I jumped, then answered, trying to sound calm and professional.

'Good morning, Ms Summers,' he said affably. 'I hope you are well. You wanted to speak to me urgently?'

'Thanks for ringing back, Mr Putnam. The urgency is my all-consuming curiosity. I understand I must pass on a message to you, but I don't know why, nor do I know what the message signifies.'

'Oh? A message from whom?'

'From Queenie Brooke-Bennet. Apparently.' There was a long silence and I wondered if we'd been cut off. 'Mr Putnam? Are you still there?'

'Yes, I'm here, I was just *surprised*... You say it's a message from Miss Brooke-Bennet?'

'Well, not directly, obviously, but I'm following her posthumous instructions. I understand that if I ever obtained certain information, she wanted me to inform you. I gather this message, which seems to be coded, is very important. Sorry to sound so mysterious, but I don't know any more, just the words I'm supposed to pass on to you.'

'Would you hold on while I check the file? I do remember now you come to mention it, that Miss Brooke-Bennet left me some unusual instructions. I believe I have some sealed envelopes... Would you bear with me a moment, please?'

There was another silence, then Putnam came back, sounding slightly breathless.

'Sorry to keep you, Ms Summers. I do indeed have some envelopes which Miss Brooke-Bennet left with instructions. One is to be opened in your presence, after you have given me the password, which I am to check against the contents of the other envelope.'

'Password?'

'That was how Miss Brooke-Bennet expressed it, as I recall. The envelopes are to be witnessed as sealed and intact, then opened in your presence. We'll also need one other person as a witness.'

'Shall I come into the Colchester office?'

'You could do that, but in view of the unusual circumstances, I would quite like to come to Wyngrave Hall, if that would suit you? I imagine one of your housemates would act as witness? Will someone be at home today?'

'Oh, yes. At least two others, possibly three. Given half a chance, they'll hand round popcorn.'

Mr Putnam chuckled politely. 'We need someone who is not related to you or Miss Brooke-Bennet.'

'My housemates are all friends, not relations.' As I said the words, I was momentarily choked. With pride, I think.

'Very good. Shall I come to Wyngrave then with the relevant paperwork?'

'Please. As soon as possible. The suspense is killing.'

'I must admit, Ms Summers, I never expected to have to deal with this eventuality. Miss Brooke-Bennet and I discussed it, in a somewhat *elliptical* way, and at the time it all seemed rather unlikely. I'd quite forgotten her instructions until you reminded me. How did you say you came by the information?'

'I didn't, and I'd rather not go into any details at the moment if you don't mind. It's... complicated. Did Queenie say I had to explain?'

'On the contrary. The letter I have in front of me says no explanation is expected or required. The only stipulation is, you must relay the *exact* words contained in the sealed envelope, and *only* those. Miss Brooke-Bennet indulged in some heavy underlining here! If you're able to do that, I shall play my part and inform you of the significance of the – ah – password. If you are not able to supply the correct form of words, I'm afraid I'm not permitted to offer any kind of explanation.'

'I see. Well, actually I don't see at all, but I do understand that I have to repeat some words to you and I think I know what they are.'

'You're confident, Ms Summers?'

'Oh, yes. My source is impeccable.'

'Excellent. Well, I could be with you later this morning. Would eleven o'clock suit you?'

'Yes, that's fine. Just one witness is required?'

'Yes. *Compos mentis* and so forth.'

'And sighted, I assume.'

'Oh, yes. He or she needs to witness the opening of a sealed envelope and read the contents. Miss Brooke-Bennet wanted to ensure there could be no interference with the arrangement she'd set up.'

'Thanks, Mr Putnam. I'll see you at eleven.'

'I look forward to it. This has been a most unusual and interesting bequest to deal with.' He chuckled again. 'Miss Brooke-Bennet was quite a character.'

Not to mention, I thought to myself, a devious control freak. If it was Queenie's intention to make me feel like a contestant in a game show, she'd succeeded.

'Let us hope, Ms Summers, that matters will be concluded to your satisfaction.'

'And Queenie's,' I added. 'Thanks, Mr Putnam. 'Bye.'

Bridget had the longest association with Wyngrave, so it seemed appropriate to ask her to act as witness. I also thought it possible that one day I might share Horatio's story with her. She'd sensed the existence of Queenie's "imaginary friend" and as it was Bridget who'd found his remains and the money box, I felt she had a right to the whole story, whether or not she believed it. I knew Bridget well enough now to feel confident she wouldn't ridicule an account of my experience. Rosamund was another matter. As Sylvia had actually seen Horatio, it felt right to invite her to be present at the opening of the envelope, which meant Rosamund had to be there too. We should *all* witness the conclusion of Queenie's extraordinary machinations. We'd shared the discovery of a skeleton and might share the burial of those bones. Wyngrave was our home. I didn't own it, I lived rent-free – indefinitely, uncertainly and subletting. We were pretty much all in the same boat and should share any developments.

I found Rosamund and Bridget drinking coffee in the kitchen. I didn't explain – how could I? – but asked if they would meet me later with Mr Putnam in the Great Hall.

Bridget looked alarmed. 'We aren't going to be evicted, are we?'

'Oh no, I don't think so, but to be perfectly honest, I don't know what it's about. I'm just following rather strange instructions.'

'From beyond the grave?' Rosamund asked with a smile. I gaped at her, speechless. 'I mean, Queenie's been dead a long time now, but somehow the old girl still finds ways to affect our lives.'

'Doesn't she just!' I said, relieved. 'But maybe all that's about to stop. Have you seen Sylvia? I know she wouldn't want to miss out.'

'She was toddling round the garden a while ago. Well wrapped up,' Rosamund added. 'I offered to sit with her, but she said she was fine and wanted to find a quiet spot to "sit and contemplate." I took the hint.'

'You'll probably find her sitting on a bench in the orchard,' Bridget said. 'Get her moving if you can. There's a real nip in the air this morning. Which reminds me, Jane, I'd like to dig that grave before winter sets in. As soon as you know where you want it, I'll get cracking. If you don't want the bones to be disturbed ever again, we should bury them at a good depth and mark the grave somehow.'

'That's exactly what I want to do, if you don't mind all the digging.'

Bridget shook her head. 'I dug the poor bugger up, so I'd like to help lay him to rest. It's the least we can do,' she added.

'Thanks, I really appreciate it. I'd better go and find Sylvia. See you both in the Great Hall at eleven.'

'With Colonel Mustard and the Lead Piping,' Rosamund murmured as she cleared away the mugs.

Sylvia was sitting on a bench in the orchard, looking like a movie star. Her hair was hidden under a fetching Cossack hat, she wore a silver fox fur coat and very large dark glasses. She preferred to shield her eyes now when she was outdoors, but her face was lifted up to the weak autumn sunshine. I knew she'd hear me as I approached over the fallen leaves, so I called out, 'Good morning, Sylvia. You look as if you're waiting to film your big scene.'

She laughed. 'Come and join me. We must make the most of this sun while we can.'

'You're sure you're not getting cold? Bridget said you've been out here a while.'

'In this get-up? I'm warm as toast.'

'Well, I'd like you to come indoors later. I have an appointment with Queenie's solicitor. A mystery document is to be unsealed. I thought you'd like to join us.'

'Good gracious, that sounds exciting! What's it all about?'

'I don't actually know, but I came across some information which Queenie wanted me to pass on to Mr Putnam, her solicitor.'

'What happens then?'

'Who knows? We're all going to find out together at eleven o' clock. Shall I ask Ros to come and escort you?'

'Thank you, that would be very kind. I'm glad of an arm to lean on these days. Oh, Jane, before you go—' She hesitated. 'I just wanted to ask… Have you seen any more of … our friend? The handyman who wasn't.'

The question was unexpected and I deflected it while I thought very fast. 'Have you seen him again?'

'Not recently. That's why I asked. I haven't seen him since you found that old journal. Well, I say *seen*, but you know what I mean. I used to sense his presence occasionally and now I don't.'

I said nothing. I didn't want to lie but couldn't find the words to tell the truth. Sylvia saved me the trouble. 'He's gone, hasn't he? I think whatever it was he needed to do, he's done it, so he's free.

Finally at rest... I say, Jane, do you think it was *his* bones Bridget disturbed?'

'Yes, I do.'

'So our ghost was a *murder victim*,' Sylvia said in a shocked whisper. 'You know, we really ought to give him a decent burial. What's left of him.'

'That's my intention. I was wondering if you'd help me devise a little ceremony. And perhaps say a few words? You'd do it so much better than me.'

'Of course I will, if that's what you'd like.'

'Thank you.'

Just then the sun disappeared behind a cloud. The air turned cold immediately and Sylvia began to sing softly.

'He is dead and gone, lady.
He is dead and gone.
At his head a grass-green turf,
At his heels a stone...'

She sighed. 'That's poor Ophelia. Mad with grief because her father's been murdered. The song just came into my head.' She shivered and said, 'I can feel the sun's gone. Shall we go in and wait for whatever it is Queenie and Mr Putnam have cooked up for us?'

She rose stiffly, leaning on her stick, and took my arm. As we walked back to the house, Sylvia hummed Ophelia's song.

I'd found the relevant speech from *Hamlet* online and printed it out. Putnam had alarmed me, insisting I must repeat the exact words, no more and no less. I worried I hadn't remembered what Horatio had said, but I didn't think I could or ever would forget. The more I stared at the lines, the cleverer I thought Queenie had been. She'd even managed to include my mother's name, which surely wasn't a coincidence.

If thou didst ever hold me in thy heart...

I hadn't held Queenie in my heart. I hadn't known her, yet I disliked her, hated her even, when I was young. And now? I had Queenie to thank for Horatio. If I hadn't inherited the portraits, I would never have met Jesper. I owed my friendship with Bridget,

Sylvia and Rosamund to Queenie. Her wish to atone had enriched my life beyond anything I could have imagined. But was it a desire to atone, or was it a last throw of the dice as she faced death, an attempt to solve a centuries-old murder?

And that final injunction… *In this harsh world draw thy breath in pain, to tell my story.*

Whose? Horatio's? Queenie's? Or even my parents'? There were so many stories. But I was a storyteller and so was Queenie. She knew these stories would be valued by me and possibly re-told.

Queenie had given me a great deal, far more than she realised. Whatever the outcome of sharing the password, I would endeavour now to "hold her in my heart", alongside Edith, Horatio and all my other dead.

I heard a car pull up on the drive. Mr Putnam was punctual. I picked up Hamlet's speech and tucked it into my pocket. As I descended the stairs, I called out, 'Putnam's here.'

Rosamund appeared from the kitchen with a bottle of sherry and glasses on a tray. Bridget called out, 'Kettle's on,' and I heard the clatter of crockery. Not to be outdone in helpfulness, Sylvia was plumping up cushions, suggesting we put another log on the already roaring fire.

As I arrived at the foot of the staircase, I knew whatever the outcome today, this scene of happy, domestic teamwork was a memory I would hold in my heart.

Bridget served coffee while we made strained conversation about Wyngrave and the weather, making no reference to the contents of Mr Putnam's briefcase or the folded sheet of paper I had placed beside my mug. Sylvia was the only one to accept sherry. I barely touched my coffee.

After a suitable interval, Mr Putnam lifted his briefcase from the floor and said, 'Well, I'm sure you'd like to get this over with, Ms Summers.'

'Please. How do we go about this?'

'I have two envelopes. One is addressed to me and numbered "One" and the other is addressed to you and numbered "Two". Who is to be our official witness?'

As Bridget raised her hand, I said, 'Bridget Thompson.'

He made a note and said, 'Very good, Ms Thompson. I'll take your details afterwards if I may. So Ms Summers, I shall open the first envelope and compare the contents while you read to me from the piece of paper you've prepared. As you can see, both of these letters have been sealed.' He handed them to Bridget who inspected them briefly, then handed them back. 'That was done by Miss Brooke-Bennet in 2017. Ms Summers, would you like to examine them?'

'No, that's fine. Please open yours.'

He did so and took out a single sheet of paper. I recognised Queenie's violet ink and her florid hand. 'When you're ready, Ms Summers. Or of course you can just hand me your paper.'

'I'd like to read it. I want Sylvia to hear everything, especially as they're lines from a play.' There was a little gasp from Sylvia and she downed the rest of her sherry. 'I'm sure Queenie meant these words to be spoken.' Staring at the paper as it quivered in my shaking hands, I said, 'These are the words that I understand I am to repeat to Mr Putnam...

If thou didst ever hold me in thy heart,
Absent thee from felicity awhile,
And in this harsh world draw thy breath in pain,
To tell my story.'

Beaming, Mr Putnam passed his letter to Bridget for scrutiny. 'You will see, Ms Thompson, that Ms Summers read what is written on my sheet. No more, no less.'

Bridget nodded, dumb with astonishment.

'It's from the last act of *Hamlet*,' Sylvia explained. 'Right at the end. He knows he's dying. And so did poor Queenie.' Rosamund leaned over, took the empty sherry glass and set it down, then held her grandmother's hand.

'Now I am to give you *your* letter, Ms Summers. You're not obliged to read it aloud—'

'Oh, but she *is*,' exclaimed Sylvia. 'I have to know what it says!'

I smiled and said, 'Mr Putnam, would you be kind enough to read Queenie's letter? I want everyone to hear what it says, but right now, I'm not sure I'm up to deciphering her handwriting.'

'Of course. It will be my pleasure.' He broke the seal, took out two sheets of notepaper and read.

Wyngrave Hall
August 30ᵗʰ 2017

My dear Ms Summers

If you are reading this you are now the owner outright of Wyngrave Hall, its surrounding land and outbuildings. Congratulations! There are no conditions. The property is yours to sell, let, even demolish if the planners allow. All ties between your family and mine are now severed.

Some thought I led a wicked life. Some even said so. I lived selfishly, but I hope you will now concede, I did what I could for Felicity's child – certainly a great deal more than I ever did for poor Felicity. I had no greater gifts to impart than Wyngrave and its mystery which, as I hoped, you have solved.

I could ask for forgiveness, but I do not. Wyngrave comes to you unencumbered, with no obligations. Perhaps now though, you might find it a little harder to hate me.

I'm sure I died unmourned, but now that you know the story – all the stories – I hope you will remember us. The dead. Some of us long dead. Thankfully, the stories remain. Theirs. Mine. Yours.

Good luck with whatever you decide to do with Wyngrave and the rest of your life.

Yours very sincerely,
Quintilia Brooke-Bennet

When he'd finished reading, Mr Putnam folded the letter and handed it to me. There was dead silence. No-one even moved. It was he who broke the tension saying, 'Well, I think congratulations are in order, Ms Summers,' then he looked at his watch. 'I'm sure you will have a lot of questions, but I should be getting back to the office. There's a lot for you to – ah – *digest*, so I'll leave you in peace and perhaps you'll give me a ring later? We can go over the details then.' He turned to Bridget and handed her a form. 'Ms Thompson, would you complete and sign this please? No hurry. Whenever it's convenient.'

'Would you like to take my letter with you?' I asked faintly. 'Or I can run upstairs and make a copy.'

'Thank you, but I believe I have sealed copies of everything in the office. I suspect Miss Brooke-Bennet duplicated everything, but I couldn't open my letters until you'd opened yours.' He smiled. 'She was surprisingly efficient.'

As he gathered up his papers, Bridget rose and said, 'I'll see you out, Mr Putnam.'

He bade us goodbye and followed Bridget to the door. She closed it behind him and returned to her seat. Stunned silence reigned until Sylvia burst into peals of laughter. 'Oh, Jane, I'm sorry, but I just can't believe it! You're a millionaire! For all I know, a *multi*-millionaire!' She snapped her fingers. 'Just like that!'

'Only if I sell.' I looked up from Queenie's letter to see two pairs of eyes focused on me and Sylvia's, blank and brimming with tears. 'And I won't. This is my home. And yours. We've made something very special here and I see it as a project, an experiment that's ongoing. If one of you leaves,' I said, careful not to look at Sylvia, even though I knew she couldn't see me, 'I'll advertise for someone else. After all, if I don't sell Wyngrave, I'll still need the rent.' Sylvia laughed again and I saw the others relax. 'The real significance of this development is, I can use the money from the sale of my London flat to get all the things done that we planned. Fix the leaking roof. Renovate the cottage—'

'Install central heating that *works*,' Rosamund pleaded.

'Wouldn't that be wonderful?' I replied. 'And now the money will be there. For everything we want to do. I didn't touch my half of the proceeds, in case things didn't work out here and I needed to buy another flat.'

'Ever the optimist,' Rosamund said.

'I was just being realistic. To be perfectly honest, I didn't rate our chances of making it work.'

'Neither did I, Jane. Take no notice. I'm just teasing because I've no idea how to react to this extraordinary turn of events. What *is* this mystery you've solved?'

'If I told you, Ros, I don't think you'd believe me.'

'Oh, go on!'

'I will explain one day, but not today. I want to concentrate on this great gift. To *all* of us. As I won't need to buy a property now, I can invest in this one.'

Rosamund looked at Bridget and said under her breath, 'Bet she puts the rent up,' and we all laughed.

'Death duties will be horrific,' Bridget said.

'I know, but I've given Jesper four portraits to sell. He said they'll raise a lot of money and there are others I could happily part with.'

'There's also a piece of land you could sell,' Bridget said. 'Well away from the Hall, but usefully close to the road. A builder could put a couple of bungalows on it.'

'I'll find the money somehow. I dare say I'll end up cash-poor, but I'll be asset-rich,' I said, looking round at my three housemates. 'And I'm not just talking about this building.'

'Oh, Jane,' Sylvia said in a tremulous voice. 'I'm so happy for you. For *all* of us.'

'So am I, Sylvia.'

Rosamund patted her grandmother's hand. 'It's okay to cry, Gran. I think we'll all be blubbing in a minute.'

'You know,' Sylvia said with a sniff, 'Queenie didn't create much happiness when she was alive – rather the *reverse* – but she's made up for it today, hasn't she, the dear old thing? We should raise a glass to her tonight, don't you think?'

'Well, it just so happens,' I said, 'that I took the precaution of chilling some champagne. I thought we'd either be celebrating or drowning our sorrows.'

'Champagne?' Sylvia exclaimed. 'Oh, I didn't think the day could get any better, but it just *did*!'

'Bridget, would you do the honours? I haven't the strength.'

She sprang up and headed for the kitchen. 'Champagne coming up.'

As she left the room I said, 'On a more sombre note, I wanted to let you know that Bridget and I have decided to bury the remains of... the dead man in the grounds. Somewhere pleasant, but well out of the way. Now I own the land, I feel even more convinced it's the right thing to do.'

'Oh, definitely,' Sylvia said. 'You know, Bridget and I could have responsibility for laying fresh flowers on his grave. I think I'd like to do that.'

'That's a lovely idea, Sylvia. Thank you for offering.'

Bridget reappeared bearing a tray of brimming glasses and handed them round, putting a flute carefully into Sylvia's hand with the consideration that had become habitual to us all.

'I think we should drink to him too, poor man.' Sylvia said. 'What a terrible end he met.'

'It certainly was a horrible death, but actually, it wasn't the end. Not really.' Before anyone could question me, I raised my glass and said, 'To absent friends.'

'Absent friends,' came the solemn echo and we all drank.

'And *I'd* like to propose a toast,' Sylvia said, dabbing at her eyes with a tissue, 'to our dear friend Jane, to whom we owe so much.' Bridget and Rosamund exchanged a look that escaped Sylvia, but not me. 'To Jane, and friends old and new, present and absent.' She raised her glass and we drank again.

As we sat beside our crackling fire, I glanced round the Great Hall, searching, but I saw nothing, sensed nothing. A log shifted, then fell. Sparks danced, then flew up the ancient chimney.

It was over.

Later I rang Jesper.

'Did you leave a bottle of champagne outside my bedroom door this morning?'

'I thought you might need it later. One way or another.'

'Thank you. We did.'

'Mr Putnam came up trumps?'

'Queenie Brooke-Bennet did.'

'How exciting! Tell me all.'

'Well, very briefly, I now own Wyngrave Hall.'

'Is this a joke?'

'No.'

'But, Jane, that's *wonderful!*'

'Isn't it?'

'I shall take the opportunity to send in my bill, which will look peanuts compared to the inheritance tax.'

'I shall just have to ask you to sell more portraits for me.'

'Oh, that's a pity.'

'I'll need the money. I want to restore Wyngrave to its former glory.'

'No, I meant I was hoping to terminate our professional relationship, so we could… pursue one of a different kind.'

'I might be a millionaire, Jesper, but I'm not sure I can afford your principles.'

'I miss you, Jane.'

'You left my bed six hours ago!'

'Exactly. Six *hours*,' he groaned.

I laughed and said, 'I miss you too.'

'Come to London.'

'I will.'

'Tonight.'

'No, I'll be celebrating with the girls. Take me out to dinner tomorrow night. Somewhere special. Where millionaires go.'

'You're on.'

'Speak tomorrow?'

'If not before.'

'Bye, Jesper.'

'Bye, Jane.'

The winter was busy and happy, apart from the day we interred Horatio's bones. Jesper joined us for the ceremony and, unable to read now, Sylvia spoke all the words from memory. Being an old trooper, she didn't cry, but I did. Sylvia had chosen some appropriate quotations – all Shakespeare, she explained – and when she said, in ringing tones, *'Heaven take my soul and England keep my bones!'* I could no longer hold it together. We took it in turns to throw a trowelful of soil into the grave, then Sylvia said, *'We are Time's subjects, and Time bids be gone.'*

She took Rosamund's arm and they led us back to the Hall in silence. We left Bridget to fill in the grave and, as I leaned on Jesper's arm, I heard the slow, rhythmic scrape of her shovel, followed by the sound of earth falling.

We lived in cheerful chaos for weeks as new central heating was installed and the roof was repaired. Bridget supervised the refurbishment of the old cottage and the work was completed by the end of the year. We began to discuss who might rent it.

When Bridget asked if I knew Rosamund's fortieth birthday was actually New Year's Eve, I insisted we throw a party. Bridget and Sylvia backed me up and, still a little reluctant, Rosamund agreed. So on the last day of 2019 we threw a party to celebrate the New Year and Rosamund's birthday.

The date was significant for quite another reason, though at the time we had no idea. On the day we celebrated forty years of Rosamund's life, China alerted the World Health Organisation to dozens of cases of "viral pneumonia" in the city of Wuhan.

And so it began.

EPILOGUE

These days are dangerous.

Henry VI, Part Two

April 30th, 2020

Hi Alison

Me again. I never thought I would be glad you're dead. I'm not really, but I am glad you didn't live to see this. Covid-19.

I don't know where to begin.

It started in China, but we didn't take any notice. China is so far away and there was so much going on here at Wyngrave – major renovations and new relationships – but I began to feel frightened when I saw what was happening in Italy, particularly in Lombardy, where Maeve and Giacomo live.

Giacomo has lost half his family. All the old. All the weak. Maeve caught it too and was very ill, but she survived. The situation in Italy was unimaginable. 1000 new cases every day. They ran out of space to store corpses and people to bury and cremate them. It was medieval. Coffins were stacked in churches with plastic bags of the dead's belongings. Relatives weren't allowed to touch anything.

Things aren't as bad here yet, but they are very bad and likely to get worse. At least we're <u>finally</u> in lockdown now, thank God. Rosamund went back to hospital nursing, which was possibly suicidal. NHS staff are now dying of Covid. The selfless dedication of NHS workers is just awe-inspiring. Ros had already nursed a lot of elderly, critically ill and terminal patients and she wanted to use her specialist skills, but knew if she did, she'd be endangering us, especially her grandmother. So now Ros lives on her own in the renovated cottage in the grounds. We can't even see it from the house. When we do see her, it's only through the window. We leave groceries on her doorstep, cooked meals and special treats. Bridget leaves bunches of spring flowers in jars on her doorstep.

Ros and Bridget have been a couple for months now, but they have to stand either side of a closed window and talk to each other on their phones. Sylvia used to do the same, so Ros could see her, but Sylvia got so upset, not being able to touch her granddaughter. To my dying day – which might come sooner than expected – I will never forget seeing Sylvia's palm pressed against the windowpane and Rosamund's, matching, on the other side, both of them sobbing inconsolably. Now they just speak on the phone every day.

Remember Live Guy? Jesper. He had to choose. He had to close his London gallery and he could have come here, especially as Ros had moved into the cottage, but he chose to lock down with his mother who's elderly and lives alone. She's moved in with Jesper and I don't see him except on Zoom calls and on the little videos he's made about conserving paintings. He's got quite a following now on his YouTube channel. Lots of people leave comments to say they find it calming, watching faces emerge from underneath all the dirt and varnish. Jesper's enthusiasm for his subject is a joy to see and he manages to inject some of his dry humour into the proceedings. I sit in bed and watch the videos over and over. Sometimes I touch him on the screen.

After Jesper chose his mother (he had to and I wouldn't have allowed him to do anything else), he proposed. When I stopped laughing, I realised he was serious. Then I cried. (Everyone cries so much these days.) I said if we both survive, I will marry him. I told Bridget and she was thrilled. She said, "I want to give you a big hug, but we probably shouldn't." We just stood there, smiling at each other until our faces ached.

I told Sylvia, who of course cried, then we all got drunk together. Not Ros, because she lives in isolation, but I left a bottle of wine on her doorstep with a note saying, "We're engaged!"

We started planning our wedding outfits, just for fun. Sylvia insists she's honorary Mother of the Bride. She's now my responsibility, especially if Rosamund dies. We had a very depressing conversation about it, but it's all sorted now. I write and look after Sylvia. Bridget feeds everyone, including Ros, and keeps the household ticking over.

Sylvia is terrified – not for herself, but for Ros. When she's had too much sherry, Sylvia says she's buried a daughter and shouldn't have to bury a granddaughter. She's already lost a lot of friends to Covid – all elderly, many living in London, where things are bad. I try not to think about Jesper's chances. He's very fit, but fit people are dying too.

Guess what? I've taken up gardening! Bridget's teaching me. I'm also busy writing. I had an idea for a new series about an Elizabethan actor and a female portrait painter. She spies for Queen Elizabeth I and recruits him when he's at a loose end because plague has closed the theatres. (Needless to say, I came up with this idea pre-Covid.) Jesper is teaching me about Tudor portraiture on Zoom. I think I'll be able to write authentically about plague now.

We're full of plans for when it's all over. That's how we keep going. We're prisoners and we're frightened, but we make plans for our future. I don't doubt we all prepare for worst-case scenarios in private. Jesper's mother said she'd like to read her eulogy while she's still alive, so he wrote one and read it to her. She said, if that was really how he saw her, she could die happy.

Every day I count my blessings, which are many. I'm alive. So far, I'm healthy. I have Jesper, Sylvia, Ros and Bridget. No one could ask for better friends, and if you have to be under house arrest, Wyngrave Hall is a good place to be. Bridget leaves me notes about what to look out for in the garden. It gives us something to talk about and I'm learning a lot.

Spring has been so beautiful. Bridget planted bulbs on Horatio's grave. (Remember Dead Guy?) There's a bench and I go and sit there for a while most days. It's surprising how you get used to the cold and damp. I suppose we all associate fresh air with safety now. First there were snowdrops, then crocuses. Now there are narcissi, daffodils and hyacinths. The flowers give me hope. There's a very simple gravestone. It just says, "1603. Fortune, good night." I don't know when Horatio was born, but that's when he died. (The quote is from KING LEAR. Dead Guy was called Horatio Fortune.) He was "locked down" here for over four hundred years, so I really shouldn't complain. Strange to think he's free now and we're not.

I'm sitting beside his grave now, Alison, writing to you in my head. I shall pick a few flowers – not from the grave, there are plenty elsewhere – and take them in for Sylvia, who is a bit "under the weather" as she puts it. I don't think she's ill, just very old and frightened. Sometimes she can't think of a reason to get out of bed. She's almost completely blind now, but she'll be able to smell and touch the flowers.

I long to smell and touch Jesper. I wrote him a love letter, sprayed it with my perfume and sent it. The moment I heard it land in the post-box, I wanted the ground to open up and swallow me, I felt so embarrassed. To my amazement, he sent one back. It smells of him. I don't think I'm imagining it. I don't really care if I am. We all have to imagine a lot of things nowadays. At night I stroke the mattress, as if Jesper's there. I fall asleep holding my own hand, pretending it's his.

I must go indoors now and check on Sylvia, take her some flowers.

Goodbye, Alison. Hope you're okay, wherever you are. Stay safe. That's what we say now. And we really mean it.

Love always,
J
xxx

AUTHOR'S NOTE

The quotations at the beginning of each chapter and throughout the book are by William Shakespeare.

Kronberg Castle in Elsinore, Denmark is the setting for an annual open air Shakespeare Festival.

Some people mentioned in this book did exist (Elizabethan actors, composers, artists), but the novel's characters and events are products of my imagination.

ACKNOWLEDGEMENTS

For their help and encouragement, I would like to thank Helen Abbott, Beth Davis, Jane Dixon-Smith, Gregor Duthie, Clare Flynn, Amy Glover, Philip Glover, Bill Marshall, Susan Patrick, Kathy Wainwright, Anne Williams and Jan Williams.

For the art conservation background, I owe a debt to Philip Mould's books, SLEUTH and SLEEPERS, and the YouTube channel of *Baumgartner Fine Art Restoration*.

Also by Linda Gillard

HOUSE OF SILENCE

Selected by Amazon UK for the Top Ten Best of 2011 *in the Indie Author category.*

Orphaned by drink, drugs and rock'n'roll, Gwen Rowland is invited to spend Christmas at her boyfriend Alfie's family home, Creake Hall – a ramshackle Tudor manor in Norfolk. Soon after she arrives, Gwen senses something isn't quite right. Alfie acts strangely towards his family and is reluctant to talk about the past. His mother, a celebrated children's author, keeps to her room, living in a twilight world, unable to distinguish between past and present, fact and fiction.

When Gwen discovers fragments of forgotten letters sewn into an old patchwork quilt, she starts to piece together the jigsaw of the past and realises there's more to the family history than she's been told. It seems there are things people don't want her to know.

And one of those people is Alfie.

REVIEWS

"HOUSE OF SILENCE is one of those books you'll put everything else on hold for."
CORNFLOWER BOOKS blog

"The family turns out to have more secrets than the Pentagon. I enjoyed every minute of this book. It's written with considerable panache and humour, despite the fact that there's a very serious underlying thread to the book – how do we, as individuals and families, deal with tragedy?"
Kathleen Jones, author of
MARGARET FORSTER: A LIFE IN BOOKS

EMOTIONAL GEOLOGY

*A passionate, off-beat love story set on the Scottish island of North Uist,
short-listed for the* Waverton Good Read Award *in 2006*

Rose Leonard is on the run from her life. Haunted by her turbulent
past, she takes refuge in a remote island community where she co-
coons herself in work, silence and solitude in a house by the sea. A
new life and new love are offered by friends, her estranged daughter
and most of all by Calum, a fragile younger man who has his own
demons to exorcise. But does Rose, with her tenuous hold on sanity,
have the courage to put her past behind her?

REVIEWS

*"The emotional power makes this reviewer
reflect on how Charlotte and Emily Brontë might have
written if they were living and writing now."*

Northwords Now

*"Complex and important issues are played out in the
windswept beauty of a Hebridean island setting, with
a hero who is definitely in the Mr Darcy league!"*

www.ScottishReaders.net

STAR GAZING

Short-listed in 2009 for Romantic Novel of the Year *and* The Robin Jenkins Literary Award, *the UK's first environmental book award.*

Blind since birth, widowed in her twenties, now lonely in her forties, Marianne Fraser lives in Edinburgh in elegant, angry anonymity with her sister, Louisa, a successful novelist. Marianne's passionate nature finds expression in music, a love she finds she shares with Keir, a man she encounters on her doorstep one winter's night.

Keir makes no concession to her condition. He's abrupt to the point of rudeness, yet oddly kind. But can Marianne trust her feelings for this reclusive stranger who wants to take a blind woman to his island home on Skye, to "show her the stars"?

REVIEWS

*"A joy to read from the first page to the last...
Romantic and quirky and beautifully written."*

www.LoveReading.co.uk

*"A thinking woman's romance that lingers in the
memory long after the last page has been turned."*

New York Journal of Books

*"A read for diehard romantics with a bent
towards environmental issues."*

Aberdeen Press & Journal

UNTYING THE KNOT

Marrying a war hero was a big mistake. So was divorcing him.

A wife is meant to stand by her man, especially an army wife. But Fay didn't. She walked away – from Magnus, her war hero husband and from the home he was restoring: Tullibardine Tower, a ruined 16th-century tower house on a Perthshire hillside.

Now their daughter Emily is getting married. But she's marrying someone she shouldn't.

And so is Magnus...

REVIEWS

"This author is funny, smart, sensitive and has a great feel for romance... Highly recommended!"
RHAPSODYINBOOKS blog

"Another deeply moving and skilfully executed novel by Linda Gillard... Once again, she had me committed to her characters and caught up in their lives from the first few pages, then weeping for joy at the end."
AWESOME INDIES book blog

A LIFETIME BURNING

Flora Dunbar is dead. But it isn't over.

The spectre at the funeral is Flora herself, unobserved by her grieving family and the four men who loved her. Looking back over a turbulent lifetime, Flora recalls an eccentric childhood lived in the shadow of her musical twin, Rory; early marriage to Hugh, a handsome clergyman twice her age; motherhood, which brought her Theo, the son she couldn't love; middle age, when she finally found brief happiness in a scandalous affair with her nephew, Colin.

There has been much love in this family – some would say too much – and not a little hate. If you asked my sister-in-law, Grace why she hated me, she'd say it was because I seduced her precious firstborn, then tossed him on to the sizeable scrap heap marked 'Flora's ex-lovers'. But she'd be lying. That isn't why Grace hated me. Ask my brother Rory.

REVIEWS

"An absolute page-turner! I could not put this book down and read it over a weekend. It is a haunting and disturbing exploration of the meaning of love within a close-knit family... Find a place for it in your holiday luggage."

www.LoveReading.co.uk

"Probably the most convincing portrayal of being a twin that I have ever read."

STUCK-IN-A-BOOK blog

THE GLASS GUARDIAN

Ruth Travers has lost a lover, both parents and her job. Now she thinks she might be losing her mind.

When death strikes again, Ruth finds herself the owner of a dilapidated Victorian house on the Isle of Skye: *Tigh na Linne*, the summer home she shared as a child with her beloved Aunt Janet, the woman she'd regarded as a mother. As Ruth prepares to put the old house up for sale, she discovers she's not the only occupant.

Ruth realises she's falling in love again – with a man who died a hundred years ago.

REVIEWS

"As usual with Gillard's novels, I read THE GLASS GUARDIAN in almost one sitting. The story is about love, loss, grief, music, World War I, Skye, family secrets, loneliness and a ghost who will break your heart."
I PREFER READING book blog

"A captivating story, dealing with passionate love and tragic death... An old, crumbling house, snow falling all around, and a handsome ghost... Curling up with this book on a dark night would be perfect!"
THE LITTLE READER LIBRARY book blog

"The ending? Beautiful and completely satisfying. I cried tears of joy."
AWESOME INDIES book blog

CAULDSTANE

"If you live in fear, you fear to live."

When ghostwriter Jenny Ryan is summoned to the Scottish Highlands by Sholto MacNab – retired adventurer and Laird of Cauldstane Castle – she's prepared for travellers' tales, but not the MacNabs' violent and tragic history.

Lust, betrayal and murder have blighted family fortunes for generations, together with an ancient curse. As the MacNabs confide their sins and their secrets, Jenny learns why Cauldstane's uncertain future divides father and sons.

But someone resents Jenny's presence. Someone thinks she's getting too close to Alec MacNab – swordsmith, widower and heir to Cauldstane. Someone who will stop at nothing until Jenny has been driven away. Or driven mad.

Hell hath no fury like a woman scorned. Especially a dead woman.

REVIEWS

"Absolutely modern and gloriously gothic... There's a remote and decrepit Scottish castle, (with a curse attached, of course), a wicked stepmother, a feisty but emotionally vulnerable heroine, more handsome men than you can shake a sword at, and a very dangerous ghost."

Kathleen Jones, author of
MARGARET FORSTER: A LIFE IN BOOKS

"The castle is a character in its own right, as evocative as Manderley, and a perfect setting for this gothic tale of love and the struggle between good and evil."

I PREFER READING book blog.

THE MEMORY TREE

Its hollow heart holds a century of secrets.

1916

A man without a memory walks away from the battlefield, while a young woman grieves beneath the tree that will guard her secret for a hundred years.

2015

Ann de Freitas doesn't remember what she witnessed when she was five. The truth lies buried in the beech wood, forgotten for forty years. Can love unlock Ann's heart and mind?

Connor Grenville is restoring the walled garden where his grandmother, Ivy used to play. Before her death, she tried to destroy the family archive. Who was Ivy trying to protect? And why?

When a storm fells an ancient beech tree, revealing a century-old love hidden in its hollow heart, Ann and Connor begin to sift through the past in search of answers. What they discover changes everything.

REVIEWS

"A moving dual-time story, THE MEMORY TREE, celebrates the power of love to overcome the darkest memories and deepest losses. Linda Gillard once again draws us into a moving and compelling story of characters forced to choose whether buried memories should ever see the light. THE MEMORY TREE will keep you spellbound."

Lorna Fergusson, award-winning author of THE CHASE.

"A nostalgic, romantic, and emotional read rooted firmly in reality. It is quite simply breath-taking."

BREW & BOOKS REVIEW

"If you've read Linda Gillard's work before, you'll be enchanted by this one. If you haven't - well, this really wouldn't be a bad place to start."

BEING ANNE book blog

HIDDEN

A birth… A death… Hidden for a hundred years.

1918

"Lady, fiancé killed, will gladly marry officer totally blinded or otherwise incapacitated by the war."

A sense of duty and a desire for a child lead celebrated artist Esme Howard to share her life and her home – 16th-century Myddleton Mote – with Captain Guy Carlyle, an officer whose face and body have been ravaged by war. But Esme knows nothing of the ugliness that lurks within Guy's tortured mind, as he re-lives, night after night, the horrors of the trenches.

As a child grows within her, Esme fears Guy's wrath will be turned on them both. A prisoner in her own home, she paints like one possessed, trusting that one day someone will hear her silent cries for help.

2018

When Miranda Norton inherits Myddleton Mote and its art collection from a father she never knew, she decides to move on after the end of an unhappy marriage. Inviting her extended family to join her, Miranda sets about restoring the house and turning it into a thriving business.

When someone from Miranda's past returns to torment her, an appalling act of vandalism reveals the Mote's dark secrets, hidden for a hundred years.

REVIEWS

"An ancient moated house, a shell-shocked war hero, a female artist caught between the desire to honour her husband's sacrifice and her own free spirit - the ingredients for a page-turning read. Linda Gillard always delivers."

CLARE FLYNN, author of *The Pearl of Penang.*

"A powerful and atmospheric dual-time story. The way the secrets of the past and the central mystery are resolved had me breathless... HIDDEN is storytelling at its very best. I loved every moment."

ANNE WILLIAMS, *Being Anne* book blog

Printed in Great Britain
by Amazon

38326167R00158